Pecan Pies and Dead Guys

The Southern Ghost Hunter Mysteries
Book 7

NEW YORK TIMES BESTSELLING AUTHOR

ANGIE FOX

This edition published by arrangement with Moose Island Books.

Pecan Pies and Dead Guys

First Edition

ISBN: 978-1-939661-56-2

CHAPTER 1

I raised a hand against the blazing summer sun and stepped out onto the back porch of the home that had been in my family for five generations. August in Sugarland, Tennessee, meant hot, humid days, beautiful pink and white bougainvillea in full bloom, and last but not least, a mischievous skunk—one who liked to roam the great outdoors instead of staying inside at this time of year.

"Lucy!" I tapped her bowl on the top step, waiting for her squat black-and-white furred body to come churning around the side of the house. "Lucy, lunchtime!"

I could hardly keep her inside. My little girl was on the prowl for young male skunks leaving the nest. In Lucy's mind, those boys had no manners, and she liked to run them off whenever they wandered too close to her favorite hiding spot under the porch.

"I have *fruit*," I cooed, offering up the bowl. Most days, the mere word had her wriggling in rapt anticipation.

Bees buzzed. Birds chirped. But no Lucy.

That was odd.

I waited for my eyes to adjust to the bright outdoors and

scanned the shade between the clay pots of geraniums lining the steps. She sometimes liked to hide among them and then pop out at the young skunks like a carnival funhouse act. The poor little trespassers would jump three feet in the air before hightailing it off our land.

The way Lucy turned a circle and fluffed her tail after, well, let's just say she enjoyed it.

Still, I wasn't so keen on her antics. One of these days, she was going to get a good spray instead of the last laugh.

I strolled down the porch steps, my sandals clacking against the dry wood, keeping an eye out for her. No matter how busy Lucy was, she usually came running when it was time for lunch. Today, I had ripe bananas topped with powdered Vita-Skunk. Yum.

I stopped at the bottom of the steps and peered into the shadowy depths under the porch. No Lucy. I straightened and scanned the yard.

Of my two housemates, Lucy's need to get out and about caused me a heck of a lot less trouble than Frankie's. But causing less trouble than Frankie wasn't a challenge. Frankie "The German" was a gangster from the 1920s who'd worked hard and played harder. These days he haunted my ancestral home, but during his life, he'd been quite the tough guy about town. He and his South Town Gang had been responsible for a string of crimes stretching from Chicago all the way down here to Sugarland, but it was in our town where he'd breathed his last.

Not that being dead stopped him from being a pain in my rear sometimes.

Soon after I'd met Frankie, I learned he could lend me his energy and allow me to step into the spirit world. It was both a blessing and a curse.

My borrowed ability had allowed me to become a professional ghost hunter when my chosen career as a graphic designer hit the skids.

My new job kept food on the table and Lucy in skunk treats, but it led to some sticky situations as well. If I was tuned into the other side and some ill-tempered gangster decided to shoot me, the bullet could kill me for real.

Frankie called it the price of doing business. I called it an occupational hazard. He'd already been shot and killed. I'd rather avoid it.

Naturally, he'd forgotten to shut off his power last night, so I was vulnerable to whatever the other side decided to throw at me.

I paused at the bottom of the steps and looked out to the wooden shed past the pond, a place I'd bought just for the gangster so that he—and I—could enjoy a bit of privacy. I half-expected to see a few moonshine runners parked out back.

Yes, it bothered me. This wasn't simply a house or a few acres of property. This was my home. This was my family legacy, entrusted to me by my grandma, and she wouldn't have approved of Frankie's shenanigans.

I set Lucy's lunch bowl on the bottom step and checked under the lush hydrangeas flanking the stairs, hoping to see a sweet black-and-white head emerge from amid the thick green leaves. But she wasn't there.

Strange. I sat back on my heels.

Everything seemed quiet today, which wasn't always a good sign.

I smoothed my sundress. "Lucy!"

She usually came when I called. The fact that she didn't today had me...concerned. Not *worried* per se. I wasn't some helicopter pet mommy.

Still, one of these days, she was bound to run into a boy skunk who wouldn't bolt. Then what would she do? I wasn't sure she had a backup plan in case her posturing didn't scare the stripes off each and every one of them.

"Baby girl!" I stood and walked around the side of my home, running a hand along the wall as I went. I'd inherited the historical antebellum house from my grandmother after my mom made it clear she was going to live out her dream of traveling the country in an RV with my stepfather. Last we'd talked, they'd hit the brakes in Washington State, enjoying a much cooler summer than we were having here.

I searched for a fluffy skunk tail among the native Tennessee wildflowers blooming against the side of the house. The red and orange firewheels, velvety yellow goldenrod, and bright purple chicory grew on their own, and since they were so beautiful, I left them to it. Unfortunately, there was still no sign of my skunk.

Lucy better not have wandered far. I didn't mind her tapping into her animal instincts, but I at least wanted to know she was safe.

Maybe she was snoozing under the apple tree. It was a nice, warm day for it. I needed to stay positive. There was no reason to worry.

Yet.

I set off for the apple tree and along the way spotted a ghostly buffalo nibbling at the tall grass where my property met a soybean field.

Frankie needed to keep my power *off* when we weren't working.

In the beginning, he'd been reluctant to share his energy. If he used up too much, he'd begin to lose body parts, starting at his feet. The missing parts always came back. Eventually. But it was never fun.

Ever since he began dating Molly Fletcher, though, a sweet young woman who'd passed away in the late 1800s, he'd had juice to spare.

Last night, he'd woken me from a dead sleep and asked me to help him cheat at poker. He wanted me to look over his buddy Suds's shoulder and then tip Frankie off to what cards Suds held.

"Absolutely not," I'd snapped, my typical store of grace and kindness at low tide thanks to the very early—or very late—hour.

4

I was a morning person, not a night owl. "I'm not going to stumble around my own kitchen like a fool in order to help you cheat at cards."

"I help you all the time," he'd countered. "And this is the thanks I get."

Frankie helped when coerced, and he never did things the right way. I'd told him such, and our conversation had gone downhill from there.

"Lucy!" I called, scanning the yard.

Not a creature stirred. Even the squirrels and birds had hunkered down for the hottest part of the day.

Waves of heat made Frankie's shed look like a mirage.

If only.

I pressed on.

In the gangster's defense, it wasn't his fault we were stuck with each other. My ex-fiancé had given me the urn full of his ashes as an offhand gift, and I'd mistaken it for an antique vase. I didn't have a lot of decorations in the house, and I'd been determined to make do.

My first step in cleaning up the old vase had been to shake out the grit in the bottom. Loose, ashy dirt is excellent for garden soil. Only it turned out I'd dumped most of Frankie's mortal remains under my favorite rosebush. To his dismay and mine, by the time Frankie turned up to yell at me, I'd watered him right into the ground, tying him to my property.

It had been an honest mistake.

We'd tried to separate his ashes from the dirt, but it hadn't worked. For now, at least, Frankie remained stuck here. The only way he could leave was when I carried the smidge of ashes that remained in his urn beyond the property line, usually in the interest of solving a murder. Lately, he'd taken to entertaining his gang and his girlfriend in my backyard, but I didn't see any sign of ghosts in the shed today.

And Lucy wasn't under the tree.

I stayed well away from Frankie's shed over on the far side of the water. Lucy wouldn't be anywhere near it. Lucy had taken an instant and active dislike to Frankie. The gangster pretended he didn't care one way or the other, but I could tell it irked him. The last place she would be was anywhere near his shed.

I made my way down toward the pond, my sandals sliding a bit on the grass. Sometimes Lucy liked to paw at the fish that bubbled up to tease her.

The air down by the pond was so damp it stuck to my skin, but I wasn't some Johnny-come-lately Yankee. My grandma always said summertime down South gave us girls the kind of dewy glow Northern ladies had to use makeup to get. Plus, the heat made my blond hair curl instead of falling straight. No product needed. Although today, I'd tied it up off the nape of my neck to keep me a little cooler.

I walked down to the edge of the water and scanned the tall grass for any sign of movement. "Who wants some skunk treats?" I called.

"Pipe down!" a familiar voice rasped behind me. That didn't keep the shock of it from nearly pitching me into the water.

I spun around. "Frankie!" He knew better than to sneak up behind me. Not that he cared.

He wore the clothes he'd died in: a pin-striped suit and a fat tie. Water dripped from his white Panama hat and ran in rivulets down his sharp, scowling face. To my astonishment, the water disappeared as soon as it fell away from him. It was as ghostly as he was. "You're blowing my cover," he snapped.

"I'm looking for my skunk," I countered. "Since when does taking a swim count as hiding out?"

"Don't be cute." He whipped the hat off his head and shook the water out, his momentary distraction displaying what he typically tried to hide: the perfectly round bullet hole in the center of his forehead. "Quit prowling around the pond," he added, planting the hat back on his head. "That investigator is after me."

I knew the one. "De Clercq," I clarified.

Frankie nodded.

We'd met Julien De Clercq on our last adventure. He'd been working to take down the mob when he died, and Frankie had been on his hit list. However, after we'd helped him solve his case a few weeks ago on the Sugarland Express, he'd agreed to get the charges against Frankie dropped if we assisted him on a case here in town that had stumped him for nearly a century. It was a good deal as far as I was concerned. "We want him to contact us," I assured Frankie. "Once we put his final case to bed, he'll be off your back. He may even go to the light. Play your cards right, and you could get rid of him for good."

Frankie glanced over his shoulder as if the investigator would pop up any second. "It's not that easy. What if we got lucky last time? I mean, if a top-notch detective like De Clercq can't find the answers, what makes you think I can?"

"You have me." It wasn't bragging. We might have our rough patches, but we did make a pretty solid team.

He huffed. "If you're going to talk nonsense, I'm leaving." He turned and glided out over the pond.

"Wait," I said. Naturally, he didn't listen. "Have you seen Lucy?" I called.

"Like that skunk would give me the time of day."

"Keep an eye out," I urged.

He turned to face me, holding onto his hat as he sank feet-first into my pond. "I can tell you with one hundred percent certainty that Lucy has not been sleeping with the fishes." I gave him my sternest glare, but he merely smirked, the water up to his chin now. "I'll let you know if I spot a swimming skunk. In the meantime, you don't see me."

And with that, he disappeared without even rippling the surface of the water.

I planted my hands on my hips. Fat lot of help he was. I was truly starting to worry about Lucy. She'd been an injured, wild skunk when I'd rescued her. After she recovered, I'd tried to release her into the wild, but she'd kept coming back. It seemed she preferred the petting and the cuddling and the cuisine. That skunk ate better than I did. If her mission to terrorize the male wild skunk population went sideways, she wouldn't have any idea what to do. And I'd be lost without her.

No. I couldn't think that way. I wasn't done looking. I started around the pond toward the little patch of blueberry bushes on the other side. If those couldn't tempt a roving skunk, nothing could.

The bushes were new as of this past spring, a gift from Lee Treadwell, one of my first ghost hunter clients. His family's stately mansion had stood uninhabited for decades. Well, uninhabited by the living, at any rate. It housed plenty of spirits, and to say that they'd caused Lee a whole heap of trouble would be understating it.

In the end, after we'd banished an evil spirit and reunited the ghosts of Lee's deceased ancestors, Lee had promised me all the fresh fruits and veggies from his garden that I could eat. I'd gladly taken him up on it, and when he offered to plant a few berry bushes at my house as well, I jumped at the chance. Ghost hunting was rewarding, but it didn't pay much, and my graphic design business had breathed its last thanks to our town matriarch's poisonous word of mouth. I'd been eating a lot of ramen until Lee came along. And as I drew closer, I saw I wasn't the only one appreciating our new bounty.

I rushed the last few steps, so relieved to see Lucy, ninja skunk and blueberry connoisseur, sprawled beneath the largest bush, fast asleep. Her tail twitched as if she were in the middle of a splendid dream, and berry juice stained the white streak under her chin purple.

I smiled as I crouched down next to her. "Looks like someone went hog wild," I murmured, reaching out to stroke her soft, fuzzy belly. Lucy didn't even stir. "It happens to the best of us." I'd have to put her bowl of bananas in the fridge and save it for dinner.

I glanced back at the house.

She seemed comfortable on the ground, but maybe I should pick her up and bring her inside with me anyway. She might wake up on the way there, but Lucy never turned down a cuddle, and once she was inside, she could settle down on my futon to finish her nap. Having her snuggled safe in bed would do more for me than for her at this point, but I didn't think she'd mind.

I stretched both hands out to pick her up, only to pull back at the last moment as my cell phone rang. I fumbled in my pocket for it and smiled when I saw the number. It was Ellis, my boyfriend.

Ellis and I had a sweet, fun, and somewhat complicated relationship, seeing as he was my ex-fiancé's older brother. It wasn't as crazy as it seemed. Or maybe it was. But Ellis and I were good together. He was strong and kind, and he had dimples that could make a girl rear back and clutch her heart. But it was more than that. Ellis Wydell was the most considerate man I'd ever met.

Then there was his brother...

Beau Wydell was the sort of man who'd been born on third base and thought he'd hit a triple. He'd been charming at first. But he'd also gotten drunk and hit on my sister the night before our wedding and then expected me to marry him anyway.

Of course, I'd refused. And when I didn't show up at the altar, he went ahead with the reception and mocked me in front of the whole town.

Shoving his smug face into our wedding cake had definitely been cathartic. But his highfalutin mother, Virginia Wydell, hadn't seen things my way. She'd sued me for the cost of the wedding she'd planned, the one that never happened. I'd about lost my house until Frankie came along, and chance led me to take my first ghost-hunting job.

Ellis had been the only member of his family willing to give me the benefit of the doubt after what happened between Beau and me. He'd also been my first official ghost-hunting client, and in the aftermath of solving the haunting at his Southern Spirits restaurant, we'd decided to give a relationship a try.

Over a year later, we were still going strong, and I was determined to keep things that way, no matter how many veiled insults and backhanded, Southern-style putdowns his mother dished out. Virginia might be used to ruling the town, but I wasn't having any of it in my personal life. Ellis was worth any discomfort.

I answered the call with a smile. "Hey, you'll never guess where I found Lucy—"

"Verity." The seriousness in his tone pulled me up short. This wasn't a lighthearted chat-over-his-lunch-break type of call. Ellis never sounded like this unless something bad had happened.

"What's wrong?" I stepped away from Lucy so I wouldn't wake her. "Are you okay?"

"I'm fine," he assured me, and I breathed a little easier. Of course he was fine. Ellis was a gifted police officer. He knew what he was doing. Still, his tone was clipped, on edge. "I'm at a crime scene, and I need your help."

Oh my. There was only one kind of crime scene where I could possibly tell Ellis anything he didn't already know. "Who died?"

"No one you know. Or at least I hope not." I could hear the wind whipping on the other end of the line. We didn't have so much as a breeze where I stood. "Verity," Ellis said, pulling me back to the present, "I'm at Wilson's quarry, and I need you to get down here right away."

CHAPTER 2

"Oh no." This didn't sound good. "Was it a murder?"

"We're not sure yet," Ellis said. He sounded frustrated. "That's what I'd like your help figuring out. It's...odd. The victim was found at the bottom of the ravine shortly after daybreak. You know how to get here?"

"Yes. Of course." Who didn't? We used to toss rocks off the edge of the ravine at Wilson's quarry when we were kids. Back then, sharp drop-offs felt fascinatingly dangerous. But after my adventures with Frankie, in which I'd nearly met my death twice on two separate cliffsides, I found them to be more frightening than fun.

"There's no obvious evidence of foul play," Ellis continued, "and the coroner's taken a look and ruled it an accident."

"But you don't buy it." Ellis had good instincts when it came to these sorts of things. And I didn't have a lot of faith in our local coroner. Raymond Thornberry was as stingy with his time as he was with his tips at the diner. He and I had disagreed earlier this summer on a cause of death, and I'd been right. If Ellis's gut told him there was something fishy going on, he was wise to investigate.

"Trouble is, I have no evidence. I thought if you could come here and tune in to the other side, you could give us some insight into how this poor girl died, maybe point us in the right direction. It'll have to be fast, though. Ray wants to remove the body, and he's getting impatient."

"I'll be there as soon as I can," I promised. On a day like today, I could understand why the coroner was in a hurry. A body wouldn't last long in heat like this.

I could almost hear Ellis's tight grip on the phone, the way he gritted his jaw. "Thanks. The quicker, the better. It's not just Ray giving me grief."

I could believe that. It was no secret in town that I could talk to spirits, thanks to an unfortunate 911 call that had recorded me confessing my unusual ability, coupled with the investigative talent of our local eager-beaver reporter, Ovis Dupree. He should have retired twenty years ago, but he was as keen to hunt down a hot story as a person half his age. A woman who spoke to the dead? That was juicy news as far as Ovis was concerned.

At least half the people in Sugarland thought I was a kook making up a crazy talent to get attention, and a good many of those people worked with Ellis.

He believed in me, of course. It would be hard not to after the things we'd been through together. But he'd never gone out on a limb to bring me into an active investigation before. I wouldn't disappoint him. "I'll head out now. Where is the scene?"

He told me to head to the south entrance to the quarry off Tilbert Road, and I promised I'd be there in a flash.

It looked like Lucy would get to sleep under the blueberry bushes after all.

I hurried back to the pond. I might be tuned in to the ghostly realm, but if I wanted to do my best job, I'd need Frankie along. He possessed the kind of insight a person could only get from nine decades on the other side.

"Frankie," I said, toeing the water, not wanting to shock him like he had done to me.

A fish bobbed to the surface, swished its tail, and splashed back into the depths of the pond.

"Frankie," I called louder. "Paging gangster Frankie Winkelmann."

"Do you *mind*?" his strained voice sounded in my ear.

Oh, good. I had his attention. "Listen. We have a new job, and it starts now."

"Hiding out is a full-time job. Especially when you're around."

"Cute."

Only I didn't have time for banter. Ellis was waiting at a murder scene.

I tucked an errant strand of hair behind my ear. "I mean it, Frank. I need you back on shore. Now." It wasn't like I could drag the gangster out of the pond.

Touching Frankie would give us both a huge shock. Worse, it would send him straight down through the muddy bottom when I needed him focused and working with me.

Just my luck, Frankie had a flair for the dramatic.

He rose out of the depths like the ghost of Davy Jones, water cascading down his hollowed-out cheeks, his coal-black eyes hot enough to burn a hole right through me—if I'd been intimidated by that type of show. Unfortunately for Frankie, we'd been through too much for me to be scared of him now.

"Ellis has a new case," I told him. "There's a dead lady in a ravine waiting for us."

"There's a dead guy right here who asked you to leave him alone," Frankie growled.

"I can't do it without you." As I said the words, I realized I was right. I didn't know how to tell a natural death from a murder. When people died, their souls left traces behind. Frankie knew how to read them, but I didn't. I couldn't do a good job for Ellis without Frankie there.

The gangster shook his head slowly. Then the whisper of a grin tugged at his upper lip. He had me over a barrel, and he knew it. I swear he had a sixth sense for the minute he could begin to capitalize on, well, anything.

He drifted across the pond toward me, his feet trailing in the water. "You want to make a bargain?" he prompted, his innocent tone not fooling anybody.

Bargaining with Frankie was like trying to teach a cat to fetch a ball. It was intelligent enough for the task, just completely disinterested in playing along.

I planted my hands on my hips. I'd already built him a shed. I'd already let him invite his friends over, a disproportionate number of whom had tried to off me after we'd stumbled into their hideout.

I'd already tried to give him his freedom, but we hadn't figured out how to do that yet.

In the meantime, Ellis was relying on me. He'd gone out on a limb to involve me in this case, and I was going to honor that by doing my best for him.

I sighed and dropped my arms. It was time to live dangerously. "What do you want?"

The sudden gleam in Frankie's eyes almost made me want to take it back, but the clock was ticking, and the stakes hadn't changed. We stared at each other in silence for a moment before he broke out in a broad smile. "How about I help you now, and you'll owe me a favor to be named later."

It was like making a deal with the devil. Only I didn't have a choice. "Done," I said quickly before I could change my mind.

He tipped his hat to me. "It's a pleasure doing business with you." His good humor faded fast. "Now get me out of here before De Clercq sees me."

And just like that, I realized I'd done him the favor.

CHAPTER 3

I fetched Frankie's urn from the house and placed it next to me on the passenger side of the 1978 avocado green Cadillac I'd inherited from my grandmother.

The gangster glided straight through the door, straightening his tie with one hand as he took a seat. He'd tucked the other hand in his jacket, most likely gripping his revolver.

"Let's get out of here," he said, keeping an eye on the yard.

"As you wish." I *ka-chunked* my relic of a car into gear and steered down the side drive, bouncing over the gravel.

I didn't relish the idea of getting up close and personal with a recent murder scene—or spending the afternoon with Frankie— but if it meant I could help Ellis gain some insight, it would be worth it. I took us down the long driveway from my house and turned left onto a country road that led to another, slightly more rural route. I hadn't been this way in years. Most of the time when we were kids, my sister and I had ridden our bikes to the quarry, cutting through yards and fields. Heck, driving probably took longer.

As we lurched over the dirt road that led down toward the quarry, we passed the old McNairy farm stand and a peach grove. There was no sign for Tilbert Road, but I saw two patrol cars parked on the shoulder next to a pecan orchard. A narrow dirt road between them led into the grove. Part of the quarry lay beyond. This must be it.

Tree limbs slapped the passenger windows of my car as I tried to park as far off the road as I could.

"Remind me never to let you drive the getaway car," Frankie muttered as a particularly large branch popped against the window by his head.

"You'd have to drag me into the driver's seat and tie me to the wheel," I said, mostly satisfied with my parking job.

Frankie pulled his hat down firmly. "Let's get this over with."

The walk through the orchard turned out to be the best part of my day. The trees were tall enough to cast a lot of shade, but the nuts weren't quite ripe enough to have fallen en masse yet, so there wasn't much to slide on underfoot. I'd never taken the time to appreciate it as a kid. "What a pretty place," I mused.

"What a weird place," Frankie said, his hands shoved into his pockets, his shoulders hunched. "You'd think there'd be a ghost or two wandering around a plot this big, but I'm not seeing anybody or anything."

I brushed a hand against a branch laden with green leaves. "Maybe you're just the dominant ghost here."

Frankie snorted. "I can't haunt everywhere at once, sweetheart." He shook his head. "No, if there were a spirit here, these trees would probably look a lot smaller. Or there wouldn't even be an orchard. How old is this place?"

"You should know. You're from Sugarland."

He scanned the trees. "I didn't exactly hang out in pecan orchards."

True. "I think it was here when my grandmother was a girl." Although I couldn't be certain. I almost wished there was another ghost here just so we could see the history of the land. Experiencing the other side was a bit like stepping out of a time machine. But I supposed we didn't have time for that anyhow, at least not at the moment.

A stout man in a Sugarland PD jacket carrying a camera strode toward us. I knew him on sight, the same way I knew most people in town. In this case, I'd gone to high school with his sister. "Hi, Walt." I smiled.

He frowned and kept walking.

Ouch.

Frankie drew back from him as he passed. "Ah, the first of the fuzz. At least we know we're in the right spot."

I peered over my shoulder after Walt. I knew I was a persona non grata in this town after clashing with the Wydells and coming out as a ghost hunter, but I'd hoped for a little more warmth. Then again, Ellis had broken protocol by calling me here. That wouldn't be a popular choice.

I couldn't let it get to me. I'd just have to prove Ellis right by doing a good job and then getting the heck out of here.

Still... I scanned the orchard. Frankie was right. There were no ghosts to be found. If the same was true at the ravine, that could be a problem.

Ghosts tended to be territorial. And if one had witnessed the death in the ravine, I might be able to get a first-hand account. It would go a long way toward showing Ellis and the police where to look for clues.

When Walt was hopefully out of earshot, I turned my attention to the gangster. "Frankie, if there are no ghosts here, we're not going to be able to do much, are we?" I didn't want to think it, but the fact was that without ghostly witnesses to give me insights, there wasn't much I'd be able to do that a regular detective couldn't.

He ran a hand over his mouth and chin. "Just because nobody's lurking around in the orchard doesn't mean there won't be a ghost in the ravine. People haunt the craziest places." He adjusted his hat. "I once met a gal who clocked out in rush-hour traffic. She's sitting on Highway 64 to this day."

Jeez Louise. I'd much rather haunt a pretty pecan orchard.

Another minute's walk and we reached the edge of the orchard. Shortly beyond the line where the trees ended, the ground rose for about five feet, and then dropped abruptly.

Ellis waited for us on the rise, along with another officer I recognized named Duranja. Ellis appeared relieved to see us, while Duranja scrutinized me like I held some kind of unnatural power over his fellow officer.

Ellis met me halfway and took my hand to help me up the last few steep feet. "You made it."

"I'm sorry it took so long," I said with a sidelong glance at Frankie.

Ellis released my hand and cleared his throat. "Thanks for coming." He lowered his voice. "Is Frankie here?" A moment later he shivered, and I felt the chill in the air. Frankie had hit him with a cold spot. The ghost cackled while Ellis shook it off.

"That wasn't necessary," I murmured. Frankie merely grinned.

"So, you can't go down to the actual crime scene," Ellis said. "Is this close enough?"

"It's fine," I said, peering over the edge of the cliff and suppressing a shudder. The coroner and his assistant stood at the bottom, looking rather irritated. In front of them lay the body of a woman, sprawled facedown across the rocks at the bottom of the ravine. It was a ways down, but from my vantage point, I could see where the blood had seeped beneath her, forming a halo of gore. A ghostly, burnt orange vapor curled from under her, almost like someone had draped her over a smoke machine.

"Did she fall onto something?" I asked.

"Yeah." Duranja snickered. "Rocks."

Ellis shot him a sharp look. "There's nothing noteworthy beneath the body, if that's what you mean."

"Interesting." It was normal for the newly deceased to leave a mark as the soul left the body. Death spots appeared bright white, with glowing tendrils of light reaching toward the heavens. I'd never seen this color before. "What does the orange mean, Frankie?"

He surveyed the scene. "Don't that beat all. I haven't seen an orange plume since Pinhead MacKenzie accidentally walked in front of a streetcar on Wabash Avenue." He eyed me. "That one was an accident, one hundred percent. He couldn't keep his eyes off this dame. She walked like she had a brass bell for a bottom, and—"

"So it means an accidental death?" I prodded, keeping him on track.

"Not always," Frankie said, focusing again on the body. "It means that death was a shock, but without any fight beforehand." He huffed. "With my crowd, you usually see the violence. It glows red. Almost everybody who was anybody had that. Dying a nasty death is practically a rite of passage for the South Town Boys."

"Poor gangsters," I murmured.

Frankie squinted at me as if he was trying to figure out what made me tick. "Who'd want to go because of something boring like *old age?*"

I would. I really, really would, but now wasn't the time to get into it. I passed on Frankie's insights to Ellis.

He didn't appear convinced. "It's not easy to fall off this ravine. You'd have to walk right up here to the edge and lean into it."

"Could have been suicide," Duranja suggested. "Assuming your girlfriend isn't nuts."

"Thanks for that," I told him.

"But there was no note," Ellis said, completely wrapped up in the case. "I'm not going to rule out the possibility of foul play unless we have some evidence of suicide."

"Okay, well, we don't have any ID for her either," Duranja pointed out. "Maybe she left her note wherever home is."

"Then she drove to Sugarland to die?" Ellis asked. "One of us would recognize her if she lived around here, and we don't have a car or tire tracks."

"Say she did commit suicide," I suggested, for the sake of argument. "If she meant to kill herself, would death be a surprise?" I wasn't sure. "It could have been a cry for help that didn't go as planned," I reasoned. "Or she could have been pushed. That would be a shock, yet not overly violent." I looked at Frankie. "Is there anyone dead that we can find and ask?"

He shook his head. "Sorry, babe. We're all alone here."

"We can walk the pecan orchard again," I told him. "Maybe someone will turn up."

Frankie looked at me like I was nuts. "Ghosts are supposed to start haunting a spot because you want them there?"

With a shrug, I turned to Ellis. "It seems we're at a dead end. Without any ghosts to question, all I can do is read the death spot."

He nodded, frustrated. "I understand. It's fine. It's more than we had before."

"Not much more," Duranja muttered. "And we waited, what? An hour?"

Ellis forced a pleasant expression and turned to his fellow officer. "Looks like we're done here. How about you climb to the bottom and help the coroner bring her up?"

Duranja's jaw dropped. "What, all the way down there?"

Ellis just stared at him.

"I mean, yes, sir." He began to head down, and I looked down at the poor girl again. No matter how she died, I felt sorry for her.

"Thanks for your help, Verity." Ellis inclined his head toward the orchard. "I'll walk you back to your car."

"Always the gentleman," I said, earning a smile. "I wish I could have done more."

"We did plenty," Frankie said, gliding next to us. "Personally, I think it's a little insulting that you expect ghosts to haunt a spot simply because it's convenient for you."

I ignored him and took Ellis's arm. "I enjoyed the movies last night," I told him as he guided me through the trees. We'd been spending a lot of time together, and I was starting to count this summer as my favorite despite some of the more hair-raising ghost encounters.

Tall, broad-shouldered, and scandalously attractive in his uniform, his presence made me feel a little happier despite my reason for being here.

I had it bad.

If the way he was smiling at me was any indication, he had it bad too. *Good.*

"I'm glad things are going so well," he said as soon as we were completely alone, "because I have a proposition for you." He stopped to face me and took my hands in his. He hesitated, which was unlike him. And I could tell he was about to ask me something big.

My stomach danced, and I wondered if I was going to be happy with what he had to say or not.

It wasn't as if this could be anything huge. We'd only been dating a year. We'd agreed to take it slow.

"My mother is hosting a barbecue tonight. She invited the two of us as of—" he tilted his head and gave a mock look of exasperation "—about ten minutes before you got here. It's pretty last minute."

And it was at the home of the town matriarch, the woman who'd sworn to ruin me. Then again, if I was to have any future with Ellis, I had to figure out some way to make a truce with his mother.

With that in mind, I forced a smile. "I'd love to go."

Ellis didn't appear convinced. "Are you sure?"

"I am," I said, this time with more conviction.

I could handle this. Or at least I'd like to try.

An invitation from Virginia was a positive step, and I refused to be too prideful to accept it.

"After we solved the murder on the train last month, I think your mother and I came to a new, well, sort of an understanding." I'd hoped that meant she would reach out, or that we could at least be more cordial when we inevitably ran into each other. "This is a good sign."

"Don't get too excited," Ellis cautioned, taking my hand to lead me around a jutting tree root. "Beau has a new girlfriend, and Mom wants to check her out. I think this is her excuse to get us all in the same place and torture us."

I thought back to the awkward dinner we'd had with Beau's last girlfriend. That unfortunate woman had ended up dead. At least this dinner would go better. It had to.

"I won't let your mom bait me," I vowed.

"Hold on to that thought." Ellis sighed.

My boyfriend had his own troubles with Virginia Wydell. Ellis was the black sheep of the family for following his heart and going into law enforcement instead of becoming a lawyer like his other brothers. His mother never let him forget it.

"Just be on your guard," Ellis advised. "Mom expressly warned me to keep you in line tonight. Beau's been telling mom that you might still have a thing for him."

I had to fight my urge to scoff. "Seriously?" Beau's ego knew no bounds.

"Hey, I don't invent the crazy, I just deliver the news." Ellis ducked under a lower hanging branch. The man was seriously tall.

"I still want to go. For you," I said, tugging at him. "For us," I added, succeeding in slowing him down. "Also, how does Beau have another girlfriend already?" We'd barely been home a month after the train trip.

Ellis chuckled. "You know Beau. He falls in love fast."

Boy, did he ever. He always had. When he and I had met, I'd been convinced it was love at first sight. Beau had a way of making you feel special, one of a kind. He gave the impression he would hand you the moon on a silver string if only you asked for it. I'd always been a pretty sensible person, but spending time around a hot-to-trot Beau Wydell was like being sucked into a whirlpool. "Who is she?" I asked.

"She's new in town," Ellis replied, his expression pensive. "She's been getting permits for her business for the past couple of weeks. That's how they met, I think. She needed legal advice. She's opening up a food truck. Sugarland's first."

A food truck! Well, that would be fun. Hopefully, it would inspire some more. Sugarland could use that kind of innovation. "She sounds like a smart businesswoman. Your mother must be proud."

Ellis squeezed my hand. "Don't count on it."

"I don't know, Ellis. Maybe your mother has mellowed a little." Virginia and I *did* have a moment back on the train. She'd saved my life. We'd worked together for once. "Facing danger like we did on the Sugarland Express can change a person."

"She tried to set me up with a girl from out of town just last week," Ellis said dryly.

"Sometimes the changes are subtle at first." He'd told me about that, and it was…not encouraging. But still. "You let her know that was unacceptable," I pointed out. "This could be a chance for us to start fresh."

I'd seen a glimmer of real, hard-won growth in Virginia, and if I didn't give her space to be a better person, she never would. People couldn't be put into a box and tucked away, never allowed to adapt.

If tonight didn't work out, well, at least I'd attempted to be the bigger person. "Let's try to have faith," I said, squeezing his arm.

We reached the cars. Before I could take another step toward mine, Ellis gently leaned down and kissed me. I closed my eyes and wrapped my arms around his shoulders, savoring the feeling of his lips on mine. A kiss from Ellis was better than sweet tea on a hot summer day.

"I like how you think," he finally said once he pulled away, a little breathless. "Even if it is pretty optimistic."

"Can't help it," I said, trailing a finger down his tan uniform shirt.

My grandma had taught me the power of looking at the bright side, and I was counting on that now.

Besides, optimism would give me the courage I needed to attend this barbeque.

There was still some fear, sure. But I'd wear his mother down eventually. I was more than a match for Virginia Wydell.

And I intended to prove it.

CHAPTER 4

*F*ive hours later, I steered the land yacht up the twisting road along the river bluff that led to a private driveway flanked by ornate iron gates with the letter *W* emblazoned in a smart monogram-style script. Ah, the family homestead.

The Wydells had owned their property even longer than our family had lived in my home. This estate had been in the family dating back to the land grants in the early 1800s. The white plantation-style house, with its upper and lower porches and towering Palladian windows, had been designed to appear as if it had always been here. In truth, the place had gone up in 1982, after Virginia married into the family. Word had it she'd been instrumental in razing the family's original home and replacing it with this overblown version of Tara.

She'd also gotten a special permit to bulldoze the old-growth trees on the back of the property. That way, the house looked down on the river, as well as the entire town of Sugarland.

Tonight, the gates stood open, and I drove right through.

Towering cypress trees lined the meandering drive that wound past small, carefully tended gardens of native purple passionflowers and American beautyberry.

I turned a sharp curve past a lovely grouping of magnolias, and Frankie's urn slid out of my purse and across the passenger-side floor.

"Hey, watch it," he warned.

I glanced at the mobster lounging in the seat next to mine. "You're lucky I let you come along at all."

"Sure." He stuck a hand through the window to catch the breeze. "You need a favor, and it's, 'Frankie, oh Frankie, abandon your hideout and schlep out into the wilderness with me.' But—"

"It was a pecan orchard," I reminded him.

"—I need a favor, and it's Frankie the third wheel."

Heavens. "I never called you that," I reminded him. In fact, I'd agreed rather easily to let him accompany me tonight when he popped up in the middle of my bath and scared us both half to death. I mean, what did he think I was doing in there? Painting my nails?

"You're going to have to face Special Investigator De Clercq one of these days," I said, steering past a stone wood nymph frolicking amid a bed of purple emperor flowers.

"Don't remind me," he said, turning his head to stare out the window.

Frankie had found a ghostly summons, written on official police stationery, tacked to his shed when he'd returned home from the ravine. Apparently, we'd just missed the investigator. "You can't avoid him forever."

"I'll take that as a challenge," Frankie said as we neared the circle drive to the house. Cars lined the narrow shoulder of the road. This was a bigger party than I'd expected.

We pulled past the richly blooming blue and white hydrangea bushes that crowded the circle drive and scattered flower petals over the custom brick. "In the meantime, I wouldn't mind casing this joint again. There's a lot of quality stuff in here."

26

"You are *not* to plan a robbery of this house," I warned.

"Not with De Clercq closing in," Frankie groused.

Ah, well, the investigator wasn't my favorite person, either. But perhaps police surveillance had its advantages.

Several cars stood in the driveway, including Ellis's cruiser. He leaned against the side panel, looking all casual. But I knew the truth. He'd waited so that we could walk in together.

He was still in his uniform, which was most likely deliberate. Ellis's parents vocally disapproved of his profession, so every now and then he took pains to remind them that he was doing precisely what he felt called to do.

I left Frankie's urn in the car and stepped out to greet my man.

He smiled at me and held out a hand as I drew near. "You look beautiful," he said, and I could tell by the way he looked at me that he meant it.

I laughed. I couldn't help it. "I'm wearing the same thing you saw me in earlier."

He tugged me closer. "You were beautiful then too, but your hair's down now. It's a little different."

"If you say so."

I had taken care with my hair and a little makeup. I wanted this night to go well. And as we stepped up to the porch, I said a little prayer for Ellis, for me, and for Beau's poor new girlfriend, who probably had no idea what she was getting into.

"Here we go," Ellis murmured as he rapped on the brass door knocker.

"I can do this," I reminded us both.

Virginia herself met us at the door, looking every inch the stylish grande dame of Sugarland. Her platinum blond hair dusted her shoulders in a sleek bob, her ears glittered with diamond studs, and around her neck lay a delicate gold and silver filigree cross that used to belong to me.

I stared at it as my body went numb and my brain buzzed with the desire to snatch it right off her neck.

That cross had been my grandmother's, given to her by my grandfather on their wedding day. I'd been forced to sell it to an antique dealer to pay Virginia back for the wedding that never was. Virginia, of course, had bought it. I think she only wore it when I was around, to remind me of her status compared to mine. *I nearly brought you down. I could do it again.*

It pained me deeply to realize nothing had changed.

If anything, Virginia's petty reminder was more caustic now because I'd let myself believe that she could be a better person.

"Ellis." Her smile held all the warmth of a winter sun. "And Verity. It's so nice you could make it." She exchanged an air-kiss with Ellis but didn't even offer to shake my hand. She stepped back, her green silk dress swishing. "The party is out back. You can walk through the house. And, Ellis, do say hello to some of your father's business associates, won't you? Try not to get into a conversation though. No one needs to get bogged down in the nitty-gritty of what you do, darling." Her eyes had strayed to me. "Of what either of you does."

In other words, no cop talk, no ghost hunter talk. Never mind that ghost hunting and police work had helped solve the murders on the Sugarland Express—a train that Virginia and Beau had both invested heavily in.

"You certainly didn't mind having a ghost hunter around when you needed one," I said, breezing past her.

"Leave the past in the past, dear," she said, her fingers lingering on her throat near my grandmother's necklace.

Fine talk, coming from her. But I kept walking. I'd said my piece.

Ellis, on the other hand, couldn't quite let it go. "You need to take your own advice, Mother," he said gently but firmly.

Oh my. I stopped short of the palatial dining room that led to an even more massive kitchen with a big beautiful door to the backyard. I'd come wanting peace and understanding, not a toe-to-toe debate with Virginia.

"Move on, Mamma," he said to Virginia. "Verity is trying and so should you." She gasped, but he kept going, his tone gentle, and his intention clear. "While you're at it, realize no amount of your criticism is going to change us."

Virginia stood, stunned as if she'd been slapped, her hand still at her throat. Her fingers tightened on my necklace before she let go. She blinked once, twice, as she composed herself. "While I'm not used to my own son questioning my guidance and my love," she said, "I admit you may be right—about your situation at least." She glared past him to me. "No amount of reason seems to work with you two."

Not her brand of reason at least. Her mouth tightened, the lines around it deepening, and I gave her a sweet smile in return.

Her mask of serene civility fell into place once more as Virginia directed her attention back to her middle son. "There's another matter I'd like to discuss with you before you go outside with your...Verity." She couldn't even say girlfriend. "We have a family situation that may change your attitude when it comes to rash decisions."

"Mother—" Ellis began to wave her off.

"Please." She touched his arm. "It won't take long, and I do need you for this." She gave his arm a squeeze. "Come with me to the study."

Ellis winced. I could tell he was torn.

"Go," I said. She wouldn't leave him alone until he did. And at this point, being left alone was all I wanted from Virginia.

He walked over to me. "Do you mind?" he asked, with all the enthusiasm of a man about to face a firing squad.

I didn't see how he could avoid it. "I'll be fine," I said. As he leaned down to kiss me on the cheek, I smiled and added, "She'd better not have a date for you back there."

Although come to think of it, I wouldn't put it past her.

Ellis and I shared a grin. "Hit the party and grab a drink," he said. "You could probably use one. I'll see what she has to say," he added without relish.

Whatever it was, he could handle it.

"I'll be quick," he promised.

"No worries," I said, heading out toward the kitchen and the backyard beyond. "I'm bound to find somebody I know." This was Sugarland, after all.

I stepped out back with a smile, and what I saw made me pause. I'd known from the cars out front that this was no simple family barbecue. In fact, I wasn't sure this would qualify as a barbecue at all. It was more like a garden party.

I skimmed a hand down my purple cotton sundress and thanked heaven I liked to wear dresses as a rule. As it stood, I fit in quite well. The men smoking cigars by the bar sported polo shirts or lightweight seersucker suits. A group of women admiring the old-growth sassafras tree had even braved the lawn in high heels.

Light jazz music filtered through the crowd, and my attention focused on a massive white tent in the center of the expansive backyard overlooking the river. A dozen round tables covered in ecru linens lined up like soldiers at the ready, half of them already occupied. The food was catered, with roving waiters passing out appetizers and uniformed staff manning the buffet tables.

Most interesting of all, as I stepped out among the chatting groups of partygoers, I didn't recognize a soul.

I hadn't believed such a thing could be possible. Not in our small town.

And not with this size of a crowd. There had to be at least sixty people here. I paused just short of the main tent. "What on heaven and earth..." I began.

"Refreshment?" A waiter appeared at my left, holding a tray of mint juleps so cold that a thin layer of white frost clung to the silver cups.

"Gladly," I said, taking a glass. The ginger-haired waiter sported a tightly clipped beard, though he couldn't have been more than twenty years old. "Tell me, where are you from?" I asked, nudging the decorative mint leaf aside and taking a sip.

"Silver Spoon Catering in Memphis," he said, offering me a napkin.

"Interesting," I mused, and not just because anyone from fifty miles in any direction would have given his neighborhood instead of his employer.

I tasted the perfect mix of sweet syrup, mint, and smoky bourbon. At least the big-city folks knew how to make a proper mint julep.

Virginia usually booked local businesses. Unless... Perhaps most of these people were from out of town as well? I scanned the crowd. I didn't see any of Virginia's heritage society friends, or anyone from Sugarland for that matter.

Well, I'd just have to make a few new friends and show them how friendly we were around here.

"Yikes," a soft voice said from behind me. I turned as a tall, cute girl in flowy boho shorts and a maroon T-shirt drew up next to me. Her eyes widened as she took in the crowd. "This is the weirdest picnic I've ever seen. No offense," she corrected, with a nervous glance at me, "but I feel like I came ready for ultimate Frisbee, not croquet."

"I don't know if these folks have even seen a Frisbee before," I said, hopefully putting her at ease. I held out a hand. "Hi, I'm Verity Long."

She shook it with a bright, relieved smile. "Zoey Lee. I thought this was a barbeque," she said, with a distinctly Northern twang. "Hamburgers on the grill, maybe a few hot dogs," she added longingly.

I could understand the mistake. She wasn't from around here. "A few quick things on the grill is a cookout," I explained. "Barbeque is an event. Still, Virginia—as usual—has taken it to an entirely different level."

"Well, I suppose that explains it," she said, clearly trying to get her head around it. "Please don't judge me by my lack of seersucker, pastel, or flowered anything."

"I never would," I vowed. "Still, you should know one thing about life in the South," I began, and I'd tell it to her plain. "If it stands still long enough, we monogram it."

"Yikes," she snorted.

I loved being a Southern girl, but I could see how our habits might not appeal to everyone. Besides, Zoey had her own quirky style. She wore a gleaming set of thin gold bangles on her right wrist and a pair of what looked like handcrafted cat-face earrings. She let her medium-length dark hair curl naturally down her back, and compared to most of the people here, her minimal makeup was as good as no makeup at all.

She took a sip of her white wine. "I have to admit I'm a little out of my element," she said, scanning the crowd. "My date is off placating his mother."

Holy geez. "Are you with Beau?" Virginia was the only one I could think of that would pull a stunt like that at a party.

She gave a smitten grin. "Guilty."

Wow. She wasn't like any of the surgically enhanced, nipped, and tucked girls I'd seen him with since we'd broken up. She seemed nice. Wholesome. Friendly, too.

"I'm with Ellis," I said, watching for her reaction. If she knew the story of my past relationship with Beau, she didn't let on.

"Ellis..." she said, chewing on her lip, "that's Beau's oldest brother, right?"

"Middle brother." Harrison was the oldest and a chip off the Wydell block. He was a district judge, and even when I'd maintained a good relationship with the family, Harrison had still never spoken more than a dozen words to me. "Ellis is the police officer."

"Oh, right! My uncle was a sergeant on the force in Santa Anna. He told some great stories. I'm sure Ellis has some good ones, too." She let out a sigh of relief. "I'm so glad I walked over to you. You looked like the only normal one." She gasped. "I'm sorry. That came out wrong. What I meant to say is you look like my kind of people. Which is good," she added. Color flooded her cheeks as she looked out over the garden party. "I was starting to think that my kind of people didn't exist in this place."

"If it makes you feel better, I don't know anyone, either," I said, scanning the crowd again just to make sure. I spotted Ellis and Beau's older brother in the distance, chatting up some of the guests. "Except for Harrison," I said, giving in to the urge to point to the stiff, handsome man with the dark brown hair and start of a middle-aged spread. He hadn't even looked our way. "I'm thinking these are a bunch of his out-of-town lawyer friends." Hence the froufrou catering company. And the fact that everyone appeared to be mingling in established groups. "You know what? I'm starving," I said to Zoey. "Want to go get some food and stake out a table for the guys?"

Her shoulders relaxed, and her smile returned. "I do." We started out across the yard. "Do you think we'll stumble over any ornamental peacocks or something on the way to the buffet?"

I laughed. "No, but don't walk too hard on the designer grass."

"You're kidding, right?" she asked, not sure, cracking us both up.

After a trip down the buffet line, we settled at the table farthest from the crowd with plates of appetizers for us and the guys—if they ever showed up.

Virginia had selected a Southern-style menu: mini grits and greens, fried green tomato sliders, mini buttermilk chicken and waffles, and more. It was everything you'd expect at a down-home barbeque, only a third of the size. I supposed that made it more elegant.

"This looks amazing," Zoey said, with the enthusiasm of a true foodie.

"Welcome to Sugarland," I told her.

The food was terrific, the buttermilk chicken crispy and

seasoned perfectly, the waffles hot off the grill. The baby cornbread and pulled pork didn't hold a candle to my best friend Lauralee's recipe, but then again, not much did.

Zoey and I spent a few minutes taking the edge off our hunger, and I gave her points for scarfing down our local delicacies like she'd been born to it.

"So, I hear you run a food truck," I said. "That sounds like fun."

She brightened. "It is. I tested the concept in California, but I want to settle in and make a real start here. That's the plan, at least." Zoey put down the remains of her fried green tomato slider and wiped her hands on a fancy cloth napkin. Her nails were cut short but painted with little white and yellow daisies. "I'm still working out some of the logistical details. I designed the menu and the truck to be funky and different. You need that if you're going to sell at the beaches in Ventura." Her cheeks colored. "That was the plan before my old boyfriend dumped me," she added, her embarrassment evident. "He got the condo in the split. I took my half of the equity and decided it was time to move on, do what I wanted for a change. I bought an RV, loaded my truck onto a trailer, and headed east."

"That's brave of you," I told her. Despite my very public and embarrassing breakup with Beau, I had never contemplated leaving Sugarland.

Zoey blushed harder. "I needed a clean slate. It's kind of weird, but until we broke up, I never realized how much of my life he controlled. Like, what we ate, where we went, even the kind of car I drove. It was all him."

Yikes. "That's not good," I said, pushing away my plate to focus on our conversation. "You need to be your own person."

She nodded. "I'm working on it. I was sad about him for a while, but the farther I drove, the better I felt. I explored the southwest and kept going. I liked being...free." She shook her head as if amazed she'd done it. "It did get lonely, though. And even if I had cash from the condo, it was time to settle down and find a place to open up the truck again. Then I pulled in to Sugarland," she said as if that were the be-all and end-all.

In my opinion, it kind of was. "This is a good spot," I agreed. "But why Sugarland?" I was always curious to know how outsiders saw our town.

"The people are so nice," she said. "I pulled into town just to get gas. And I was standing there, fighting with the gas cap. The thing never comes off right. An older woman with wild gray hair did it for me. Then she pretended it was nothing."

"You don't happen to remember her name, do you?" I asked.

"Maisie," Zoey supplied without hesitation. "I was a little emotional about it, which actually made her grumpy at first." She laughed. "Of course, that just made it worse. I'd been so frustrated and feeling so alone that I started crying. She didn't know what to do."

That sounded like Maisie. A heart of gold buried under a pound of gruff. "She sometimes takes a bit to warm up to new people," I explained.

"She had baby rabbits in her truck and shoved one into my arms while my RV filled up. She said it would be good for both me and the bunny." Zoey accepted a water glass from a passing waiter. "Of course, now I want a bunny."

"How could you not?" I asked. If I didn't have Lucy, I'd have brought home one of Maisie's bunnies by now.

"Maisie let me hold that little fluff of fur and love on it and snuggle." Zoey sighed. "Then she announced I was good people, took her rabbit back, and drove away. She was like a combination of Triple-A and mobile bunny therapy."

"Only in Sugarland," I told her.

Zoey nodded in complete agreement. "Then my tablet died, but I needed to buy more credit for my phone, so I went to use a computer at the library, and this incredibly nice girl took a ton of time to help me figure out where I might be able to park my RV, where to go for food truck permits, and who could supply me if I wanted to open up the truck for a day or two. She even talked her boss into letting me park my truck in the town square, right in front of the library. Way above and beyond." Zoey snapped her fingers. "She was super sweet. What was her name…?"

"Melody?" I suggested.

"Yeah, that's the girl!"

"That's my sister." That was exactly the sort of thing she did, too. Melody had half a dozen almost-degrees to her name, which came in handy at the library. She was great at research and could help people find out anything they needed to know. But what she loved, what she talked about every day, were the people she met.

Zoey gave a rueful grin. "Small world."

"Small town," I countered. "If you're planning to stay here, you'd better get used to it. Nothing stays secret for long."

Zoey shrugged. "No worries. I don't have anything to hide. I'm not that interesting."

If she only knew. The rumor mill would churn overtime when word got out she was dating Beau Wydell. I wanted to warn her—about that and about him. But I wasn't sure exactly how to put it. Or if it was even my place. We'd just met, and Beau obviously hadn't told her about me yet.

"Melody even talked to Maisie," Zoey was saying, "and convinced her to rent me space on her land to park my RV."

I snapped back to attention. "That's great." Maisie could use the company, and it seemed Zoey could use a friend.

Maisie Hatcher didn't live all that far from me. I'd helped find a small fortune that Maisie's husband had buried right before he died, and in exchange, she'd given me a loan that helped me hold onto my house until I could pay off all of my debt to Virginia. Ellis regularly went over and did odd jobs for her as well. It sounded like we'd be seeing a lot of Zoey in the future.

Zoey propped her chin on her hand. "Between Maisie, Melody, and Beau, I've got a good feeling about this town."

Maisie and Melody…yes. As for Beau? Well, with any luck her

experience would be completely different from mine. Beau had said he wanted to change, and Zoey was a stark departure from the girls he'd dated after me.

"Earth to Verity," Zoey teased, and I realized I'd spaced out on her again.

"Sorry," I said, a little embarrassed as I reached for a sip of mint julep. "I was just thinking about the town. Sugarland is a wonderful place to live." She seemed to fit right in. "I love your earrings, by the way."

"Yeah? Thanks! I know the artist. She specializes in working off pictures of people's pets. This is my childhood cat, Moe. He was the best. He used to ride around on my shoulder like I was some kind of pirate. Do you have a pet? I could give you her name. Or you could borrow these ones next time." Zoey's smile abruptly fell away. "I mean if I ever see you again." She planted her elbows on the table and leaned close. "I'm sure Beau will dump me before long. His mom hates me, and he loves his mom. She whisked him away almost as soon as we got here, and I haven't seen him since."

Boy, that sounded familiar. "Give him a little more credit. Beau might surprise you."

Admittedly, before last month I would have said something different, but Beau really was trying to change. When we were on the Sugarland Express, he'd apologized for treating me badly, and he even apologized to my sister once we got back to town. And now he was dating a fun, wholesome girl like Zoey. "I think you'll be good for him. He needs to learn how to lighten up."

Zoey smacked the table with her hand. "Oh my gosh, yes! Can you believe he only owns one pair of sneakers? And he only has that pair because I took him shopping. When I asked him what he wears on weekends, he said loafers." She snorted. "You can't hike in loafers. Of course, he'd never been hiking before, even though you have some amazing trails down along the river. So we got the sneakers. I'm working my way up to getting him in a pair of

37

Crocs," she confided, and I giggled. I couldn't imagine Beau wearing Crocs, but if anyone could get him to do it, I'd bet Zoey could.

"I would pay to see that," I told her.

"I know, right? Hey, on the subject of paying," Zoey braided her fingers together, her hands so tight her knuckles were white. "Okay, so this is kind of a weird ask, but do you know anyone who can work a few shifts with me on the food truck? The library is right on the town square, and that's going to be busy at lunch. I'll be serving Thai barbecue fusion, which I know sounds strange, but I've got all the recipes done, and it's completely delicious," she assured me. "I just need someone to keep an eye on the food while I work the window. Or someone who can take over the window while I'm busy cooking. Sort of a partner in crime."

She made a face. "I asked Virginia, but she got offended and said she didn't know anyone in food service." Zoey used air quotes around the last two words. "You'd think I was asking her if she knew any good prostitutes. And Beau drew a blank. Most of the people he knows are lawyers."

Actually... "I know the perfect person to ask," I said. "My best friend, Lauralee. She works at the diner and caters on the side. She knows a lot of people in the business." She was also the mother of four boys under the age of eight, which meant her time was at a premium, but if anyone could help Zoey figure this out, it was her. "Let me give you her number."

"Thank you!" Zoey took her phone out of her purse and passed it to me. "Seriously, you're a lifesaver. I was kind of regretting coming to this barbecue, but now I'm glad I did since I got to meet you. And—" She winced. "Please don't feel obliged, but it seems like we've got friend potential, and I really needed a friend today."

Aww. "We can definitely be friends," I said, tamping down a niggle of guilt. I'd sure like to get to know Zoey better, but I wondered if she would feel the same once Beau told her a little more about his past and my role in it. I impulsively added my number as well as Lauralee's to her phone, then handed it back. "There. Now you can call me and let me know how things go after you chat with Lauralee. And truly, I think you'll love Sugarland. It's a great town. It's just got plenty of unusual folks."

Frankie picked that moment to pop his head right out of the middle of the table, startling me so badly I almost knocked over my mint julep. "It's the fuzz," he hissed at me. "We gotta get out of here!"

"What? Where?" I looked around but didn't see anything.

"Verity?" Zoey looked at me curiously. "What's up?"

Oh, right. She was new in town. She didn't know about my ability to speak to ghosts. "I—um, I have to go to the bathroom," I told her. I wasn't ashamed of what I did for a living, but Virginia had asked me to keep a lid on it, and this wasn't the time or place to explain it. "I'll be back soon." I stood and started making my way toward the house.

Frankie darted back and forth in front of me like a moth flirting with a flame. "No, not this way, he'll see you!"

Yes, well, I couldn't turn into a flickering ball of energy like Frankie could. "I'm sure he sees me anyway," I hissed.

I stopped short as a new spirit appeared directly in front of Frankie, blocking our way.

"Inspector De Clercq," I said. There was no avoiding him now.

CHAPTER 5

*T*he inspector raised a brow and rested a hand in the pocket of his dark suit pants. He wore a matching jacket and a black hat with a brim. A pocket watch glittered on a chain over his trim midsection, and his mouth quirked under a white mustache that curled at the ends.

"Well, hey, Inspector," Frankie said, shimmering into view as if this were a friendly run-in, "it's great to see you."

"Is it?" De Clercq asked, his words clipped.

Yep, he wasn't buying it.

The sun had begun to set, casting long shadows over the yard. "Let's find some privacy," I suggested, easing toward a copse of trees shading a hammock. The guests at Virginia's party didn't need to see me talking to thin air.

"Your need for discretion is not my problem," De Clercq said, refusing to take his eyes off Frankie.

Of course. The partygoers couldn't see him, so they didn't matter and neither did I. The inspector didn't have much respect for the living, or for the opinions of women. And a woman ghost hunter? Well, last time I'd run into him, he'd made it clear he considered the whole idea absurd.

"Um, hello," a woman said, and it was at that moment I realized I stood in the middle of a circle of guests holding cocktails.

"Excuse me." I flushed and stepped aside.

"This way." Frankie glided toward the privacy of the trees.

Saved by the ghost.

De Clercq frowned, but he indulged us.

"I've been looking for you for some time, Mr. Winkelmann," he said, advancing until he backed the gangster up against the trunk of an old oak.

Frankie ran a finger under his collar. "I was outta town."

Inspector De Clercq raised a brow. "You were seen escorting a Victorian lady to the Kitty Kat Lounge for the past three nights in a row."

"That's impossible," I said. I'd taken his urn to Ellis's house.

Frankie made an iffy motion with his hand. "It's nothing," he assured me. "Merely a small penthouse attraction that we opened in your boyfriend's attic." He turned to De Clercq and added, "Her man's a cop. The lounge is part of some important police work I'm doing for the living. Research," he stressed.

More likely he'd been skimming off the bar, watering down drinks, and corrupting Molly while Ellis and I watched Netflix downstairs.

De Clercq frowned. "Did your research include..." He pulled out a notebook and read from it. "The acquisition of a bourbon still, three flappers, and a six-piece band?"

"Yes," Frankie said, in his most innocent voice.

He wasn't fooling anybody.

But I was impressed he could fit all that in Ellis's small attic. When Frankie used his dominant ghost vision, he certainly thought big.

The detective stared him down.

"Fine, fine." Frankie raised both hands in mock defense. "You

PECAN PIES AND DEAD GUYS

got me. I was throwing a surprise birthday party for George Sykes. You know, the Merchant of Death."

I did not know, and I was glad for it.

Frankie laid his palms flat out. "These things have a tendency to get out of hand."

"I can vouch for that," I promised.

De Clercq directed a stony glare at my housemate. "Out of hand to the tune of twelve cases of bootleg champagne, six pounds of silver confetti, and one pigmy goat."

"Yeah, well, he had a goat named Trixie when he was growing up." Frankie shrugged. "He loved that goat. Thought having one there would make the whole event extra special."

De Clercq gave no reaction, but I could swear I heard his knuckles crack.

This was bad. De Clercq knew all about Frankie's shady past, and he had the power to put him away for it. And since Frankie was tied to my land, that meant imprisonment in my ancestral home for the rest of his afterlife. There would be no more field trips with me and the urn, no more mysteries to solve around town. I'd have to find yet another career. Frankie would go ballistic in a month. I wouldn't last a week.

"You win," Frankie said quickly. "I was kicking back, catching a few laughs, but now I'm here, and I'm ready to make good on my bargain."

De Clercq appeared doubtful.

"I'm serious." Frankie straightened his hat. "What can we do for you, Inspector?"

"A question I ask myself frequently," the other ghost muttered.

"There's no call for that," Frankie said as if he were the one who had a right to be peeved. "You're the one coming to me. If you think I'm such a rat, why do you want my help?"

De Clercq tucked his notebook away. "Sometimes it takes a rat to catch one, Mr. Winkelmann." I saw Frankie deflate a little and felt kind of sad for him. He made a big show out of being a criminal, but a part of him had enjoyed being cast as a good guy on the Sugarland Express.

"I may not care for you personally," De Clercq said, looking him up and down, "but I acknowledge that you are talented at what you do. I need a criminal mind on this investigation."

"He does have a certain skill set," I admitted.

"We leave at once," the inspector announced.

Frankie and I exchanged a look. "Believe me, I can leave now," I assured them, and I could swear I saw Frankie wince.

It was best to get this over with. Delaying wouldn't make it any easier. Besides, apart from meeting Zoey, this barbecue had been a bust. I hadn't even gotten to spend any time with Ellis. "I just have to find my boyfriend and say goodbye. Oh, and Zoey, too."

De Clercq didn't even bother to look at me. "Your living assistant is not invited," he clarified.

"She's my ride," Frankie countered.

De Clercq wrinkled his nose as if he'd detected an unsavory odor, but he didn't argue.

Rather, he addressed Frankie once more. "I have secured us special invitations to a house party at the Adair estate." He paused and twirled the end of his mustache. "A murder will take place tonight."

"We can stop it," I said, forgetting I wasn't allowed to speak.

"Hardly," De Clercq replied, his words a bit sharper. "The man died in 1928. The details are most puzzling. Most scandalous. But I believe, with some work, Mr. Winkelmann and I can sort them out."

"Yeah, I'm good at that," Frankie said, nodding his head one too many times.

I was the one who did most of the murder solving. De Clercq was lucky to have me, even if he didn't know it.

But I wasn't in it for the dead inspector or even Frankie. A person had been killed. A unique soul with a family and a life. I hadn't been able to help the girl at the bottom of the ravine this morning, but maybe I could help the poor victim from 1928 find justice.

I said my goodbyes to Zoey, and then popped into the house in search of Ellis. I found him in the kitchen, one hand on the wall, talking on his cell.

He saw me coming and ducked his head. "I'll be there soon, sir," he said into the receiver. "Yes. Bye." He ended the call and closed the distance between us.

"I'm so sorry," he said, pulling me into a hug. "I didn't mean to abandon you out there. My mother needed me more than I realized."

She wasn't one to leave her guests unattended, either. "What happened?" I asked, sliding my arms around his waist.

"A confrontation that turned into an intervention with Beau." He grimaced. "He's skipping out on meetings at the law firm, and he's behind on his cases. He's not happy there, and it's starting to show. Dad's out of town. Harrison won't bother talking to him, so Mom appointed me the voice of reason. I told him he should do what he wants with his life."

"I'm sure that went over well," I said, catching a glimpse of Virginia out the kitchen window. She scurried from guest to guest, making up for lost time.

"Mom had a fit. Beau made it worse. I barely escaped a few minutes ago. Then I got a call from the station. The chief wants to run a couple of things by me. We still don't know who the dead girl is, except she's definitely not from Sugarland."

"That doesn't narrow it down much." Sugarland wasn't all that big. "What are you going to do?" I asked.

He sighed. "We need to locate her next of kin. Duranja is hitting dead ends. He's working a double and ready to put his fist through the wall. They called me because I have a knack for investigation."

"You do," I agreed. "You should go."

He nodded. "Maybe that will get Duranja out on the street, where he can focus and calm down."

In my opinion, Duranja would be a bit on edge on a beach vacation, but I kept that to myself. "I'll be busy anyway. Inspector De Clercq tracked Frankie down."

The corner of his mouth ticked up. "At last."

"He wants us to go out to the old Adair estate and investigate a murder from the 1920s."

"I've always wondered if that place was haunted," Ellis mused. "I've driven past it on patrol and swore I saw lights on the lawn. But when I'd stop and look...nothing." He shook his head. "Be careful," he warned.

"I always am." I never took unnecessary risks. He knew that.

Ellis drew a lock of hair behind my ear. "I'm just saying you have an uncanny knack for stirring up trouble."

Didn't I know it.

THE ADAIR MANSION stood a few miles outside Sugarland. It had been a country estate at the turn of the century, where the rich went to play. I'd only been there once before, on a dare. The entire property was closed off. No one had lived there for decades.

Well, except for the dead, it seemed.

Thick elm trees staggered in unkempt rows up the weed-tufted drive leading to the house. Their branches twisted and twined overhead, like a gnarled trap.

My car tires crunched over the gravel as I pulled to a stop at the locked front gate. The horizon glowed orange and purple with the approaching dusk.

A cold breeze tickled the back of my neck, and I exchanged a glance with Frankie as I slid out of the car.

"This house was always hopping back in the day," he said as if defending the eerie silence in the air. He ran a hand along his jaw. "I never got an invite myself, but I heard some wild things."

"You heard correctly," De Clercq said, materializing in front of us. He'd been too cool to ride in my car.

I caught a glimpse of a stone mansion in the distance.

"Come." De Clercq motioned to Frankie. "The crime will take place soon."

"Wait. Let me figure out how to join you," I said. The gate appeared solid. I'd been hoping for a rusted hinge or a few missing bars.

De Clercq floated through without a backward glance.

Lucky for him.

Frankie followed suit.

Darn it.

The fence surrounding the property was fifteen feet high, with a decorative, curlicue top designed to impale anyone crazy enough to climb it.

I tested the front gate, and it held. Just my luck, the metal was in remarkably good shape. When I was a kid, I'd been small enough to slip between the iron bars without a problem, but there was no way I was squeezing through now.

De Clercq glided down the path, drawing farther and farther away from me. Frankie floated a few paces behind him.

"Hold up," I called. I could walk the perimeter. Surely, I'd find a weak spot somewhere, but I needed time. "You're not seriously leaving without me?"

Frankie hurried back to me. "You want to make this guy mad?" he hissed, hitching a thumb at the inspector, who continued on without him. "Improvise," the gangster urged, drawing his hat down over the bullet hole in his forehead. "Go over, around, under. Just get in here and help me."

"I'll try," I called as he turned and caught up with De Clercq, leaving me alone.

An owl hooted from a branch overhead, and I found myself

strangely comforted to know that there was something else alive in this place.

All right. *Think,* I told myself as my eyes adjusted to the waning light. I was a smart Southern girl, and I wasn't about to let two ghosts and a fence get me down.

There had to be another way in.

I stepped back and studied my situation, just like my grandmother had taught me to do when the going got tough. Only night was approaching, and it was getting harder to see with the trees blocking the remaining light.

The silvery ghosts floated farther down the path toward the house.

I couldn't go under or through the fence. But the last tree on the path grew close to the gate. And I had been quite a climber in my day.

I dug the mini flashlight out of my purse and clicked it on.

The gnarled elm wove in and out of the fence's iron bars, a good part of it cast in shadow. It looked half-dead, the branches dry and weathered, but it wasn't as if I was going to get a better chance at this.

Holding the small flashlight between my teeth, I hoisted myself up on the lowest branch and breathed a sigh of relief when it held. The rough bark scratched the inside of my thighs as I drew myself up to stand and grabbed for the next thickest branch I could reach. I made it up two more before perching on a positively anemic branch at eye level with the top of the fence.

I tossed the flashlight down onto the ground on the other side of the fence. There was no turning back now.

"Be strong," I said to myself and to the branch as I eased off the straining wood and onto the top of the fence, taking extra care to avoid the sharp spindles on top. I grabbed the sides of two spindles for support and jumped down onto the flattest piece of ground I could see.

I landed with a bone-jarring crunch, but the ground held, and so did my ankles. I was in one piece. Now I just had to find the ghosts.

I retrieved my light, ignoring the burning scratches on my hands and legs. One thing at a time. I hurried through a sprinkling of trees toward the main path. Once there, I spotted my companions already halfway to the house.

"Wait up," I called as loudly as I could.

Frankie turned to me wide-eyed. The inspector continued as if he hadn't heard me at all.

"Keep it down," he muttered as soon as I'd caught up, his shoulders stiff, his posture drawn tight. "You're making a scene."

"Said the guy who brought a pygmy goat to a party," I said, scraping the hair out of my face and retying my ponytail. "How about, 'Hi, Verity,' 'Glad you didn't get impaled on the fence, Verity.'"

"I am glad about that," Frankie admitted. He drew a cigarette case out of his suit pocket. "The last thing I need is you following me around for eternity with a fence post up your—"

"Frankie!" I snapped.

He grinned. "Kidding," he said, removing a smoke and stashing his case. "Just stay cool and stick with us. The inspector isn't in the mood for games."

I noticed the inspector had stopped and waited for Frankie. The mobster cupped a hand and lit his smoke, tossing his match as we hustled to catch up.

"Can you imagine living on an estate like this?" I asked as we drew closer to the house. The mansion was lit up like Christmas morning, and the faint tinkle of piano music floated down the path. The rest of the property lay in desolate shadow.

Naturally, we veered off to the left, into the darkness, toward a tall foreboding structure looming amid the trees and choked with underbrush.

Frankie took a deep drag off his cigarette. "For once, I'd like to go to the party," he groused, smoke trailing from his nose.

I had to agree with him.

I remembered my grandmother talking about visiting the Adair property when she was a little girl. Apparently, the couple never had children. They'd wanted them desperately, but it wasn't meant to be. That didn't stop them from making their home into a place that children would love. They built a menagerie on the grounds, an exotic zoo right here in Sugarland, and opened it to their nieces and nephews and the kids in town. Entire families would visit on Sunday afternoons and make a day of it, picnicking on the grounds.

When the Adairs died, the little zoo was shut down, the animals sold, and the property slowly fell into disrepair. An out-of-town relative had inherited, but no one had lived on the estate since.

We neared a long, rectangular glass and metal building on the left side of the mansion. In the ghostly realm, the two stories of tall glass windows stood dark and silent. An elaborate iron sign above the entrance read *Adair's Magical Menagerie*.

In the world of the living, the place had lost some of its magic. Cracked glass caked with grime clung to rotting window frames. In many places, the windows had broken altogether, leaving jagged pieces of glass behind. The once-grand sign slumped over the rusty doors like something out of a funhouse nightmare.

I was pretty sure I'd seen Ellis play a game like this on his Xbox. In the game, people who entered the building usually got eaten by roving zombies. I shuddered but tried to think sensibly. *There are no zombies here. There's no such thing as zombies. Just ghosts.*

It wasn't as comforting a thought as I'd hoped.

De Clercq veered straight for the abandoned menagerie. "The crime will take place in here."

Of course it would. We couldn't have a murder inside a nice, well-lit sitting room, now could we? "We still have time to see who did it," I said, venturing closer, catching a flicker of movement in the darkness behind the broken windows and fragmented glass.

"There's something alive in there," Frankie said.

Maybe it was just a squirrel. Stranger things had happened.

An inhumanly shrill shriek split the stillness of the night. I jumped so high and so fast, I nearly grabbed on to Frankie for support. He hollered and ducked out of my reach, dropping his cigarette. "Geez, woman!"

My hands shook as I whirled to face Frankie and De Clercq. "What was that?"

De Clercq, calm as could be, stared at me as if I were off my rocker. "That was a monkey." He eyeballed Frankie. "You need to train her better."

"I'm trying," the gangster said, straightening his suit jacket, keeping his eye on me as if expecting me to pounce. Smoke curled from the cigarette he'd dropped on the ground. He retrieved it and took a drag. "You know how unpredictable the living can be."

Sure. Blame it on the fact that I had a pulse. "I figured the animals in there would be long gone."

I crept up to the doors and peered inside, and the dusty moonlight filtering through the holes in the ceiling showed me something remarkable.

Expansive cages soared at least ten feet tall in this world and in the ghostly realm. They lined the walls on either side of the doors and housed all sorts of fantastic creatures, all long dead. I made out a pair of black and white capuchin monkeys swinging back and forth from a hanging rope. Next to them, three more gray, ghostly monkeys with long silky fur and big eyes clung to a small spindly tree. They eyed their neighbors like they couldn't believe they were distantly related to those clowns.

An anteater snoozed next door, and across the way, a spotted cat paced, running its silky coat against the bars. It might be an ocelot, I wasn't sure—but whatever it was, it was ridiculously cute. And up above everything, perching in the rafters, a flock of chattering parrots.

My word. They were all dead. Although they didn't seem to know it. "I didn't expect to see animal spirits."

"Really?" Frankie drew behind me, the bitter smoke from his cigarette curling over my shoulder. "Where did you think all the horses down at the track—ah—I mean," he amended when he saw De Clercq looking his way, "all the horses those dead soldiers ride come from?"

Yes, but every animal I'd met before had been bonded to a human ghost, cared for by a person who hadn't gone to the light. These were wild animals.

"Animals have spirits just like people do," the inspector said stiffly. "True, they usually tend to move on. They are simpler creatures and not so tied to this realm." He joined us and stood on the other side of Frankie. "These animals seem to have been particularly happy and decided to stay."

"I don't know," Frankie hedged, "being penned up in a cage for all eternity don't sound very happy to me."

"How fortunate for you that you're not a monkey," De Clercq said.

Yes, well, the inspector wanted to put Frankie in a cage for eternity if we didn't solve this mystery. I pursed my lips and kept my opinion to myself for once. I didn't think the inspector would appreciate the irony.

De Clercq opened his pocket watch. "Our timing is excellent."

"Excellent for what?" I readied myself.

"For murder," he said simply.

A bloodcurdling scream split the night air. I instinctively looked to the monkeys, but I knew that they weren't responsible this time around. That had been a woman's cry.

De Clercq tucked his watch away. "It is done. Follow me," he ordered. Then he stepped right through the door.

"We could have been there." This was ridiculous. "We could

have helped! Why didn't we hurry?" I asked, trying the door handle.

Naturally, the entrance was locked.

De Clercq obviously knew the timeline by now, and he wasn't one to miss a detail like a time of death.

De Clercq paused just inside the door. I saw him clearly through the broken glass. "The dominant ghost, whom I also believe is the killer in this case, has hidden the crime," he said gravely. "We can only deal with the aftermath."

"How awful," I said. Worse, it suggested we were dealing with a very powerful ghost. I pondered that thought as De Clercq once again left without me.

It wasn't like I could climb over the doorway or through the shattered panes.

I turned the handle and banged my hip against the door in an attempt to force it open, but only succeeded in getting rust on my dress and most likely a bruised hip.

"Frankie," I pleaded, as if he could help.

Frankie let out a curse and looked to the inspector, who didn't even slow for Frankie this time. The gangster lowered his voice. "You gotta start carrying around a jimmy kit if you're going to take breaking into places seriously."

"I'm not breaking into anything," I told him in no uncertain terms.

"You'd better start," he said as if that were my only option. And perhaps it was.

I would have to use one of the side windows. Those were bigger. And full of jagged shards in my realm, not to mention solid glass on the ghostly side. Great. I gathered my skirt and kicked in the window in the ghostly realm. Glass shattered, and I cringed at the icy sensation that clung to my foot.

"Speed it up, buttercup," Frankie urged, passing through the entrance the inspector had used moments before.

Yes, well, I didn't want to slice myself open while I was throwing away the remains of my dignity.

"You should also wear more practical clothing," Frankie said from the other side as I used my generous skirt to brush broken glass off the windowsill. "I recommend black pants," he added as if I were some sort of protégé. Smoke curled from his nose. "I mean, if you're going to commit to a life of crime, doll, you ought to commit to doing it right."

Heavens. I liked him better when he left me alone to go suck up to De Clercq.

"I'm not committing crimes," I corrected, clinging to the rotten wood as I hoisted a leg over, "I'm solving one."

"Hold on to that thought," Frankie advised as I levered myself up and through the window frame.

When my feet touched the floor, I eased my rear off the windowsill and settled onto the slivers of glass below with a wince. Hopefully, none of them would poke through my sandals. I'd dressed for a date with a police officer, not a gangster.

"If you could hurry, Mr. Winkelmann?" the inspector called. He was already halfway down the central hall of the long dark building.

"You got it," the gangster assured him as I shook out my dress. "Coming right up." As soon as De Clercq turned his back, Frankie's smile vanished. "Damn, I can't wait to get this over with. I could get labeled as a snitch just for being seen with this guy."

"We haven't run into anyone you know so far," I reminded him.

"We've only met the monkeys," he said.

Good point.

"Hopefully we'll solve the case quickly, and then you're scot-free." No more inspector breathing down our necks. No more trips to strange, dark places—at least not under the threat of Frankie's imprisonment.

It was dark in the menagerie. I pulled out my mini flashlight and clicked it on.

Two different hallways loomed in front of me, one superimposed on the other. The first was the present-day mess of dirt, leaves, and glass. The second appeared the way the dominant ghost saw it. Clean, bare. Dark, as if the menagerie had closed for the night.

It made sense. The party was going on at the main house. Anyone in here now—save for us—was probably up to no good.

We followed the inspector deeper into the building. It became harder to keep my bearings with cages on either side instead of windows. From the outside, the menagerie seemed to lead to the main house. I clung to that thought as we ventured deeper.

Pale, glowing eyes stared out at me from the cage on my right. I was about to take a closer look when a low, menacing growl trickled from the cage to my left.

I swiveled, and my light landed on a ghostly mountain lion. It hissed and bared its teeth. I backed away. Fast. Straight into the cage on the other side.

A furry body screeched and rattled the bars at my back.

"Holy geez!" I rocketed back into the center of the hall. When I was tuned in to the ghostly plane, those things could take a bite out of me. Or worse.

The round, watery beam of my flashlight shook as I trained it on the path ahead.

"It's going to be fine," I reminded myself.

I hoped I was right.

I tucked the flashlight under my arm and smoothed my sweaty palms over my dress. Nearly every cage was occupied by the spirit of whatever animal had once lived there. You'd think some would move on.

Perhaps some of them just moved *out*.

I whipped around and shone the light behind me, revealing an empty corridor.

I didn't like this one bit.

A prickle of unease crawled down my spine as I ventured deeper, careful to keep my footing in the rubble. That prickle grew into a full-fledged ache in my gut when my light shone upon a cage with the door flung open.

No telling what it had contained.

"Frankie," I said quietly, "did this place ever house any big, bad, dangerous animals? Besides the mountain lion?" At least its cage had seemed solid.

"I wouldn't know. I was never invited here, remember?" he said, his image flickering into existence next to me. He'd chain-smoked his cigarette down to the nub. He was as nervous as I was.

The hallway turned a hard right up ahead, and I spotted a dark corner, perfect for something to watch us from. Or jump out of. And right now, I was vulnerable to every ghostly animal in this place. If I could see them, then they could hurt me.

"Too bad you can't dissolve," Frankie muttered, stubbing out his cigarette.

No. I was very much open to attack.

We neared the corner, and a pair of orange eyes stared out at us from the darkness.

"Oh, no, ohnoono," I said, dashing around the corner.

I couldn't go back. It was too far, and who knew what might be following us. But we had to be near the end. I clung to that thought as I hurtled forward through the darkness.

"Jesus!" Frankie cursed, on my tail. "What did you stir up this time?"

No clue.

I ran so fast I buzzed right past Inspector De Clercq.

He glared at me, but I didn't care. I whipped back and saw a wide-eyed Frankie behind me. He'd lost his hat and wrinkled his suit. He stood panting as if he needed to breathe. Of course, he didn't, but it showed how freaked out he was.

"Did you see what it was?" I asked.

He shook his head. "Only that it was massive."

"Great." I heaved out a breath.

"Are you two finished?" De Clercq snapped.

I nodded. I'd been right on one count. We were almost out of the menagerie. Only a circular wrought-iron cage stood between us and the side of the house.

The bars had been hammered to look like vines, and the top was an elaborate filigree dome. A trembling young couple emerged from behind it. The girl leaned into the man's embrace like her legs might go out at any moment. Her lipstick was smeared, and the top few buttons of his shirt were undone. It was clear that they'd been—

"These two were in the middle of a tryst when they found the body," De Clercq said, his tone crisp.

A ghostly boa constrictor coiled inside the cage with a grown man in its grasp. The wide, glistening body of the snake wrapped around his torso, shoulders, and neck. I gasped when the ghostly boa tightened its grip, scales gleaming as its thick body looped up and over the poor man's gaping mouth.

CHAPTER 6

I stared at the dead man crushed in the coils of
the snake.

"Hey," Frankie burst out. "I know that guy. That's Greasy
Larry!"

De Clercq dipped his chin. "County Judge Lawrence Knowles,"
he said, his tone clipped. "I'm sure that colorful nickname derived
from the ease with which men like you could grease his palm. We
were opening an investigation into his acceptance of bribes when
he died."

Frankie did his best to appear unaffected, but I saw the way his
eyes jumped and his features tightened. No doubt the inspector
noticed too. De Clercq rarely missed a thing.

As the investigator drew closer to the dead man and the snake,
Frankie pulled me aside.

"This is bad." He crammed a finger between his collar and his
neck as if he could feel the noose tightening. "Plenty of my guys
would have offed old Larry to shut him up, especially if he was
about to get investigated. Think De Clercq's trying to set me up?"

"If the inspector knew who did it, he wouldn't be asking for your help," I assured him. But he was right. We could be in real trouble here.

The young couple began to slink away.

"You can't leave," I told them. They were witnesses.

De Clercq directed a sharp glare my way. "They are free to go. I have questioned them extensively. For years."

Right. He'd been on this case a long time.

I watched as the young couple hurried out the door toward the house.

"Okay, I have a question," I said, earning a look of disdain from the investigator. "You said earlier that the dominant ghost has hidden the actual crime. What did you mean by that?"

De Clercq's frown deepened. "Our killer is the dominant ghost. That means we see the events through his or her eyes. This ghost has chosen to delete the record of the murder altogether."

Frankie shifted his shoulders uncomfortably. "I didn't know anyone could do that."

"It's rare, but possible if the killer is a psychopath," the inspector said, "capable of divorcing himself or herself from the actual crime so completely that he or she can make the memory of the event vanish. And since in this case, the killer was also the only witness, we can't see the event, either."

"Oh my," I murmured. That was new. "It must take a ton of energy." Especially since this ghost had kept the truth hidden for decades.

De Clercq stood stiffly. "Some ghosts use their power to go poltergeist. Some are able to move objects in your plane. Our killer uses a considerable force to dominate this place and block out the memory of the past."

"So Greasy Larry suddenly appears inside the cage with the snake," Frankie said, his gaze flicking back toward what remained of the crooked judge.

De Clercq gave a sharp nod. "We see him enter the menagerie at 9:02 p.m. We see nothing more until he is dead at 9:18 p.m."

Frankie nodded slowly, no doubt fearing the worst. "That snake works fast."

"What else happens during that sixteen-minute period?" I asked. "Maybe we should have gone to the party at the house to see who was missing."

The inspector directed a withering look at me. "I've tried that." He thawed slightly and shook his head. "The party inside is a separate event. It's based on the combined memory of every guest who attended. It's the same ghosts, but the events do not progress exactly the same as they did that night in 1928. Memories can be...imprecise."

Through the windows I saw party guests spilling out onto the lawn, some into the menagerie itself, most of them still holding their drinks. Excited chatter filled the air. Night had fallen, and fireworks shrieked up into the air to light up the sky with glittering sparks. Someone cheered.

"The party will go on," De Clercq said with disdain. "It always does."

That seemed almost callous. Then again, the ghosts had been living with this death, and De Clercq's investigation, for nearly a century.

Back to the problem at hand. "We can't nail the killer in the act," I said, thinking out loud. "Instead, we're trying to figure out who lured the crooked judge into the boa's cage."

I was pretty sure it wasn't the young couple. De Clercq said he'd questioned them already.

"No one lured him to his death," the inspector corrected, "at least not in this cage. Look at his hands."

Only one of them was still visible. I leaned in a little closer and frowned. "There's blood under his nails. He struggled with someone." He'd fought for his life, poor man. Fought and failed.

"Now look at the snake," the inspector prompted. "There are no marks on it."

I was about as close as I wanted to get to that snake, ghost or not. It was preoccupied now, but I didn't want to take any chances.

"The snake isn't the only thing that wrapped itself around Mr. Knowles's neck tonight," De Clercq continued. "When the snake uncoils from the body, it will be quite obvious to the trained observer that the killer strangled the victim and then dumped him in the boa cage."

Frankie pulled another cigarette out of his case. "Who'd be that flashy?" he asked, almost to himself. He balanced the cigarette on his lip as he lit up. "Give me a gun and a pair of concrete boots any day."

De Clercq raised an eyebrow at him.

"You wanted shady," the gangster reminded him, taking a long drag and blowing out the smoke.

"So where do we start?" I asked.

Inspector De Clercq inclined his head. "You don't start anywhere," he chastised me. "Mr. Winkelmann and I will enter the den of iniquity behind us."

"I'm coming too," I said, not about to let him lose me this time.

"Is she always this way?" De Clercq asked Frankie.

"No," the gangster said as we exited through an open door near the house. "She's usually worse."

Whatever. It didn't escape me that the inspector could have led us inside through the door that was open to the living. He'd deliberately tried to cut me off.

Best for him to figure out right away that it wouldn't be so easy.

A pair of ghostly spotlights roved across the front of the white stone mansion. The windows on the other side had been thrown open, and raucous piano music filled the air. Ghostly 1920s cars lined the driveway, and I didn't miss how Frankie ran a covetous hand over the sleek body of a Rolls Royce.

"Don't get distracted by the shiny," I told him under my breath.

Inspector De Clercq cleared his throat as we neared the front door. "This is the Adairs' annual Red Hot Ritz. They hold it every summer, and it lasts for three nights. That is how long we have to solve this murder before our chance is lost for another year." He eyed Frankie. "If you can't prove yourself before the party ends, I lock you up for good."

No pressure there.

He pulled a pair of stiff paper invitations from inside his jacket and handed one to Frankie. They presented them to a man in a tuxedo at the door, who waved them through. I slipped in with them.

"Miss," the man in the tuxedo called.

I kept walking. He couldn't expect a living girl to see the dead.

My bluff paid off, and he didn't follow. I certainly didn't look back. There was plenty to see in every other direction.

I'd just walked into a raging party.

And if I'd been dead, I'd have been severely underdressed.

The vast front hall was packed wall to wall with girls in sparkling beaded frocks and men straight out of *The Great Gatsby*, in white slacks and dapper striped jackets. A glass fountain in the center of the space trickled merrily with pink champagne, judging by the flutes the guests were using to scoop it up.

This was amazing, a piece of Sugarland history, and I stood in the middle of it.

Ghosts smoked and laughed and danced to the music and, heavens, I couldn't even see the piano through this crowd. Whoever sat banging out the notes had to have fingers of steel to keep up this kind of volume.

Double staircases wound up either side of the main room, with more guests toasting, teasing, and taking turns sliding down the wide banisters to the floor below. An enormous crystal chandelier hung from the ceiling, caught here and there with balloons and bits of tinsel. Clinging to the base of it and swinging around for all they were worth were two capuchin monkeys. One of them had stolen a cigar. The other one chewed on what looked like a diamond bracelet.

Because, why not?

At least I knew the monkeys hadn't committed a crime. As for the rest of this crowd? Well, I couldn't imagine how we were going to suss out a killer.

I narrowly dodged a giggling woman who stumbled past me with a man hot on her heels. "How on earth are we supposed to keep the witnesses straight, much less figure out who did it?"

"You see my problem." De Clercq nodded grimly. "I have been gathering clues about this murder for nearly a century, and I've narrowed the possible killers down to five guests."

"Then let's get this party started," Frankie said, grabbing a champagne flute off a passing tray.

A handsome ghost with pale, slicked-back hair and a dark black suit stood in the corner by the bottom of the right-side staircase, watching us with cold fury.

"Is that one of our suspects?" I asked, pointing him out. If looks could kill, I'd be just as dead as the rest of them at this party.

As soon as I called attention to the hostile ghost, he disappeared.

"Who?" the inspector asked, turning his head a second too late.

A confetti cannon fired from the second-story landing, spraying the cheering crowd with thousands of bits of glittery paper. I ducked my head at the brush of the ghost confetti against my skin. It felt like cold rain.

"Our first suspects are the hosts of the party," De Clercq said, ignoring the confetti on his shoulders. He tilted his head to indicate a glamorous couple in their prime. They held court by one of the open windows, surrounded by fawning admirers. "Mr. Graham Adair and his wife, Jeannie."

I did a double take when I saw them. Graham was a slender gentleman sporting a top hat and a mustache with twice the curl of De Clercq's, while Jeannie had shoulders broad enough to stop a linebacker. She was resplendent in a sleeveless, sparkling tiered dress with fringes so long they brushed the floor. The Adairs were about the same height. In fact, with her high heels, Jeannie might have had an inch or two on her husband.

As I watched, the lady of the house wrapped one swirly end of her husband's mustache around her finger and tugged him into a kiss. They kept at it so long that I had to look away with secondhand embarrassment after her jeweled fascinator fell to the floor.

"She's certainly not shy," I said.

That didn't mean she was a killer, although she and her husband had the means to commit a murder. As the owners of the estate, the Adairs spent the most time here and had the most familiarity with the grounds and especially the menagerie.

But they seemed so happy together, so carefree. How could people who looked like that be murderers?

Of course, I'd learned the hard way that appearances counted for nothing when it came to who might willingly end a life.

"Now for our next suspects." De Clercq led us into the next room, smaller than the entrance hall, with about the same number of people and piano music rising clear above the din. A petite, glamorous woman with a feather boa looped over her shoulders danced on top of a table with a debonair man in a tux, swinging each other around so vigorously I was afraid the fragile furniture would break underneath them.

In fact, the table *was* broken—I could make out the pieces lying on the ground in real life. In the spirit realm, however, it stood upright and did its duty as a tiny dance floor. The dancer saw me staring at her, winked, and blew me a kiss before spinning into her next turn. Another lady, wearing nothing but a sparkly G-string and some strategically placed feathers, dangled from a swing fixed to the ceiling, swooping just low enough to exchange kisses with the guys if they jumped a little. And oh, how they jumped. The floor vibrated with their ups and downs.

De Clercq pressed on as if the spectacle meant nothing to him. "Over there is Mr. Shane Jordan, a diamond dealer based in Memphis."

He pointed to the man I'd seen glowering at the bottom of the stairs.

So he was a suspect.

Shane Jordan had directed his attention elsewhere, and I used the opportunity to observe the man with pale, slicked-back hair and a cutthroat attitude. He appeared stiffer, sharper than a lot of the people here—less like he'd come to this party to kick back and hang loose. He held a tumbler in one hand and gesticulated with the other to the gentleman standing next to him. And I noticed he kept his back to the wall.

"There—" De Clercq pointed across the room to the woman dancing on the table "—is another of our suspects: his lover, Marjorie Phillips." As we watched, her partner spun her around and threw her over his shoulder into a flip. She landed with a shimmy and a grin—in high heels, no less. My feet hurt just looking at her.

Frankie whistled. "Dang, look at the stems on that one. You think she can get 'em up over her head?"

"Frankie," I chided, "you've got Molly, remember?"

"Sure, yeah, but...I mean, I've got eyes, too. I'm not *dead*."

Well. "Actually—"

"How do you tolerate such blatant impertinence from your assistant?" Inspector De Clercq asked, with a pointed glare at me.

Frankie pressed a hand theatrically to his chest. "It's a struggle sometimes, it really is."

I'll give you a struggle. I gritted my teeth and kept it together. Now wasn't the time.

"Mrs. Phillips was a professional dancer before her marriage," De Clercq said.

No kidding. "Is that her husband up there with her?" I asked. If so, they were a handsome couple.

De Clercq shook his head. "No. His name is Marcus Phillips. He is our final suspect, and I've yet to locate him this evening."

"Hey, is this Marcus fellow a gambler?" Frankie prodded. "Because I hear a roulette wheel rolling from here."

"Frankie," I began. This wasn't the time to get distracted.

"I bet that's where Magnus is," the gangster concluded, with absolutely no proof whatsoever.

"Marcus," I corrected.

"I'll go look," Frankie assured us. He threaded his way through the crowd, heading for the next room.

"You don't even know what he looks like," I called after him.

I tried to follow but had a difficult time navigating the ghostly crowd. I didn't like to come into contact with spirits, and they didn't like touching me either. The sensation was cold and invasive and miserable for everyone involved. But apparently, these spirits hadn't encountered too many live people, because I was buffeted on all sides the moment Frankie and the inspector weren't flanking me anymore.

"Excuse me," I called out, sucking in my stomach, trying to make myself as thin as possible. "Can I just—please, I need to get through here."

Most of the ghosts ignored me, which was—well, it wasn't what I was used to. I guess they had better things to do than chat with the living when it was so fun being dead. Except for one. I noticed him immediately, working his way through the crowd toward me.

He couldn't have been more than thirty-five, and he looked like he'd stepped straight out of an old black-and-white Hollywood movie, with chiseled features and wavy, Gary Cooper hair that curled at the ends. He wore a crooked grin, and his dark hair was just messy enough to give him an air of frivolity despite his tuxedo jacket. He wore his collar open, with no tie. And when his smile widened, well, I found myself grinning back.

"Hey," he said, stopping right in front of me. "You're a girl."

"Are you always this observant?" I teased.

"Ha." He dipped his chin, recovering. "No. I mean a *living* girl." He was so focused on me, he sloshed champagne out of his glass. It hit my foot like dry ice burning.

"Watch out," I warned, dodging backward, praying I didn't run into another ghost.

He advanced, fascinated, swallowing up all the space between us. "You can see me," he said, unable to let it go.

"It's a gift and a curse," I said, trying to keep my distance.

He wasn't getting the memo. I backed away farther, feeling my heart thunder in my ears, the blood pumping through my veins. I didn't realize how far I'd retreated until my back hit the wall.

"It's amazing," he pressed, close enough for me to see the slight furrowing of his brow as he trapped me.

"Please," I pressed. I didn't want to be rude, but I couldn't let him touch me. "You're making me uncomfortable." The trick was I had nowhere to go—not unless I wanted to go through him. And, oh my, I truly didn't.

"I'm sorry," he said, jerking his head away. "That was—" He held up a hand and stepped back sharply. "I wasn't thinking." He held out a hand. "Marcus Phillips," he said. "Please don't think I'm a sap."

"I don't," I said, unsure of the slang, but willing to give him the benefit of the doubt. "Verity Long," I added, giving him a wave. "Forgive me if I don't shake your hand."

"You're forgiven if I am," he said ruefully. The handsome ghost gingerly planted his back on the wall next to mine and shoved his hands into his pockets. "I just haven't spoken to the living since… well—" he shrugged a shoulder "—since I was living."

"I'm still getting used to this whole thing myself," I said. It wasn't his fault I'd taken him by surprise. "Looks like I picked a good party."

Good for me, at least. I'd just located my final suspect.

"I never miss it," he said, his lips twisting into a wry grin as he looked out over the crowd. His attention landed on Marjorie Phillips dancing on the table.

"Your wife is beautiful," I told him.

He let out a sharp breath. "She knows it," he said uncomfortably, watching her lean up and plant a lingering kiss on her dance partner's cheek. "She won't dance with me. Not lately, anyway. But I promise you, I'm good." He recovered and gave me a wink. "Come on," he said, holding a hand out to me. "Let's you and I give those two a run for their money."

"I can't do that," I said, backing away.

"Why?" he asked. "Don't you dance?" He grabbed for my hand.

"Stop!" I tried to snatch it back but was too late. A full-body shudder rocked me. I felt the cold, invasive sting down to my bones and fell to the hard marble floor. "We can't touch!"

"Sweet Jesus!" The ghost reared back like I'd bit him.

"What was that?" A nearby ghost recoiled as if he'd felt the aftershock, too. He straightened his glasses. "I swear I felt my heart beating just now," he said, noticing me for the first time. His ringed fingers reached for me.

I raised my hands defensively. "Frankie," I hollered.

But he was long gone. Marcus, who'd taken the force of our contact full-on, looked ready to keel over. Naturally, De Clercq hadn't stuck around.

"Hey there, honey," a feminine voice said next to me. Before I could open my mouth, Marjorie Phillips shimmered into existence between me and the dead man in glasses. She cradled his cheeks and pushed up onto her tiptoes to kiss the tip of his nose. Then she shoved his face away with one hand. "Show's over, sweet cakes." She eyed Marcus, who was bent over a few feet away from me, breathing hard and staring at his hands. "You too, darling. I think the live girl's had enough."

He looked past her to me. "I'm sorry," he said before fading away.

Marjorie watched him disappear, raising a slender cigarette holder to her lips.

"You'll have to forgive my better half," she said, taking a drag. "Marcus isn't always good at reading a lady's signals."

"He just wanted to dance," I said, hoping she'd take him up on it later. "I appreciate the help with the other one, though," I added, rubbing the cold out of my shoulders. "My name is Verity Long."

Her lips quirked. "Aw, aren't you polite? Marjorie Phillips," she said, blowing smoke, acting casual. But I saw the way she studied me. She was trying to figure me out. It was only fair. I was doing the same to her.

"Your husband was a complete gentleman," I said. At least he'd tried to be.

She lifted a slim shoulder. "He has his moments," she said, matter-of-fact. "As long as he lets me have mine."

She fanned herself with her boa while I tried to get a handle on that statement. "But you love him, don't you?" I asked, regretting the words as soon as I said them.

Marjorie laughed. "Sure I do, after a fashion!" She ran a finger under the strand of pearls wrapped around her throat. "We grew up together—him, Graham Adair, and me. We've been friends since we were babies."

He sure hadn't looked at her like a friend.

Marjorie turned a glare on a pair of flappers who ventured too close. When they'd gone, she took another drag of her cigarette and blew smoke out her nose. "Marcus has always been there for me. In fact, he got me out of a nasty situation back in New York in '26, so when he popped the question, I accepted." She shrugged. "He says he needs me, and I guess that's true." She forced a laugh. "I'll take friendship over relationship drama any day."

"It...sounds nice." If a marriage of convenience could ever be nice, which I wasn't at all sure of.

"Aw, honey." She brought the cigarette to her lips and blew

smoke into the hazy air. "Don't sound all sorry for me. You got a fella?"

"I do."

"He treat you right?" She winked. "Give you what you need, make you feel happy?"

I didn't even have to think about it. "Yes, he does."

"Good for you. It's lucky when you can find that kinda deal in one package. Me? I've got to reach a little farther for it. I've got dear old Marcus for stability, a dozen different dance partners for fun, and when it comes to having a little excitement—" she nodded her head across the room "—I've got my Shaney."

He stood about ten feet away, next to an ice sculpture of an angel, arms crossed, glowering so ferociously I could have bottled that expression and used it to remove paint. "He doesn't look very pleased right now."

Marjorie's mouth tightened. "He hates this party, says it makes him itchy." The faint lines around her mouth deepened. "Your detective friend makes us relive Red Hot Ritz every year. The same people, the same party, the same murder." She let out a breath and gave a small smile when she saw my surprise. "Oh, sweetie, it's not your fault. I know you're with the jerk, but he'd do it every year with or without you."

"Once he solves the murder, I think he'll move on and let you all live in peace," I told her, for what it was worth. "I could use your help to make that happen."

Unless she was the one who'd killed Greasy Larry.

Marjorie took a long drag, then blew out enough smoke to make my lungs burn and my head spin. "I don't have anything new to say, sugar."

Suddenly she was speaking as if I were a stranger at a party. And I supposed I was. Our moment of understanding had evaporated. She'd shut down on me.

She tilted her head. "Honey, you look as though you could use some fresh air."

It would help if she stubbed out her cigarette, or if her husband hadn't been so keen on dancing. "I've got a job to do," I said, refusing to let discomfort sideline me.

When I interacted with the other side, ghostly bullets could hit me, ghostly train crashes could crush me, and apparently an overabundance of ghostly cigarette smoke could make my head pound and my lungs ache.

"Just take a minute until you feel like yourself again. Let me walk you to the window, okay?" She led the way through the crowd, deflecting the few spirits who seemed interested in me until I finally reached an open window. This one didn't even have glass in the land of the living. I stuck my head out into the fresh air and inhaled deeply, the sweet scent of grass better than a cold glass of lemonade on the Fourth of July.

Marjorie studied me with a little smile on her face. "I don't know what De Clercq is up to, but I for one think it's nice to have someone living at this party," she said. She leaned against the window frame. "Definitely keeps things interesting."

"I appreciate your help," I said. Even if she viewed me as a lab specimen. Feeling more myself, I straightened my back and turned to face her. "Do you mind if I ask you a few questions about the murder that took place here tonight?"

"I figured it was coming." Marjorie tilted her head toward the driveway. "But I think you're going to want to answer the questions that copper has for you first."

I frowned. "What copper?"

I looked outside just as a flashlight shined right into my face. "Oh no," I winced.

Through the spots in my vision, I saw an officer standing in front of a police car, its red and blue lights flashing. It didn't look like Ellis from here. And when he spoke into his radio, I knew for a fact it wasn't my man.

"Yep, the caller was right. There's a trespasser inside the house. Yeah, I'll bring her in."

Yikes.

I wasn't trespassing. Well, yes, I kind of was inside a house that wasn't mine. And I did get in by climbing over a locked fence. While I'd always prided myself on following the law, not breaking and entering no matter how many times Frankie suggested it, I seemed to have some explaining to do.

CHAPTER 7

*D*uranja approached with the ease of complete authority, and I knew I was in trouble. For one thing, he hadn't been too happy with me this morning. And for another, he looked up to Ellis, and he'd been gunning for me ever since I'd become responsible—at least in his eyes—for the changes he'd seen in his friend and mentor.

I'd best come right out with it. I ducked out the window and stepped onto the patio, with my hands up for good measure.

"It's not what it looks like," I assured him. I wasn't doing anything wrong. Not really.

He stood in front of his car, backlit by the headlights as he ran the beam of his flashlight over me like an inspection. "So I didn't just see you walking out of a vacant house you don't own."

"Well, of course you did," I began. "But—"

"A house you didn't have permission to enter."

The ghosts had engraved invitations, and I was Frankie's plus-one, although I didn't think he'd want to hear that. I settled for a simpler explanation. "It wasn't locked." At least the front door hadn't been.

He barked out a laugh as he cut the distance between us. "The gate looked pretty solid to me." My mind raced as he strolled up the stairs, keeping an eye on me the entire time like I was a flight risk. He stopped just short of me. "I had to use the key left to the county."

Okay, so maybe I had climbed a tree to get in. He ran his light over the scratches on my shins and hands. "Is there something you want to tell me?"

I lowered my hands to my hips. "No. I'm ghost hunting," I said quickly. "Ask Ellis. I told him I'd be here tonight. There's no harm in it. I'm just investigating the property—"

"Ask Ellis," he repeated, with no small amount of scorn. "You would have to bring him into it." He stood over me, and I realized all over again how tall he was. "Don't use the good name that he built to do—" he waved a hand at the mansion "—this."

"I know it looks bad," I began.

"Do you?" he snapped, reaching behind his belt for his cuffs. Oh, geez. He was going to arrest me. "Do you realize how big a problem this is? The girlfriend of an officer, breaking and entering."

I held up my hands as if I could somehow ward him off. "This isn't necessary."

"Then you have the gall to use him to try to get yourself out of trouble," he said, snapping the cuffs open. "I don't know if you get this," he said, jaw tight, "but Ellis has worked his ass off to make it where he is. When he joined the force, the old guard was suspicious of the rich kid playing cop. His family sabotaged him from the other end. He had to keep his mouth shut and his butt in line until he proved everybody wrong. I joined the force five years in, and he was still fighting. Now he's got the trust. He's got the respect. And you're blowing it all to hell."

"I was helping him this morning," I said, voice catching because the last thing I wanted to do was hurt Ellis, and dang it all, Duranja was making sense. "He called me because I can see things you guys can't."

Duranja held up a hand. "I don't know what you think you can do, and I don't care. I don't." He closed his eyes briefly, clutching the cuffs in one hand. "You don't know how much I want to arrest you right now."

"Then do it," I said, holding out my wrists. I was tired of being blamed for things I couldn't control. If Duranja wanted his revenge, he could have it.

He stared me down. "Don't tempt me." The officer took a deep breath and snapped the cuffs closed without me in them. "The only reason I'm not is that it would make Ellis look bad. Again. But I swear, if I catch you doing this one more time, I'm going to nail you to the wall."

I nodded, relief coursing through me. I hadn't realized how much I feared the metal handcuffs until Duranja clipped them back into his utility belt.

"Come with me," he ordered, gesturing with his flashlight.

"I will," I promised. "One second." I took a step back toward the house. I wanted to tell Frankie to talk with Marjorie, see if we could learn more from her about our suspects.

"Now," Duranja snapped, reaching for the cuffs again.

"Right. Yes." I dug into my pocket for my car keys and showed them to him.

He made me ride in the back of the police cruiser as he drove me to my car parked outside the gates by the old elm. Then he watched me get in and drive away.

How was that for lack of trust?

Still, I understood his point. And his frustration. I had technically broken into the Adair estate, an event that would have left me mortified a year ago when I'd first met Frankie. But it wasn't a private home or business. It was an abandoned property. And I hadn't intended to take anything. Truly, there was no harm.

I bumped over the road leading away from the house and the gated part of the property. Frankie's urn rattled on the passenger seat next to me.

As soon as I crossed the property line, he'd be dragged out of the party and into the car with me. No doubt, I'd have to hear about that.

Not only would I yank him out of the investigation, but I had also made it nearly impossible to go back.

Worse, I couldn't stop thinking about what Duranja had said. Ellis trusted me. I loved that about him, and I took pride in the fact that we had such an honest, healthy way of treating each other. He believed in me and put himself out on a limb for me. I did the same for him.

This morning, when he'd needed help, I was glad to respond. I'd taken it for granted that Ellis and I were a team. I hadn't fully realized how his faith in me would impact the career he loved so much. Or the price he might have to pay for me being a ghost hunter.

I turned left onto Rural Route 7, and Frankie materialized next to me with a curse. "You have the worst timing."

"I'm starting to think so," I said, clutching the wheel as the darkened landscape whizzed past.

"I was up five large in the middle of a hot streak," he groused.

My grip tightened on the wheel. "You should have been talking to our suspects."

"The Adair fellow was right next to me. People let all kinds of things slip when they're at the tables."

"Like?"

He grinned. "Like Marjorie Phillips was paying off the judge."

I almost missed the curve in the road. "You mean she was bribing the judge we found dead?"

"Yep." Frankie gave a curt nod. "Greasy Larry. Although you have to realize that isn't exactly rare."

"Yes, but what would a socialite like her have to do with a crooked judge?"

"That's for us to find out," he concluded. "Probably you," he added, running a hand over the window ledge. "I have a feeling her lover would snap me like a twig if I so much as talked to her."

I'd give him that.

He tilted his head back. "The inspector's gonna be real sore I got yanked out early tonight."

True. "Tell him we'll make it up to him tomorrow night." I'd just have to figure out a way to get back into that mansion without getting arrested.

The next morning, I awoke to a knock on my back door. I squinted against the bright sunlight and checked the time. Almost nine thirty.

The knock sounded again.

"Coming," I said, easing past my skunk, who'd curled up next to me on my futon. Lucy blinked sleepily as I drew my robe from the edge of my purple couch and hurried to greet my visitor.

I opened the door, ready to apologize for my disheveled state, but I didn't see anyone. No car in the gravel drive. Not a soul on the porch. Although, I wouldn't know that for sure since I'd made Frankie turn his power off when we returned home last night.

I stepped out onto the porch and nearly put my foot into a pecan pie.

Strange.

Yes, it was a tradition in the South to express your feelings with food. Joyful news, sad tidings, or even an invitation to gossip came in the form of casseroles, cakes, and pies. But I hadn't done anything to court the grapevine this week. At least I didn't believe so.

I bent and picked up the pie, still warm from the oven. I could smell the sweet brown sugar and creamy butter. Heaven.

I stepped out onto the porch and searched to see if the

mysterious pie benefactor had left on foot. But I saw only green grass, my peaceful pond, and Frankie's shed.

Hmm...

Why pie, if it didn't come with small talk, condolences, or congratulations?

I took my gift into the kitchen and placed it on the counter.

"Well, Lucy," I said to my little girl, who had toddled out into the kitchen, still bleary-eyed, "it seems we have a breakfast treat."

I opened my utensil drawer to fetch a knife and a pie server. I'd have a big slice. She could have a nibble of crust. I was about to dig in when my phone buzzed.

I fetched it from the charger next to the futon and checked the number. My stomach sank. It was Ellis. I'd meant to call him first thing. He should hear about last night from me. He should know I cared about what had happened and that he didn't need to be worrying about me, but it seemed I was too late.

I brushed my hair back behind my ear and took the call. "Hey, you."

"Verity." Ellis's voice was flat, almost no inflection. "I found a strange note on my desk from Duranja this morning."

Yikes. I strolled into the parlor. "I meant to call you first thing, but I just woke up. I was out late last night."

"So I hear."

I sat on the edge of the purple couch. "It's not as bad as it sounds." I explained to him about the tree and the suspects at the party, and the body we found in the boa cage. "I didn't mean to get caught," I finished.

He gave a long sigh. "I understand your work is important. I understand you got wrapped up and didn't think it was a big deal to walk into an abandoned property, but, Verity, you have to work within the law."

I realized that. "I'm usually really careful," I said, "only Frankie's afterlife depends on me solving this case."

"There's always something dire happening on the other side." Ellis exhaled, frustrated.

Didn't I know it? "This time, it's even more personal," I said, eyeing the plastic trash can in the corner of my formerly glorious parlor. It contained the dirt from my garden that had mixed with Frankie's ashes, the rosebush I'd been watering when I rinsed them in, and Frankie's urn, like the cherry on top.

My life was so strange now, so different. I wouldn't trade it for the world, but Ellis had to realize: "I'm flying by the seat of my pants here."

"I know," he said simply, his tone warming. "You're a good person, Verity. And you're excellent at what you do. But if you break the law, my hands are tied. Duranja did you a favor last night. If it had been one of the other guys, you wouldn't have been so lucky."

I placed my feet up on the couch, using the arm as a chair. "I'm not sure I'd call it lucky. Duranja tortured me a bit."

"Good," Ellis quipped before growing serious once more. "If you do go back to that property, you will be arrested for breaking and entering. Duranja has arranged for a patrol to drive by every night. And if you get caught, there's a chance you'll have to go in front of my brother, the judge."

Harrison didn't like me much. Virginia had poisoned the family against me. I drew my feet closer to me. "I understand what you're telling me, Ellis. I do." If I had any hope of being a part of his family, heck, of once again being a respected member of the community, I couldn't be committing crimes, however innocently.

I stared out past my empty front room, through the window to my expansive green front yard. "I'll figure out a way to legally investigate the Adair estate." Somehow.

Preferably by tonight.

"I hope so. There's not much I can do to help you," Ellis said.

"I know." He was only looking out for me. "How are you doing?" I asked him. "Any leads on the girl in the ravine?"

"Not yet," he said, sounding tired. "I was at the station until midnight trying to trace her identity but haven't had any luck. There's no missing persons report, no abandoned vehicle found nearby, nothing."

"Could she be a drifter?" I wondered. "A hitchhiker, maybe?"

"That's what Duranja thinks, although we didn't find a backpack or any personal items except for a photo in one of her pockets. It was her in the middle of what looked like a happy family, and it's not an old picture. Someone cares about this girl, I'm sure of it. I just haven't figured out who yet."

"That's sad." Her family would mourn her. They might not even realize something was wrong yet, but they'd be missing her soon.

Of course, she might have had a falling-out with her family or been on the run for some reason, but that didn't mean they didn't care.

"The death has officially been ruled an accident," Ellis continued, "but it doesn't sit right with me."

"I wish the death spot had been more useful."

"I'm going to keep at it," Ellis vowed. "At the very least, I want to get this poor girl back to her family."

"I know you do." Ellis was a good police officer—dedicated, thorough, and uncannily insightful at times. It was interesting to see him work on an investigation like this. "You'll find them. I'm sure of it."

"I know I can't keep you from working your own case," he went on, "but try to find a way to do it legally. That's all I'm asking."

That was the trick. "I know that the land around the property belongs to the city, but who owns the mansion itself? The Adairs didn't have any children, but they had to have named an heir."

"Let's see." I heard him tapping on his keyboard. "The property records database has one name in it: Eliza Jean Adair. It looks like she's a niece, and her home address is in New York City."

"Does it include a phone number?" This could be my big break. I just had to convince a woman I'd never met to let me into a property where she couldn't supervise me or know what I was doing there.

"There's nothing listed. Her occupation says art dealer, but there's no mention of any specific gallery, so that won't help much either. I could try—" He paused as someone called his name on the other end of the line. A few moments of muffled conversation went by before he came back on and said, "I have to go. Someone drove a car into Mr. Mackelhenny's pasture and took down the fence. Now there's a small herd of cattle wandering toward Main Street."

I smiled a little. "Sounds like a job for Ellis Wydell, animal wrangler extraordinaire."

He snorted. "I couldn't wrangle a bunch of earthworms, much less a herd of cows. I'm just going to keep the cars back."

"Good luck with that. I'll talk to you later?"

"Definitely." He ended the call, and I sighed with relief. That hadn't gone well, exactly, but it hadn't gone terribly either. I'd known Ellis would be upset. Heck, I was upset, too. I didn't want to break the law. But he'd spoken to me reasonably, laid out the facts, and asked me to change things.

Which I would.

I even had an idea how to do it.

It was amazing what Google could get you these days. Five minutes on my phone led me to a website for Elements Gallery in Brooklyn, where Ms. Adair was listed as the sole owner and proprietor. There was also a phone number.

I slid off the arm of the couch and stood. Somehow, I sounded more proper when standing.

"What do I say to her?" I asked Lucy.

The skunk blinked up at me with big black eyes.

"I should be myself," I told her. "That's what I always tell you, isn't it?"

But I could hardly call her up and say, 'Hi there, Eliza Jean, I'm a ghost hunter from Sugarland who needs to solve a murder that happened back in 1928 during one of your aunt and uncle's bacchanals, so do you mind me traipsing around your family home for the next two days so that I can keep my gangster ghost out of prison?'

She'd most likely call me a crank and hang up right after 'ghost hunter.'

But I did have one more tool in my box.

"I've got it." I gave Lucy a pat.

She rubbed up against my leg, as if to say *way to go, girl.*

I smiled and tapped in the number.

Someone picked up on the third ring. "Elements Gallery."

"EJ Adair, please," I said, more confident than I felt.

Fake it until you make it.

The phone clicked, and for a second, I thought the receptionist had hung up on me.

Then a slightly raspy voice said, "EJ here. How may I help you?"

"Hi there, Ms. Adair." I scooped up my skunk and held her close. "My name is Verity Long, and I'm calling on behalf of the Sugarland Heritage Society."

I was a card-carrying member. And after all the trouble I'd gone through solving their ghost issues, they could help me with one of mine. I strode toward the mantel in the parlor, the half-truth tumbling out of my mouth as I walked. "I'm researching the history of the Adair estate property and was wondering if I might have your permission to look around."

"The... oh, heavens, that old place?" EJ's brassy Brooklyn accent faded, and I detected the hint of a Southern drawl. "Good grief, I haven't thought about the estate in years. It's still standing, then?"

I stroked Lucy on the head. "It is. The exterior is absolutely lovely, I can see why it was the toast of the town back when your aunt and uncle lived there."

When EJ spoke again, her voice was warmer. "It was a popular place. Uncle Graham and Aunt Jeannie loved company, and they pulled out all the stops when it came to parties."

And then some. I leaned against the wall next to the mantel. "Between the beautiful house and menagerie, the Adair estate is one of the most interesting and unique properties in all of Sugarland. I'd love to learn more about it." Lucy wriggled, and I let her down. "If you don't mind, it would be helpful if you could give me permission to enter the house. I could document the inside as well as the outside." She didn't respond, so I added, "I'd be more than happy to share what I've learned. I'm not interested in moving or taking anything, I just want to see it up close."

"Oh. Well, I...sure, I suppose it would be nice to see how everything compares these days. I haven't been there myself since I was in junior high. All I have to go on are old pictures."

"Pictures?" I braced a hand against the wall and seized on her remark like a catfish snapping at a crawdad. "Do you have any of the animals? Like, say, a boa constrictor?" If she had pictures of the boa's cage, then I could compare it to what we were seeing at the party and tell if the dominant ghost was manipulating the scene in some way.

"I believe I do. I loved that boa when I was a child."

I wanted to hug her through the phone lines.

She chuckled. "I once asked my parents if I could sleep in the snake cage, but they weren't willing to leave me alone with Sir Charles, and I refused to let them kick him out of his home."

"Sir Charles, the snake?"

"Oh yes. I used to play with that old snake all the time." I could hear the smile in her voice. "I have a picture of my eighth birthday party with him looped all over me while I put a birthday hat on him. It used to give my mother fits, but he was such a gentle creature."

85

I'd have to take her word on that. "Would you mind emailing copies of those photos to me so I can use them to put together a presentation for the board of the heritage society?"

"Oh, not at all, not at all. I'd be happy to." She paused. "It's nice to see you taking an interest in the old place. That's what I like about small towns. You're proud of your history."

"It's fascinating," I said honestly. "And I very much appreciate your help with this." I gave her my email address, as well as the number of Ellis's police line to call and leave a message giving me permission to look around. That way there could be no question I was allowed to be there.

"Can I also get a gate key?" I asked, going for broke. "A house key would be helpful as well." The entrance to the house hadn't been locked, but I wouldn't put it past Duranja to correct that.

"I'll have my assistant send them overnight, and in the meantime, I'll let the city know you can use their key."

We thanked each other, and I hung up with a smile on my face.

Perhaps I'd celebrate with some pie. I headed back to the kitchen just as a knock sounded at the front door.

I was sure popular today.

I rebelted my robe, smoothed my hair, and hoped that whoever was at the door didn't mind seeing me in my pajamas after ten o'clock on a weekday.

It might even be my mysterious pecan pie benefactor, returning to talk or to at least accept a thank-you.

But as I neared the front window, my face fell. I recognized the champagne-colored Cadillac parked out front, the precisely bent elbow visible through my side window, and the second impatient knock.

Virginia Wydell.

$\mathcal{V}$irginia stood on my porch with the stiff-backed grace of a woman who had crossed the railroad tracks and found the other side even worse than she'd imagined. She looked fancy enough for church in a red sheath dress, kitten heels, and a light, cream-colored cardigan covering her shoulders. Armani sunglasses and her traditional, enormous pearl studs completed the look, elegant without trying too hard. I kind of hated her for nailing it.

Her lips, a perfect red to match the dress, curved in the world's tiniest smile. "Verity, dear, have I caught you sleeping the day away?"

I held my chin high and did my best to pretend I wasn't in my robe sans slippers.

"Not at all. I was working on a case."

"I suppose your ghosts don't care how you present yourself," she said pleasantly, stepping into the foyer.

She removed her sunglasses and appraised the foyer and adjoining front room with an expression I could only think of as 'Wicked Witch of the West surveying the results of tornado damage.'

"My goodness." Virginia spun in a slow circle, taking in the devastation she had wrought. All of my grandmother's furnishings—from the handwoven rugs to the Sheraton mahogany hallway table, to the sconces my great-grandfather had commissioned—were gone.

"I see you've decided on a minimalist decorating scheme."

"I'm getting back on my feet," I reminded her, leading her into the front room and toward the parlor, the traditional place for receiving guests and the only room in the house that had any furniture to speak of.

She took in the pale shadows on the walls where family portraits had once hung, and I was almost tickled when she startled at the trash can next to the carved marble fireplace in the back parlor.

It was hard to surprise Virginia Wydell, but Frankie's trash can might have managed.

She made no mention of it, though.

I led her to the purple velvet couch I'd earned in exchange for a ghost-hunting job. "Would you care to sit?" I asked as if I were offering up a spot on my verandah.

She eyed the used piece of furniture like it might bite her, and then hastily covered her social gaffe. "I'd rather not. I don't want to stay too long."

Thank goodness. The sooner she was out of here, the better. "What can I do for you?"

She turned to face me, her lips pursed. "You can stop using your influence to entice Beau into making bad decisions."

"Excuse me?" What was she even talking about? I hadn't spoken to Beau since we'd made a semi, sort-of peace on board the Sugarland Express. "I'm not sure what you mean."

She gave me a hard look. "You might be fine with your joblessness and your bohemian lifestyle, but Beau is destined for bigger things. I don't know what kind of hold you have on him.

I've never understood it. But I won't have him jeopardizing his future to impress you."

"Believe me, I'm not impressed," I said quickly before I'd had a chance to think. "I mean, whatever's wrong now, you can't put it on me." Beau was his own person. In spades. He had done some soul-searching when we were trapped on that train, and while it hadn't been fun to be on the receiving end of his ire, I was proud of the way he'd pulled himself together.

Virginia sniffed. "Verity, honestly, do you think I don't remember the role you played on the train last month?" Her bracelets rattled as she gestured. "Encouraging Beau to walk all the way to Gatlinburg, and at such a time?" *While there were murderers afoot,* her eyes accused.

"It was his idea, and he did a good job." Beau had come through for us surprisingly well. He'd not only brought the police, but he'd also rented a van to transport all the passengers to the next station. It was the sort of thoughtful, self-aware action that the old Beau wouldn't have even considered.

"He should never have been put in that position in the first place," she spat, her temper flaring.

She turned her gaze to the ceiling, and her attention snagged on the wires hanging where my grandmother's favorite antique chandelier should be. I'd sold it to pay back my debt to her, and she knew it.

She advanced until she was directly underneath the devastation she'd wrought. "My son is a good boy, or he was until he met you."

I wasn't even sure which son she was talking about but didn't believe it wise to ask.

"Your boys are grown. They can do what they want."

She served me a brittle smile, clearly struggling to maintain her decorum. "It's plain to me that you've had a heavy hand in encouraging Beau to shirk his duties, to change who he is. Come now, dear, you've already secured another foothold for yourself into the family. Why must you add to the drama?"

All I wanted was a quiet life with Ellis. "Beau is the one making waves for once, and I'm glad to see it."

"What?" she demanded. "Beau has let three of his clients go," she said as if he'd jumped naked into traffic. "He's given them to a junior partner."

"What does that have to do with me?"

She looked like she'd like to bop me over the head with her clutch. "If he keeps this up, he's going to lose status at the firm. This all started on the train, and you know it. Now Beau is acting as though he can zip around and do a bit of this, a bit of that, and expect to have some modicum of respectability at the end of the day. Ludicrous as it sounds, I think he's holding you up as an example to follow."

"I can't control your son," I told her. "Never could. Never will."

Virginia narrowed her eyes, one hand rising to her throat. A moment later, she drew my grandmother's cross out from under the edge of her dress, her fingers resting lightly against the delicate filigree. "Someone is steering the ship, and it's not Zoey." She gave me a long, hard stare. "Beau says she's quite taken with you. But then, you both seem to enjoy making minimum wage, so I suppose you have that in common."

I stiffened. "If you're going to stand here and insult me, you'd best get on with your day."

She closed her eyes briefly. "I apologize."

She almost sounded sincere. I wasn't sure what to do with that.

"You have to understand," she said, regrouping. "I know you care about Beau. You must see that he's ruining his life! I mean, first, it's you and this—" she waved her hand around the room at the signs of my desperation as if she hadn't been the cause of it "—and now a woman without a home, a woman whose life's ambition is to run a *food truck*, for the love of God. What kind of woman is that for Beau? She's not even from Tennessee! She looks like she time-traveled here from some hippie commune in the sixties."

"Virginia, I don't have enough influence over Beau to dictate to him what sort of woman he should date." I mean, honestly. "It's none of my business." *And none of yours, either.*

I didn't say the last part, but she reacted like she heard it anyway, squaring her shoulders and gripping the cross so tightly I was afraid she would break the chain.

"It's not the sort of thing you would understand, I suppose," she said at last. "You don't have children. You don't know what it's like to see them throw away all their hard work and potential on distraction and frivolity. You don't know what it's like to watch them grow, to mold them into people you can be proud of, only to see it all begin to slip away. And for what? An upstart, ambitionless food truck owner, or a woman who says—"

Virginia stopped herself before anything else slipped out, but I knew what was on the tip of her tongue. I had been a decent enough catch back when I was Beau's fiancée, with my family history and my respectable job. Now it was an embarrassment to be associated with me.

Well, I felt the same about her. I couldn't imagine the amount of pressure her sons had been under growing up in the Wydell mansion, surrounded by so much pomp and circumstance. My family wasn't perfect, but my parents hadn't doled out affection like it was a prize to be won, either.

"Are we finished?" I wanted to be out of my pajamas by noon.

"I want your word on this," Virginia insisted. "That you won't encourage Beau in his ridiculous delusions. He's a lawyer, and a good one. He's going to take over his father's firm someday. *That's his future.*"

I hated to tell her, but… "It's not up to either of us."

She clutched the cross. Hard. "Do you truly want to go toe-to-toe with me again?"

No. Not again in this lifetime.

Virginia made up the rules as she went, and I never saw it coming. I couldn't anticipate that level of viciousness. I never would have predicted my home's destruction, almost losing it, watching her wear my grandmother's necklace.

I wouldn't put it past her to sell it just to spite me.

I might not see it on her neck anymore, but I'd also never see it again.

Virginia calmed. She must have seen her message had been received.

Loud and clear.

She released her death grip on the cross, folded her hands over her clutch, and said, "I believe it's time for me to go." Then she turned and walked out without another word. The door clicked shut behind her.

I stood for a moment, recovering. I realized I was shaking.

I could handle this. I was a strong woman, too.

She wasn't in control of my life or anyone else's.

A moment later, a hard clang rang out from the kitchen. I hurried back to find Lucy standing over the pie pan, which lay facedown on the floor. She looked every bit the guilty skunk.

"Lucy!" I rushed over and picked her up, holding her away from the food. "Bad girl!"

I didn't even know how she'd gotten up on the counter. Yes, I did. Melody had lent me her stepladder so that I could dust up high, and my skunk was using it like a stairway to heaven. At least it didn't look like she'd gotten any of the pie. She didn't need to be rewarded for bad behavior.

I let her out into the backyard and cleaned up the mess.

As outrageous as Virginia's accusation had been, she had one thing right. Beau was searching for something outside his usual sixty-hour-a-week lawyer life. I sincerely hoped he found it. I couldn't imagine going through life feeling like you were in the wrong place.

And as I took a bath and readied myself for the day, I made a point to feel grateful for my home and my job. I might not have much furniture or a clue as to who killed that judge in 1928, but I'd figure it out somehow.

In fact, my sister, Melody, might be able to help or at least give me a place to start.

I called up the library's front desk, but instead of my sister, I got the library director, Sheila Ward. "Melody's off getting lunch at the food truck out front," she explained. "So is everyone else who is supposed to be working here." She didn't sound as annoyed as she might have. "As soon as one of them comes back in, I'm going to visit it myself. It smells delicious."

Good for Zoey. She hadn't wasted any time getting her food truck up and running. My stomach rumbled just thinking about it. "Thanks, Sheila. No need to leave a message."

I'd visit my sister in person. Zoey too. And maybe I could get some lunch while I was at it.

I DROVE into town with my window down and the radio blaring country and western tunes. I didn't usually turn on the radio when Frankie was riding with me, because he had opinions with a capital O about modern music, and none of them were good. It felt like a treat to be able to listen to a man sing about taking a pretty girl for a ride in his pickup truck.

I passed the trendy brick-faced stores that I couldn't afford to shop at anymore with barely a pang—although come heck or high water, I was treating myself to a truffle selection from the Candy Bar for my birthday. At last, I ended up on the edge of the town square.

Sugarland, like lots of the towns founded during that era, built most of the main city buildings in basically the same spot. The old justice department, the town hall, and the library hemmed the square. The buildings were made of gleaming white limestone quarried from the south end of town. Red limestone accented the doorways and windows, and the library had two tall red columns flanking a pair of large wooden entry doors. I felt a little like I was walking into a castle every time I entered it.

But the library could wait. I parked and set my sights on the orange and red food truck reading "Tuk Tuk Thai Grill" standing in front of it. Melody wasn't there. She must have finished eating. But a few other people stood out front, inspecting the menu and chatting with Zoey, who leaned down from the window and held court like she was having the time of her life. She'd tied her dark hair up in a bun, and she looked bright and energetic in a sleeveless blue blouse with a beaded collar. We exchanged a wave, and she interrupted her other conversations long enough to shout, "Hey! Lauralee, check it out, Verity's here."

Lauralee's familiar face popped up next to Zoey's a moment later. "You found us," she said with a grin. "Hang on, I'll meet you at the back."

A second later she opened one of the rear doors and stepped out of the truck. She wore a familiar red and white cherry-patterned apron and held a bunch of greens that I didn't recognize in one hand. "Smell these," she ordered, extending them toward me. I complied with a smile. They smelled mild and sweet and vaguely lemony.

"What is that?"

"Fresh lemongrass," she said. "Isn't it lovely? Zoey's got an amazing recipe for the most delicious barbecue sauce, and I thought it would be mostly curry-flavored given the Thai influences, but no! The base for the glaze is lemongrass!" She sniffed the herbs herself with a happy sigh, and then put them back on the counter in the truck.

"You two hooked up fast." I was glad to see it, although I'd only meant to give Lauralee's number so my friend could recommend possible coworkers for Zoey.

"It was fate," Lauralee announced. "Zoey called me last night and told me she wanted to do a test run at lunchtime today, and could I spare a few hours to help prep the food so she could handle the counter?" She planted a fist on her hip. "I would have been working the diner today, but the owner keeps hiring his wife's cousins, and they cut my hours back again, so this was the perfect fill-in. Thank you for recommending me to her. I think this could be exactly the third job I need."

That's right, she had her catering business as well. I wanted to send her on a trip to the spa just thinking about how much work she put in every day. "I don't know how you find the time for everything you do, a husband, four boys, and yourself."

"Love what you do, and you'll never work a day in your life," Lauralee replied. "How's that for a pithy platitude?" She grew serious. "I do fine. It's hard, of course it is, but at least with this job I'm learning something new."

I opened my mouth to reply, but Zoey beat me to it. "Two barbecue chicken satays and a side of fried okra with the teriyaki dipping sauce!" she called out.

"Whoops, order up," Lauralee said. "I have to work, but can we—"

"We'll talk later," I assured her. "Go, go." I walked back around to the front of the truck, where the two guys Zoey had been chatting with were now talking to each other. She waved me over.

"Hey! You caught us at the end of the lunch rush."

What constituted a 'rush,' I wondered. "Were there a lot of people?"

"Like, around twenty or so? Which isn't huge, but for a first day I think it's pretty good." Zoey tossed her head to the side, cat earrings swinging. "People seem to like it. Lauralee is amazing with the food, and I needed the help so I could work the window. I'm hoping the word of mouth will build things up even more for tomorrow. It's like you said, right? People talk in a small town. Here's hoping the talk will all be good."

Her enthusiasm was infectious. "I'm so glad." Bringing two talented, hardworking women together left me with a warm glow, which dampened when I remembered the visit I'd just survived. "Hey, you should know—Virginia is on the warpath. She ambushed me this morning. She might go after you next."

Zoey retucked her hair behind her bandana. "I can handle her."

She had no idea. "That's what I said at first, too." What I'd always tried to do. "Be careful. She can surprise you."

Zoey tilted her head. "She'll come around once she gets used to the fact that I'm not going anywhere." She smiled. "Beau came back to me at the party last night, and we spent every minute after that together, even when his mom tried to drag him away again. He's got my back."

Famous last words. I knew that nothing I could say would convince Zoey otherwise, though. She'd learn about tangling with Virginia Wydell the hard way like I did. And if she was going to stick with Beau, a tangle was inevitable.

"How much have you and Beau talked about his past?" I asked, easing into yet another unpleasant topic. She needed to know the whole truth, at least about Beau and me.

"He tells me everything," she said, with a wry smile.

Well, maybe not everything.

It wasn't my business to get in the middle of it, but I didn't see how I could avoid it. "You see—"

"I need you inside," Lauralee called to Zoey. "Your stove knobs are sticking and the heat's getting high."

"Just a minute!" Zoey called back to her.

"Real quick," she said to me, "I got permission from Maisie to build a fire pit out of some spare cinderblocks on her property, and I'd love it if you and Ellis could come and join me and Maisie and Beau for a cookout tonight."

She must have seen the reluctance on my face, because she

hastily added, "I'll do the cooking. You guys just bring yourselves." She paused. "Wait, your boyfriend's got a brewery, right? So bring yourselves and some beer."

That would not be the place to tell her my news, although I hoped Beau would have a talk with her once he knew she was planning an event like this.

"I—"

"Please," she said as Lauralee called for her again.

"I will," I said, lifting a finger between us to contain her squeal, "if you tell Beau he has to talk to you about how he and I met and...everything else."

"Fine," she said. "Everybody knows everybody, right?"

Not as well as I'd known her boyfriend.

I'd have to make sure Ellis was free. "I also can't stay late," I said as she rushed to join Lauralee. I absolutely had to be at the Adair mansion tonight.

"No worries there," she promised, climbing into the back of the truck "If I go to bed later than ten o' clock, I'm blasted the next day." She waved at the smoke coming out of the rear doors. "Whew! Yeah. That stove is acting up. The food looks good, though."

"Oh, I'd never burn a skewer," Lauralee joked.

Lauralee sounded so happy.

And having Zoey around for company probably made a world of difference to Maisie, too.

Beau would be the better for knowing her as well.

Now if we could all just get along...

"Drop by tonight at seven," Zoey said, leaning out the back of the truck. "This'll be so much fun."

"I hope so," I told her.

At least the smoke had begun to clear from the back of the truck.

"Here," she turned and came back with a plate of steaming chicken satay. My mouth watered at the aroma of garlic and curry powder as she tucked a lime wedge on the side.

"Made just like that place you loved on our weekend in Memphis," Lauralee called from behind the stove.

Zoey beamed at me as she handed it to me. "On the house." She winked. "Now relax and enjoy. You'll see. Everything is going to be fine."

CHAPTER 9

$\mathcal{T}$hat evening, Ellis and I set out for Maisie's, with Frankie in the backseat of Ellis's police cruiser. The gangster appeared oddly comfortable behind the metal security screen. I supposed he'd seen enough of the back of squad cars.

"Sorry we have to drag you to the bonfire first, Frankie," Ellis said, turning onto Rural Route 7. He couldn't see or hear the ghost, but he liked to be polite.

The gangster merely scowled. "It's better than hiding in a lake for eternity."

I turned to Ellis. "Zoey promised me she was going to ask Beau about our past," I told him, "so this could be a shorter party than we're expecting."

He shook his head. "I can't believe Beau didn't tell her he was engaged once."

I crossed my arms and leaned back in the seat. "He might have told her that, but he certainly didn't tell her who the girl was."

"And here I thought *The Jerry Springer Show* had been canceled," he mused.

Meanwhile, Frankie hunched back against the seat, staring out the window at the violet sunset sky like it held some sort of answer.

"You should have brought Molly along tonight," I said. To the bonfire at least. She always had a calming effect on him.

He brushed imaginary lint off his suit coat. "She visited me at the bottom of the pond this afternoon but got mad and went home early. She was asking too many questions."

"She'd be welcome," I said, not that Frankie ever waited for an invite from me. "In fact, if you want, we can go back and—"

"No," Frankie snapped. "I don't want her around another murder investigation."

Ellis turned onto the highway, and we sped toward the east side of town, my hair blowing in the wind from the open window, Frankie's hairdo frozen in place for eternity.

"Frankie," I began. I hated to see him struggle with Molly.

"Don't you see?" he shot back. "I can't take her. You saw what that mansion was like."

"You take her to speakeasies." I left off the part about the one in Ellis's attic.

Frankie scowled. "I trust the bootleg gin swillers. The swells are a different story, especially with a killer on the loose."

That made absolutely zero sense. "She hangs around killers all the time. You, Suds, the rest of the South Town Gang, you're all—"

"Hey!" Frankie sounded terribly affronted. "That's completely different! We're not psychopaths. You heard what the inspector said."

Put that way, I could see where he was coming from. "And now she's mad at you," I said sympathetically.

"Mad. Sad. Disappointed. And I didn't even lie to her. You'd think I'd get some kinda points for that." He glared down at the floor. "This is why I never got into a relationship before. It's too hard to stay on top. You pull a job, and you either win or lose, no in between. But being with Molly, sometimes I feel like there's nothing but in between."

Aww...I felt sorry for the crusty gangster. "You want what's best for her. She'll understand that."

"From your lips to God's ear, sweetheart." He shut down after that, and when I glanced over at Ellis, he was looking at me with a bemused expression on his face.

"What?" I asked, bracing a hand on the windowsill as we began to bounce over the dirt road leading to Maisie's property.

"I'm trying to figure out your conversation from context," Ellis said, steering. A thick forest rose up on both sides of the road. "It's an interesting challenge."

"Tell him he's as useful as a trapdoor on a canoe," Frankie drawled.

I started to laugh, then faked a sneeze to try to cover it. The gangster rarely showed his Southern side.

Ellis shot a look over his shoulder toward the backseat. "He just insulted me, didn't he?"

Frankie spread his arms out over the back of the seat. "This is why you make the big bucks, copper."

MOMENTS LATER, we arrived at Maisie's house. Maisie had been living by herself out on this remote, wooded property ever since her good-for-nothing husband died almost fifty years ago. Her blue jalopy truck sat on a patch of gravel in front of her small weather-beaten home. Tonight it was joined by two other cars: Beau's silver BMW coupe and Zoey's red and orange painted food truck, still looking bright even in the dying light.

Off to the left about a hundred feet, only partially visible through the trees and brush, was a tan RV with the word *Moonbeam* painted along its side in glow-in-the-dark paint. A canopy extended from the top of it to shelter a little sitting area, which was bathed in the warm glow of firelight.

"Hey." Frankie brightened. "I forgot about the old lady's backyard."

Beyond Maisie's house stood a stretch of haunted woods. I'd braved them on a previous adventure and barely made it out.

That didn't seem to matter to Frankie. He vanished into the night, quick as a ghost.

Ellis and I left the car, him with a six-pack in hand. He'd brought his newest beer, a dark, caramelly stout brewed in bourbon barrels. He'd tested it on me the last time I'd visited his place, and wow, was it ever delicious. I could only handle about half of one before it went to my head, so I'd be abstaining tonight. But his brews were going to be a hit. Maybe Beau would drink three and confess everything.

It'll be okay, I reminded myself as I held my hand out to Ellis. We were going to enjoy a lovely evening with my ex, his current flame, my man, and Maisie, who had absolutely no filter.

Hopefully, Maisie would be too busy talking about baby bunnies to talk about me.

"You look nice," I said, leaning into Ellis as we made our way to the fire pit. He wore a dark blue T-shirt that clung just enough to his biceps to make it hard to look away.

"Verity!" Zoey caught sight of us and waved both arms above her head like she was bringing a plane in to land. "Over here!"

Oh boy. She clearly had no clue what had happened between her boyfriend and me.

Darn it, Beau.

He was going to make me tell her.

We joined the three of them. Zoey looked adorable in a zigzag-patterned black and white romper, while Beau could have stepped out of the pages of a golfing magazine. He hadn't quite gotten the whole "outdoor casual" thing yet, although I was pleased to see him in sneakers. That showed effort.

Maisie sat on a log in front of the fire. She stood as fast as a woman half her age, her wild auburn hair flying around her head like a halo as she wrapped me in a bear hug.

My ribs creaked at the force of it.

"Verity," she drew back, "I hope you're ready to eat. That one —" she pointed at Zoey, who winked back "—has been working on this meal all afternoon."

"Maisie let me raid her herb garden," Zoey said as if it were the greatest treasure in the world. And for a foodie, perhaps it was. She busied herself turning a half-dozen skewers of meat roasting over the fire pit's flames. "She also let me steal her fondue forks. I didn't even know people ate fondue anymore."

Maisie shrugged one skinny shoulder. "How should I know? I got them as a wedding present and used 'em to break up the soil in my garden for years. What have you brought there, Ellis?"

"Beer," he said, handing the six-pack to his brother before coming over to greet her himself. "How's the rabbit hutch holding up?"

"Nobody's escaped from it yet," she said. "I can't ask for better than that. You said you brought beer?"

"Strong beer," I cautioned.

"Nine percent alcohol by volume," Beau noted, turning over a bottle in his hands. "That'll knock you out for the night."

"Good thing I live close," Maisie joked. "Crack one open for me."

Beau took care of it while Ellis and Zoey said their hellos. Beau passed a beer to me to give to Maisie, then asked, "One for you too?"

"Oh, no, thanks." I shook my head. "I've got to work after this."

He waggled the bottle at me. "Are you sure? I don't think the ghosts care if you have just one."

"I care," I said. I wasn't about to go to the Adair mansion tonight at less than one hundred percent.

He didn't press any further, which was new. Beau had never exactly pressured me to drink when we were together, but it used to be that when he did something, he automatically assumed that other people wanted to join in, whether it was drinking, skinny-dipping, or cow tipping. I hadn't been there for the cow tipping myself, but there were pictures. It was one of the few bad decisions Beau had made that he'd allowed to be documented.

Someone had carried Maisie's rickety red leatherette chairs out to sit on. The plates were paper, and the air smelled pungent, almost musky. Cottonwood didn't make for a pleasant fire unless it was totally dry, which these logs apparently weren't. But dinner ended up being lovely. Zoey talked a lot about her first day with the food truck and exchanged heart eyes with Beau, who didn't pick a fight with Ellis—a minor miracle all on its own. She asked questions about Southern Spirits, too, including the specials menu, which Ellis was using to try new dishes.

I mostly sat back with Maisie and let her take me through the rabbit photos she'd whipped out of her pocket. They were old-fashioned Polaroids, thick and stiff. I didn't even know you could find film for those cameras anymore.

"They're growing so fast," I said as she held out what had to be the thirtieth picture of her bunnies in their new hutch, courtesy of an afternoon of Ellis's time. Well, more like a full weekend. Ellis wasn't a born handyman, but he'd learned so he could help Maisie and others in town who needed an extra hand.

It almost made me forget about what lay in store tonight with Beau. Almost.

All too soon Maisie went to bed—after declaring she had to "check on her lil' darlings" first. Ellis, because he was a gentleman, escorted her back to her house while Zoey packed away the leftover food and Beau tossed another log onto the fire. He seemed antsy, ready to jump out of his skin.

I walked over to him. "You didn't tell her about us."

He shot me a nervous half-grin. "She doesn't need to know everything about me."

Maybe not, but this was a big one. "If you're going to date her, you have to be honest." I took a drink of water. "If you don't tell her tonight, I will."

"You're bluffing," he shot back, not sounding at all sure of himself anymore.

"You know I'm not."

"The thing is—" he began.

"Miss me?" Zoey breezed past me to snuggle up to Beau.

He caught my gaze from over her shoulder and gave a small smirk. "Like you wouldn't believe," he said, nuzzling her hair.

Yes, well, Zoey derailing the conversation didn't mean he was off the hook.

Perhaps he hadn't changed so much after all.

A moment later, Ellis joined us. "It's getting late," he announced. "Verity and I need to head out soon."

Beau gave a sharp nod as if deciding something. "Before you go, there's something I need to say." He pulled up a log to form a small grouping.

Zoey held his hand.

"All right." This had to be it. I took a seat next to Ellis, facing Beau and Zoey.

When we'd all settled in, Beau took a deep breath.

He planted his bottle on the ground, leaned his elbows forward onto his knees, and looked at me. "I have something to say."

He should be addressing Zoey, but okay. "Let's hear it."

Ellis swirled the last of his beer and shared a glance with me.

"As you both know, I've done some soul-searching over the past year and a half since Verity dumped me."

Zoey's face fell. "You dated Verity?" she asked, her voice barely a whisper.

Beau patted her on the leg. "We were engaged."

Zoey's features tightened. She tried to twist a brave smile out of a tight-lipped frown, but she looked more like she was about to cry.

"I'm sorry," I said, quashing the urge to hug her. She might not even accept that from me right now. "I wanted to tell you, but it seemed like something you needed to hear directly from Beau. I didn't want to get in the middle of you two."

"And I didn't realize you'd run into her so fast," Beau said, his tone purposely light as if that would diffuse Zoey's hurt. "Hey, what can I say? This is Sugarland!"

"You're an ass," Ellis said.

"You were engaged to Verity," Zoey repeated, her voice taking on a hard edge, her attention moving to me as if I'd planned the whole thing.

"It wasn't my place to say anything," I said, feeling awful and guilty and wrong. I should have found a way to tell her. But I didn't know she'd find out like this.

Beau, for his part, appeared as if a weight had been lifted. The jerk.

"Anyway—" Beau shrugged off the discomfort he'd caused "— I've been doing some soul-searching, and I've come to a decision. You're the first people I'm telling apart from Zoey."

"Who obviously isn't in on everything," she interjected, taking a hearty swig of beer.

Beau ignored her. "I thought it was important to start with the one who opened my eyes." He looked straight at me when he said the last part. Zoey noticed too, and I wanted to punch him. He hung his head, then brought it back up again. "I've found my true calling in life." He said it like a man going to war, come hell or high water. "I'm going to be an eclectic folk artist!"

None of us spoke for a long moment.

"Well?" Beau prodded as if expecting applause.

Ellis was the one to finally break the silence. "I'm not sure what that is," he confessed.

Thank heavens he said it first. I had no idea either.

Beau stood. "It's surrealist self-expression through found-object meta-construction, imbued with local Southern flavor," he said, his fingers brushing Zoey's shoulder as he stood. Maybe that impressed her, but I had no idea what it meant. Fortunately, Beau had pictures on his phone. He passed it over to us. "Take a look!"

I scrolled through slowly, taking in the self-expressive meta-objects. They looked a lot like Beau had scavenged some cheap wood scraps and twisted branches, nailed bits of metal or cloth to them, fixed them to poles like the world's most avant-garde scarecrows, and gone to town with some spray paint. Blindfolded. Possibly while drunk.

No wonder Virginia had been alarmed. I was starting to see her point.

"I rented a barn to use as a studio," Beau continued excitedly. "It's why I've been taking some time from the firm lately." He took a drink of beer. "I have to work in natural light, there's no way to get the colors to blend so perfectly otherwise."

"He is talented," Zoey reluctantly agreed, cooler than she had been before. Beau would be lucky if his relationship recovered.

Ellis flipped to another picture. Beau looked over his shoulder. "Ah, yes. I call that one *Magic in the Moonlight*."

It looked like a black and yellow blob. Was the black supposed to indicate phases of the moon, or had he run out of the neon yellow paint? "What is this fringe?" I asked. It hung from some of the yellow blobs.

"Horsetail to symbolize the moon's ties to nature," Beau said as if it were obvious.

Ellis quivered with choked-off laughter, and I silently willed him to keep it under control. "This is...so different from any art I've seen before," I said, handing the phone back.

Beau beamed. "I know! It's a totally unique artistic avenue, and I have Verity to thank for it."

Not me. Not ever. "I don't remember telling you about

horsetails and moonlight," I said to him, and to Zoey. I'd deny ever seeing the moon if it meant I had to take credit for this.

He dragged his log over and sat directly across from me. "I understand now why you didn't want to be with me."

"Let's not do this," I managed, my eyes on Zoey, who stood behind him, seething. I didn't blame her.

Ellis wasn't laughing anymore, either.

"You wanted everything out in the open," Beau reminded me.

"Don't put this on me," I warned. "I ended things. Permanently. Because of what happened right before the wedding." I glanced up at Zoey. "You owe your girlfriend the truth. After that, let's let the past stay in the past."

"Don't you see?" Beau prodded. "It all comes back around!"

Oh, it was coming around, all right.

"I wasn't being my true self," he continued. "It frustrated me, and I acted out. I ruined everything."

"Beau—" I began. He was about to ruin everything again. At least for him and Zoey.

"I couldn't handle being real," he plowed forward, "I couldn't face getting in touch with my deepest emotions." Beau touched a hand to his chest, still looking straight at me. "After what happened on the train and seeing you living your own life so genuinely, with no apologies for what you believe in—it lit a fire inside me, Verity. It made me realize that life is short, and if I'm going to live a life free of regrets, then I need to follow in your footsteps."

"Let me get you moving," Ellis said, shoving Beau's log out from under him with one foot.

Beau stumbled and stood, shooting Ellis a dirty look.

"You may want to watch out for Mom while you're at it," Ellis continued. "She's not the artsy type."

"Unbelievable," Beau said, his attention returning to Zoey. "Ellis thinks he's the only one in the family who should get to do what he wants, who can date who he wants. And Verity used to be my biggest supporter."

"Like Zoey is now," I said, making a giant leap, but I didn't care. My chance for a new friend might be shot, but I'd be darned if I'd sit by and watch him mess up with the only good girl that had come into his life in a long time. "Just do me a favor and don't tell your mom this was my idea."

After her visit today, I didn't think I could take that kind of heat.

Ellis ran a hand through his hair, a nervous tell I only knew from our occasional poker nights. Frankie had insisted I learn how to play. "So, Beau, is there much of a market for this kind of art?"

"West Coast collectors are getting into Southern eclectic right now," Zoey said, her words stiff. "It's going to be the new thing."

"But it's not a thing yet?" Ellis pressed. Here was the cop coming out. He was trained to peel back the layers of a story until he found the reality hiding at the bottom of it.

"Not yet," Beau said, his anger cooling. "I'm on the cutting edge. Check this one out." He handed the phone back. "I think it's my best sculpture so far."

The centerpiece was shaped like a fat snake with three heads, and each head was something different: a hubcap, what looked like a bent wine barrel ring, and the detached blade of a saw. Each one was painted a different color—red, aqua, and brown. I think there might have been shards of glass involved, that or glitter. And the polka dots were...wait, had those been *glued* on? It looked like one was about to fall off.

"Wow," was all I could say at first. "Very memorable. Do you have any buyers yet? Or an agent?" It was possible. Just because his sculptures weren't my taste didn't mean other people wouldn't like them. I leaned more toward classic design rather than hubcaps and glitter. "What are you doing to sell your work?"

"I'm waiting for the art dealers to catch up with *me*," Beau said as if that were the goal of every artist. "They don't understand what I'm doing yet, but that's because it's so unique. You're an artist. You get it," he said as if my past as a graphic artist would prepare me for that sort of thing.

Newsflash: it hadn't. I'd worked for businesses who'd needed my logos and designs to sell their own products. It wasn't about wild self-expression. It was about making my clients look good.

"Besides," Zoey grabbed another beer and took up Beau's cause, "art critics and agents don't matter."

"It seems like they might if an artist doesn't want to starve," Ellis said.

Beau huffed like Ellis had no idea. "When the world is ready for my work, it'll sell so fast I won't be able to keep it in stock." He drained the rest of his beer. "Of course, maybe I'll have my own gallery by then."

"You totally will," Zoey said, leaning over to kiss his cheek. "I believe in you, baby." She glared down at me. "Even if Verity doesn't."

Lovely.

It was good that he had her support, at least. "Well, this is great," I said. "You can be a lawyer and an artist. Keep working at the firm, use the barn on the weekends, and eventually, the right buyer will come along who can properly appreciate your work."

Beau frowned. "It's not like it's going to take years to establish myself as an artist, Verity. People make it big every day."

As the only one of us who'd worked as a professional artist in the group, I had to disagree. "I'm just saying, building a client base takes time. It's not a bad idea to keep your day job until your art covers the bills."

Beau looked as if I'd slapped him. "Are you saying you think I can't do it?"

"Not at all." I stood, considered placing a comforting hand on his arm, and thought better of it. "I'm just urging a little bit of caution."

"Do you live a life of caution?" he demanded. "No!" he answered before I could respond. "So don't expect me to either. You're being a hypocrite, Verity."

"And you're being an ass," I told him.

He walked away, toward the fire. I thought that was the end of it until he spun to face me. "You know what? I'm going to prove you wrong." He pointed his beer from me to Ellis. "Both of you."

"Please don't do anything rash," I cautioned.

He pointed his bottle at me. "I'm quitting the firm tomorrow. I'm going to take up art full-time."

"Hold up, little brother," Ellis cautioned.

But Beau was on a roll. "I'm going to spend all day in the barn working on my creations, contemplating the message and meaning each piece yearns to convey. I'll raid dumps and secondhand stores and give new life to other people's thrown-away dreams. I'm a *dream* maker. *This* is my true path."

"It is." Zoey beamed. "I'm honored to be a part of it."

I was horrified just to be on the periphery of it.

My only hope was that maybe he'd leave me out of it. Maybe he'd take full credit. Otherwise, my life was over. Virginia was going to kill me.

CHAPTER 10

"*J*'m as good as dead," I said to Ellis half an hour later as we drove toward the Adair estate.

"No," Ellis said, turning onto the long road that led to the Adair mansion. "My mother can't possibly blame you for Beau losing his mind."

I was pretty sure there was no limit to the things that Virginia Wydell could blame me for.

"Being dead's not that bad," Frankie mused. "At least when you're not tied down to a bunch of dirt under some dame's rosebush."

"Thanks for the reminder," I said. And then, trying for a bit of levity, I added, "Sounds like you had fun at Maisie's."

He chuffed. "The World War One veterans have a shooting range going in the woods out back. Crack shots, all of 'em, but I held my own. It was a hoot. You'd have had a lot more fun watching blindfolded trick shots than you did talking art with your ex."

"What's he saying?" Ellis asked, glancing at the empty backseat like he could see Frankie gushing.

"He thinks I'd have more fun if I actually *were* dead."

"You might," Frankie insisted.

Ellis laughed. "I heard the dead have it easy."

We both knew better.

Just then Ellis crested a hill near the old pecan orchard. He slowed as we passed, no doubt thinking about his case.

Seeing the rows of pecan trees also reminded me of the strange pie I'd received on my porch this morning. "Ellis," I began, telling him the story as the car bounced down the familiar weedy path toward the old mansion.

He shot me the side-eye. "That is the strangest thing I've heard since five minutes ago," he said. Then, growing serious, he added, "You'd think somebody would take credit for a home-baked dessert. Let me know if anything else weird happens."

"I will," I promised.

Although for me, weird was a daily occurrence.

Ellis slowed as we neared the overgrown estate. It appeared as formidable as it had the night before, only this time we had permission to be there.

"You have the keys?" Ellis asked.

"Of course," I said, fishing in my pocket for the key ring I'd picked up at the records office this afternoon.

I opened the gate and slid back into the car as Ellis began the long slow drive up the main driveway.

Wind moaned through the trees. It was as dark now as it had been yesterday, but this time, inexplicably, it felt as if we were being watched. The tall grass bent and swayed as another gust, a stronger one, hit us from the side and whipped toward the house.

The wind felt almost like something was moving within it, taunting us.

"Stop here," Frankie said, just when we passed a particularly gnarled old elm.

I repeated his request, and Ellis parked in the middle of the road halfway to the house. "What's going on?" he asked, keeping the engine running.

"I'm not sure," I said, watching the ghost step out of the car. "Maybe we're making a discreet entrance."

But as I stepped out into the night, I got the distinct feeling someone had spotted me.

The wind fell quiet, and the air around us stilled.

The gangster glided toward the front of the car.

"I'm here as a friend," I said to no one in particular, peering into the shadows. Ellis joined me, the car door snicking closed behind him.

"What do you see?" Ellis asked.

"Nothing yet." I didn't have Frankie's power. When I turned my attention from the shadows by the road, I saw Frankie frozen in front of the car, the headlights shining straight through him.

"What's wrong?" I demanded.

Ellis reached behind his belt for his gun, but that wouldn't help us. Not against the dead.

Frankie stood in the middle of the path, eyes wide, his lower jaw drawn tight.

"Are you okay?" I joined him. "Do I even want your power tonight?"

Without it, I couldn't see any ghostly threats. Then again, when I wasn't tuned in, they couldn't hurt me, either.

"Take it," he said, zapping me.

"Wait." I held up a hand at the same time.

But it was too late.

The power sizzled over me, racing down my body. It felt like diving headfirst into a vat of pure energy. Every nerve in my body crackled as I tried to adapt.

"Verity!" Ellis caught me, steadying me. He held me close. I must have looked awful.

I pulled away. "I need to be able to move fast."

"Right." He let me go.

As hard as it was to be hit with Frankie's ghostly juice with no warning, I was more afraid of what I'd see next.

"I—" My breath stopped in my throat, choked off out of fascination, awe, and—it had to be said—a little horror.

We'd stopped just short of, well, nothing I'd ever seen before, this side of the veil or on the other.

"These ghosts win," Frankie said, serious as a funeral. "They win at life *and* death."

"I wouldn't go that far," I said, glad at least I wasn't in mortal danger.

The gangster watched, fascinated. "I've never seen so many people running around in their underthings in my life, and I've been to Newport Beach in the summer."

"Not underthings," I said. "Togas."

Frankie furrowed his brow.

"Remind me to play the movie *Animal House* for you sometime."

He shuddered. "I don't do talking pictures. But I think I could do this," he added, warming to the scene unfolding in front of us.

The mansion was lit up as it had been the night before. The entire front lawn had been transformed into a bizarre kind of obstacle course, with false trees built from papier mâché dangling real fruit from their branches, enormous shells full of water—or alcohol, it was hard to tell—rising out of frothy clouds of netting, and men chasing women around with heart-tipped arrows in their hands, laughing their heads off while the women giggled and dodged.

The men wore togas long enough to brush the ground, while the women were clothed in what looked like belted slips, with lace-up sandals and glittering laurels around their foreheads.

"Better?" Ellis asked, seeing my expression.

"Much." We had a lot of work to do. I couldn't afford to get distracted. Still, I slipped an arm through Ellis's. "I think we're about to step into Drunk Olympus."

CHAPTER 11

I spotted Marcus standing next to Graham on the front steps of the mansion. Drinks in hand, heads together, they reminded me of a pair of fraternity buddies. Graham laughed heartily at something Marcus said, and the taller man nudged his host before adding a comment that sent them into a new round of guffaws.

Jeannie sauntered up to the men, dolled up in a much fancier version of the tiny tunic that most of the women wore. A cloak of peacock feathers draped from her shoulders down to the ground, and more feathers—these glinting with diamonds—formed a halo around her head. Not to be outdone, Marjorie strode arm in arm with her host and friend, wearing a glittering gown that displayed her entire back and a long trail of rhinestones down her spine. I could tell by the knowing look the women exchanged that they were up to something.

"Ready?" Graham prodded, like a kid at Christmas.

"Always," Jeannie purred.

The men stood next to a large statue draped in white cloth. And when Graham nodded at his friend and his wife, the women took their places on either side of it, like *Price is Right* models.

"Something's going down," Frankie said as Graham raised a hand.

The crowd murmured. Several people began to clap. The women whipped the cloth away to reveal an enormous donut-shaped metal cylinder on a tall stand.

"What the what?" I began.

It glowed, kicking off tiny sparks.

More cheers erupted.

Jeannie gave her beaming husband a kiss on the cheek. Marjorie did the same, and as Marcus leaned to whisper in her ear, I watched her face fall. She tried to paste on a new smile, but it was raw and forced. Marcus smirked, and I wondered what he'd said to his wife.

Graham Adair strode behind the strange, sparking contraption and withdrew a long wand from the base.

He raised the wand into the air and—*crack!*

The sparks became a sizzling bolt of lightning connecting his hand to the glowing ball. The watchers shouted. I winced before recognizing that our host wasn't only unharmed, he was cackling with a showman's glee.

"Bow to me, the king of the gods, Zeus the Thunderer!" he cried.

The crowd roared and clapped.

I couldn't help it. I clapped too. It was amazing. Spectacular. I was so glad to be here. I had to rein it in. I was investigating. But, oh, my goodness. I was used to crumbling haunted houses with cobwebs and angry ghosts. Not...this.

Marcus kissed his wife on the cheek and left to go greet a trio of socialites. The band started up. Marjorie jumped down into the crowd and got the dancing started, and I looked at Frankie. "Yay for the 1920s," I said.

"Babe," he said, shaking his head, "you have no idea."

If last night had been a rollicking party, tonight was a complete and utter bash. The pianist had been replaced by a live—well, a dead—jazz band. The entire front lawn doubled as a dance floor. A few ambitious partygoers tried to play along on lyres and pan pipes. More guests plucked fruit off the trees as fast as the unobtrusive staff could hang it, and the shells had to be continuously refreshed with new infusions of...whatever people were drinking.

Frankie accepted a shell from a passing waiter, who was dressed in black tie with a laurel wreath on his head. The gangster dipped a finger in his drink and licked it. "Huh, fruity. Strong, too." He grinned. "These people know how to party."

"Stick close," I told him. We had a killer on the loose, a psychopath who could be all smiles one minute and deadly the next.

Besides, the inspector would be expecting insight and answers from us. For that, we needed to stay sharp.

And speak of the devil...

De Clercq strode from amid the crowd, his hands clasped behind his back, observing Mr. Adair's display with the expression of a man who had seen it all.

He frowned when he saw us. "Mr. Winkelmann, you're late."

Frankie jerked his head back toward me. "We were just enjoying the show." He joined the inspector. "What have we got going tonight?"

"This party offers us an excellent opportunity to observe and interact with each of our suspects," the inspector said. "Starting with him," he said, inclining his head toward Graham Adair, who waved the lightning rod theatrically for the crowd. "He's confident. He's clever."

"He has keys to the snake cage," I finished.

De Clercq didn't appear impressed.

He addressed Frankie. "I've conducted interrogations on this night every year for the last ninety years, so stay close and observe well." He twisted the edge of his mustache as he studied the gangster. "I'll be counting on your powers of criminal observation to uncover something I have not."

"Sounds peachy," Frankie said, glancing to make sure I had his back as the ghosts set off toward the house.

No worries there.

"We're going to start questioning," I said under my breath to Ellis, who walked briskly at my side.

"I think I can handle that," Ellis replied.

"You will not speak to the suspects," De Clercq said to me over his shoulder.

"For now," I agreed.

We didn't know what would happen once I had a suspect to speak with.

Too bad Ellis wasn't wearing his police uniform. Maybe then the inspector would take at least one of his live investigators seriously.

I respected De Clercq and his incredible powers of observation, but what he had been doing wasn't working. He was stuck.

He'd been investigating this case for a year when he died in the wreck of the Sugarland Express in 1929. My guess was he hadn't been able to rest without catching the killer. I wasn't a big fan of the inspector, mainly due to the way he liked to dismiss me as just another living girl. But if I could help him find justice and peace, I'd do it.

We followed the inspector as he walked up behind Mr. Adair. The static electric coil hummed and crackled, just about to snap. The hair on my arms stood on end, and I could feel the current down to my bones. Our host swung his wand down, and I jumped at the spectacular lightning strike. The crowd cheered. Adair held his wand aloft.

De Clercq cleared his throat.

Mr. Adair turned, impatient. "Again?" he said through a

clench-toothed smile. "I told you last year, and the one before, please wait until the end of my show."

"Murder waits for no man," the inspector said crisply. He drew his notebook from the inside pocket of his suit coat, the same notebook he'd used to catch Frankie in his lies. "Where were you last night between the hours of six and nine?" he asked Adair.

Our host lowered the wand. "You know where I was. I was overseeing preparations for the party and welcoming guests."

De Clercq ticked off the answer in his notebook. "Who can verify your claim?"

Unlike Frankie under questioning, Adair appeared bored and annoyed.

This was bad. "He's asking the suspects the same questions he always asks them," I murmured to Ellis. "Trying to catch them in some sort of inconsistency, I guess, but it hasn't worked in ninety years. I don't see how it's going to work now."

De Clercq shot me a frosty look.

I offered him a sweet Southern smile. We were here to unstick him, and if that made him a little uncomfortable, well, it was a small price to pay for catching a killer.

"That's what he brought you and Frankie along for, right?" Ellis said. "To see the things he doesn't and ask the questions he won't."

"Frankie, maybe. I think he's mostly annoyed with me." It was mutual, that was for sure. The inspector was brilliant, but he needed to change tactics. He also needed to let me talk.

"Sometimes, a repeated line of questioning will trip a suspect up," Ellis added.

"For ninety years?" I asked. That seemed like a stretch, even for the most dedicated cop.

The old detective ignored us. "Do you have a key to the snake cage?" he asked Adair.

Adair gritted his jaw. "You know I do."

This was going nowhere. We had to do something different.

We'd start by having a more open dialogue with the host of the party, even if he was a suspect. Adair might very well have done in the crooked judge, but he also knew every single person at this party, and he was too valuable to antagonize.

Before De Clercq could begin to read his next question, I stepped up. "Mr. Adair?" I smiled as brightly as I could while dodging a giggling nymph. "I have to tell you how impressed I am with your machine here. It's a Tesla coil, right?"

"Excuse me," De Clercq snapped.

But Adair's face brightened. "Ah, you know your transformers, Miss…"

"Long. Verity Long. And I don't know transformers at all." I was just impressed by them. I'd seen them once on a History Channel special. "Thank you so much for having us at your party. It must have taken a lot of work to get all of this set up."

"Winkelmann," the inspector fumed behind me, "get your live girl under control."

"Easier said than done," the gangster groused.

But I had Adair talking. And I was genuinely interested in what he had to say.

"The Tesla coil was worth the effort." He beamed. He raised the metal rod in his hand, and another bolt of lightning shot to him. "After all, how can I be Zeus without my lightning?"

"I'm never going to forget seeing you hit that coil for the first time," I confessed. It was true. Some of the things I'd witnessed on the other side were downright amazing.

"This has nothing to do with our investigation," De Clercq insisted, trying to insert himself between us. "Mr. Adair, you were seen speaking with the deceased less than an hour before he disappeared. What were you discussing?"

Mr. Adair smiled thinly. "The weather. It is about the only subject he and I could ever agree on."

"Have these discussions ever become physical?" the inspector pressed.

"No, never." Mr. Adair indicated himself. "Look at me. Larry Knowles had four inches and fifty pounds on me. I didn't become a successful businessman by ignoring the odds, Inspector. I know a bad deal when I see one."

"Hmm." De Clercq flipped his notebook closed. "That is all for now, Mr. Adair. Don't leave the premises. I'll have more questions for you later."

"Of course you will." Adair adjusted his tilted laurel wreath. "As always. Right in the middle of my champagne toast."

I winced at that. Poor guy. The inspector could use some people skills. "Maybe we'll try to wait until after your toast this year," I suggested.

"We will not," the inspector barked.

Mr. Adair dipped his chin at me. "At least you tried."

"I have a question," I said. Something that had begun to bother me. "Why invite Greasy Larry to your party if you don't care for him?" From the way Adair treated the inspector, I could see our host wasn't the type to humor those he didn't like.

Mr. Adair hummed thoughtfully. "Well, it turns out that—"

"Mr. Winkelmann, let's not waste our valuable time on flights of fancy," De Clercq said deliberately to Frankie. "Come with me." He began to head inside. Frankie looked back at me, shrugged, and followed him. I decided to stay.

"Odious little man," Mr. Adair muttered, watching De Clercq walk away. "I appreciate what he's doing, but it's pointless. Things happen as they always have. There's no stopping it now."

"What do you mean by that?" I asked. "Was there a time you could have stopped it?"

He glanced at me and cleared his throat. "No." He waved away the question. "Never mind. I misspoke." He drew me away from the coil and the crowd. "You want to know why I invited the judge?" He huffed. "I didn't. A guest of mine included him with their invitation. I've never been able to discover whom." He clenched his jaw. "It's not as if they'd admit it now."

That was interesting. I told Ellis what I'd learned, and Mr. Adair watched the exchange with interest.

"So you can see us and he can't?" he asked. "Fascinating," he added, noticing Ellis for the first time. "How did you come about your marvelous gift, my dear? Could it be replicated in other living souls?"

"I'm back! I'm back," a new voice announced. Mrs. Adair hurried through the crowd, peacock feathers swaying. Guests parted for her like the Red Sea before Moses, and she swanned over to her husband's side.

"Ah, excellent," Mr. Adair said, reaching for one of the glasses she carried.

"Ah-ah," she tutted. "Put down the magic wand first, dear. Let's not mix our pleasures when one of them is electrifying, hmm?"

He smiled indulgently at her and put the metal rod on the ground. "Always looking out for me. Thank you, Jeannie—I mean, Hera." He motioned toward me. "This is Verity Long."

"I've heard about you," she enthused, "the live girl. It's great to have someone new at the party after all these years."

"She's working with that inspector," her husband added, "although she doesn't seem to agree with his tactics."

"De Clercq doesn't like me much," I admitted.

"Then you're in good company." Mrs. Adair rolled her eyes. "I don't mean to give him trouble. I honestly don't. But that man has no sense of style, or privacy, for Heaven's sake. We're under siege here."

"For eternity," her husband added.

"He could stand to be more sensitive," I agreed. "But he is devoted to justice, if not manners." I might not care for the inspector, but he was doing his job the best way he knew how.

Just then, Ellis's phone went off.

"Sorry," Ellis said, looking at me, "but it's work. It could be about the girl's identity. I have to take this."

"Of course you do," I told him. He had his job, and I had mine. "I'll keep chatting. Don't worry about me."

The raised eyebrow I got reminded me that Ellis knew how my chats could turn sour, but he nodded and left, answering the phone with a, "What have you got?" as he walked off.

"Fascinating," Mr. Adair said breathlessly. "Is that a wireless telephone?"

That was one way of putting it. "Yes. They're quite popular nowadays."

He kept his eyes glued to Ellis like he'd pulled the hope diamond out of Al Capone's vault. "You must employ a tremendous number of operators."

"Darling, don't bore her," his wife chided with a smile. Then she looked at me. "Gadgets and gizmos are Graham's specialty. Ours was the first house in all of Sugarland to have a telephone."

"No kidding," I said. "You know, I'm supposed to take some pictures for the Sugarland Heritage Society while I'm here. Would you mind showing me?"

She beamed with pride. "I'd be delighted." She touched a hand to her chest. "It would be nice to get some good press for this old place. And call me Jeannie. Mrs. Adair was my mother-in-law."

"Would your friend mind if I watched him use his wireless telephone?" Mr. Adair asked. "I won't touch, I promise."

"He's working on a case," I said, by way of dissuading the ghost, but Mr. Adair was already floating after Ellis. "I suppose it couldn't hurt."

There was nothing but love in Jeannie's expression as she watched her husband go. "We'll be in by the telephone," she called.

"You two seem happy," I ventured as she led me toward the side of the house.

She nodded. "Oh, we are. I met him on New Year's Eve 1919, and that was it for me. I even kissed him that night. There's never been anyone for me but Graham." She made a little face as she sipped her fruity drink. "That's one reason he dislikes Larry so much. Old 'Greasy' made a play for me that same night." She snorted. "As if he had a chance."

"Did you know Larry well?" I asked, "before or after?"

"I tried to avoid him," she sniffed.

Then she might have kept tabs on his movements from time to time.

The remains of the menagerie loomed ahead. "Did Larry go in there by himself often?"

"You mean did he hang out by the snake cage?" she asked pointedly. We passed the darkened door and she gave a small shudder. "No. My theory is that he was using our house, our party for some sort of nefarious meeting. Larry was as crooked as they came."

She guided me to a side porch and disappeared through a gleaming white side door. In the world of the living, layers of paint peeled off in chunks. I dug out my house key and inserted it into the rusty lock. It opened with a creak and I entered a darkened kitchen. Pots and pans hung in racks overhead, barely visible in the light that shone through the doorway leading to a bare white servants' hall.

"Jeannie?" I called, stepping inside.

She hovered near an old-fashioned icebox.

"This way," she said, leading me away from the light.

I pulled out my mini flashlight. The glowing gray form of Jeannie Adair retreated through an arched doorway. I hurried to catch up, and there, in a tiny room off the back stairs, I found her next to an old-fashioned telephone attached to the wall.

"Ta-da," she said, going for *Price is Right* model once again. "It's not as fancy as your friend's calling device, but look." She pointed out a handwritten list of numbers framed on the wall. "We are connected to everyone in Sugarland who owns a phone."

All twelve of them.

The flowing, slanted script had faded to light purple, yet I recognized a few of the names: Adolphus Banks, the then-mayor, as well as Jack Treadwell, a Victorian-era Egyptologist I'd met on another adventure.

"I'd like to get a picture of this, too," I told her, pulling out my phone and snapping several shots.

She laughed and jumped at the flash, and then clucked in delight when she saw I was taking photographs with my phone. "My stars. Graham will bust a gut when I tell him about this." And when I backed up several steps to get the entire phone and "directory" in the shot, she even stood and posed next to them both.

"I wish someone besides me could see you," I said.

"I don't care." She posed with her hands on her hips, then in the air, then like an Egyptian wall painting. "This is the most fun I've had at this party in years."

"I hardly believe that," I said, finding myself smiling back. "You have to realize what an amazing time this is. I mean, last night, I saw monkeys."

"Ernest and Klyde." She grinned, but then it faltered. "This party's getting old," she admitted. "It's the same thing every year. We've wanted to bring in different drinks, different music, a few other guests...something. De Clercq makes us do it the same every time."

I sighed. I could understand her dilemma. I lowered my phone. "The trouble is, De Clercq needs it as uniform as possible so he can investigate." The ghostly realm was always changing, and this was the best way he could "see" the party as it was.

"It's his ego," she said, leaning against the wall. "He can't let go. De Clercq is convinced he was close to breaking this case, and then he died with it unsolved. He won't move into the light until he learns who killed the judge, and he's determined to drag us all down with him."

That was new. "You think he's trapped?"

She crossed her arms over her chest. "I know it."

No wonder he was nailing Frankie to the wall on this one, and why he was so willing to let him go if we helped solve the case.

"Who do you think killed Larry?" I asked point-blank.

She snorted, and I could tell I'd surprised her. "How would I know?"

"You must have some clue," I said. She hadn't outright denied knowing. "De Clercq asked me here to help him solve Larry's murder," I said, stretching the truth a bit. "I've solved cases like this in the past. If we put this one to rest, you can throw your party any way you like next year—or not have it at all, if you want. Is there anything you can tell me that will help bring the killer to justice?"

Her expression hardened. "Greasy Larry is dead. His killer is dead. Tell the inspector to move on. Quit the Red Hot Ritz. Let it go."

I didn't want to tick her off, not in a deserted hallway. Not if she was the killer. But it had to be said, "We're going to solve this, with or without your help."

She let out a short huff. "Talk to me after eighty more years of doing this and we'll see how you feel."

Unfortunately, I wouldn't have eighty years. If Frankie and I failed now, we wouldn't get another chance.

I started to explain, but she waved me off. "Let's go," she said, leading me into the narrow servants' hall. Gaslights flickered in simple brass sconces, casting the hall in more shadow than light. "I used to think like you did. That we'd find something new one year. That we'd make this right. Now it's like being forced to host Thanksgiving, Christmas, and New Year's Eve for one hundred and twenty people. Every year. With no end in sight." She shook her head ruefully. "Still, we persist. We entertain. After all, our reputations are at stake."

I stood still as the implication washed over me. "You're not even the dominant ghost in your own house." The killer controlled the unfolding events. And the Adairs joined in as unwilling hosts.

Then again, she could be lying to gain sympathy. Or perhaps Graham did it and he was the dominant ghost, but she just didn't know.

"It's not all that dire," she said, without emotion.

Yes, it was. If what she was saying was true, Graham and Jeannie were hostages of a sort, with their home under someone else's control for ninety years, in the middle of an ongoing murder investigation they were forced to endure, playing the part of the happy hosts.

She drained her glass. "At least Greasy Larry is dead and gone for good." She dropped the glass in the hallway and it shattered. "I hated him."

"You'd better not say that too loud," I advised.

She laughed. "It's not a secret." Jeannie glided toward me, stopping almost close enough to brush me with her feathers. "Do you know Irene Smith?" She shook her head before I could answer. "Doesn't matter. Anyhow, that woman—and I use the term deliberately because she's certainly no lady—Irene broke into my jewelry box during my coming out party and stole my Great-Aunt Emily's sapphire tiara. I loved that piece. And Aunt Emily. That's why she left it to me. I caught Irene afterward and had her arrested, but who was the judge on her case? Greasy Larry Knowles."

The air around Jeannie chilled with the strength of her anger, and goose bumps rose on my arms.

Her lip curled over wide, white teeth and her forehead creased with a frown. "He let her off with a warning after she lined his pockets. Absolutely disgusting. And then he went into the evidence locker and let his mistress wear my tiara before it was returned to me. She died on her way to a party wearing my tiara! She's now flaunting it for eternity." Jeannie turned her nose up and took a long drink. "But never at this bash."

"I'm so sorry that happened to you," I said, wary of the deepening chill. Angry ghosts could turn very dangerous very fast.

"I don't forgive easily," she said, her eyes going coal black.

Oh dear.

I found myself wanting to apologize and I hadn't even offended her.

Jeannie waved a hand and the tension dissipated. "What's done is done," she said as the air warmed. "Still, I hardly see Inspector De Clercq interrupting his afterlife to worry about justice for me."

Stealing wasn't the same as murder, but I wasn't about to point that out. "No one should get away with such blatant theft," I agreed, rubbing my arms.

She looked me up and down as if trying to decide whether I really cared. "I need to get back to the party," she said, leading me through another arched doorway, toward the sounds of the crowd.

"Lead the way," I said. "I want to get a shot of the chandelier." EJ would surely recognize that. In fact, I might get on better terms with Jeannie if she knew I had permission to be here. "Your niece, EJ, is the one who let me onto the property tonight."

She froze. Then turned.

"EJ is here?" she asked, her voice small, her eyes welling up.

"She's not," I said quickly, to avoid getting her hopes up any more than I had. "She's living in New York, but she gave me permission to be on the property because she'd like to see you and the house remembered."

Jeannie pursed her lips and hastily wiped a tear from her eye. "I'm glad *she* remembers us." She turned and continued down the servants' hall. I rushed to follow and almost ran into her when she turned back to me, composed once more. Only her chin trembled ever so slightly as she asked, "You think you can end this?"

"Yes," I said. It was a statement as well as a promise.

She considered me carefully. "If I were you, I'd take a closer look at Shane—Mr. Jordan," she clarified. "Marjorie's caught him sneaking away from her more than once, and it seems he always ends up in the menagerie."

"Did it happen last night as well?" I pressed.

She shook her head slightly. "That I don't know. But he's got his hands in all kinds of nasty business, and he knew the judge well." She closed her eyes briefly. "You'll also find that nothing makes his upper lip stiffer than a visit from your inspector."

Interesting. "Anything in particular I should ask him? Maybe a question he hasn't heard ninety times?"

Jeannie smiled at that. "Just think quick. Shane's a smart one." She straightened to her full height, a good six inches taller than me. "Now, if you'll excuse me, I have to go rein in my Zeus before he ignores his guests any longer."

I watched her go, her head held high like the goddess she portrayed. She turned the corner ahead, pasted on a smile, and walked into the party like she owned the place. I wondered what it would be like to live on such an estate, throw wild parties, and live like it was 1928.

I supposed I'd never get closer to it than I was now.

Glass shattered at the other end of the servants' hall, just around the corner from where I stood. I jumped as gray, ghostly shards skittered in my direction. "What?" Marcus barked, his tone sharp, angry. "You don't want to drink with me now, either?"

"Get your hands off me," Marjorie spat. "You're drunk."

"Suddenly you care about a little liquor?" he mocked. "That's a first. Well, rest assured, I won't get too buzzed with a live girl around."

"Now you're not even making sense," Marjorie snapped. Glass crunched just around the corner, and I wondered if she was headed my way.

"Don't be stupid," Marcus warned. "The only thing different about the party this year is the living, breathing blonde. I want you to stay away from her."

Interesting. Marcus had wanted to get closer to me last night—

too close. And now he told Marjorie to steer clear. I wondered what had changed.

"You want me to stay away from everyone," Marjorie countered.

"Yeah, well, this time, you'd better listen," he growled. "Or I'll make sure you do."

"Ouch. That hurts!"

Sweet heaven. I started for them, not at all sure what I was going to do when I turned the corner.

"Oh, sure!" she called, her voice warbling, collapsing into a sigh. "Disappear after you get the last word."

I halted, a breath short of the turn in the hallway. Shaking.

Thank goodness she was safe, for now at least. No wonder she hadn't wanted to dance with Marcus or pretend to have feelings for him.

I hesitated, debating whether to confront her with what I'd witnessed. I'd like to offer comfort if I could. I'd also really like to know what that conversation was about.

Then again, Marjorie might not welcome my interference. She was still one of my suspects, and it didn't sound like Marjorie herself knew what her husband had meant. I ran a hand along the cold plaster wall. If I wanted to keep my eavesdropping a secret, now would be the time to skedaddle.

Decision made.

I clutched my cell phone and joined the party inside the grand entryway. Marcus was right—I was the biggest variable at this party in almost a century. And I'd learn what happened that night in 1928, with or without his help, or Jeannie Adair's, or anyone else's.

The main entry held fewer partiers than the night before, probably because most of the revelers had moved the action outside.

The decorations had changed entirely. Grecian columns outlined every door, and the hanging ferns and riotous bouquets of flowers on every surface gave the place a fresh, organic look. A younger gentleman dressed as Pan trotted by, complete with hairy legs and a pair of long curving horns on his head that reminded me of an old-timey opera diva.

I took pictures of the room itself. Only my photographs showed a cracked marble floor, pedestals that held nothing but dust, and a cobwebby chandelier with nary a monkey in sight. I wondered how EJ would receive the photos, if she would be surprised at what had become of her aunt's once-grand home.

There was nothing to be done for it, I supposed. Unless these photos somehow moved EJ to return to the childhood retreat she'd left all those years ago and sink heaven knew how much into the place. I sighed. I wished she and the rest of Sugarland could see this place as I did.

But I didn't have time to fret about lost history. Not at the moment anyway. Not when I spotted my last suspect, Mr. Shane Jordan, at the foot of the stairs, in the exact same place I'd seen him last night.

The diamond dealer leaned against the wall like he was holding it up while he and a small crowd listened to a woman in a long, almost glowing, crystal-covered gown sing a song about lost lovers.

He was the only one who didn't wear a costume. His suit was black, and so were his tie and shirt. The only distinctive thing about him was the enormous diamond ring he sported on his right hand. That hadn't been there last night.

Aha. That clinched it.

I sidled up next to him. "Good evening, Hades," I said. What could he be except the god of the underworld, who was also coincidentally the god of wealth?

He glanced at me. "Not bad. You're the first person to guess that tonight." He took a sip from his martini. "And who are you supposed to be, sweetheart?"

"Myself."

He laughed. "Ah, I always love new blood at an old party." His eyes narrowed. "Tell me. What's a live girl like you doing at a dead man's bash?"

I met his gaze head-on. "I'm looking into the murder of Larry Knowles."

Mr. Jordan's expression cooled even further. "What does it have to do with you?"

"It's a long story," I told him.

"I've got time," he quipped.

Yes, but I didn't. We only had tonight and tomorrow to solve this.

I tucked a strand of hair behind my ear. "You're a diamond dealer, right?"

"Among other things." He drew an olive out of his glass. "I also hand out advice on occasion to people who need it. So listen up, honey. Don't dig into something that doesn't concern you. You might attract the wrong kind of attention, and then?" He popped the olive into his mouth. "Next thing you know, you're cut down by a vengeful god while still in your prime."

My pulse quickened. "Is that a threat?"

He smirked as he chewed. "Scurry away now, Arachne. I'm trying to listen to the music here."

"Shaney." A delicate arm looped around his as Marjorie came into view. A gold cuff wound up her bicep to her shoulder, and jeweled hearts dangled from it. "Don't go frightening the girl, it's rude. She's just doing her job."

He grunted. "Her job doesn't concern me."

"Such a grump." Marjorie pressed a kiss to his cheek, then straightened up and looked at me. "Why don't you come with me, sugar?" she said with a smile. "We can go have some girl talk."

"I'd like nothing better," I said, irritating Shane Jordan by casting him a dazzling smile. He wasn't going to intimidate me. Then I fell into step next to Marjorie and hightailed it out of there.

I hadn't expected to see her so quickly, especially after her husband had forbidden contact. It seemed Marjorie was quite the rebel, at least where Marcus's interests were concerned. Good. That guy needed to learn he couldn't boss her around.

We eased out into the main hall and found a quiet spot behind a ghostly statue of Cupid. "Thanks for the smooth exit," I said. "I didn't want to show weakness around a man like that."

"Smart." Marjorie lifted her champagne glass to her lips and took a sip. "Shaney's not a bad guy, you know. That inspector buddy of yours gets him riled like nobody's business."

"He's not my buddy," I said quickly.

Marjorie gave me a commiserating look. "Treating you like a useless dame, is he?"

"You could say that."

She nodded. "Yeah, I know the type. They love to bark orders, but they never listen to a word you have to say. Then they wonder why they get no respect." She shook her head. "That's why you've got to love yourself first." She indicated her outfit, consisting of a long dress ruched at the waist, a sparkling heart-shaped pendant, and another one to match it on a pin holding up her hair. "Aphrodite, goddess of love. Who better to look after herself?"

I was sorry she felt so alone, but after hearing Marcus in the hall, I didn't blame her. "Some guys are good," I assured her.

"I saw you taking pictures," Marjorie said, changing the subject. "Jeannie said they're for EJ."

"Her niece," I said. "Did you know her?" I asked. "Wait. Of course you did. EJ said she came here all the time when she was growing up."

Marjorie deposited her empty champagne glass on a nearby plinth. "She called me Aunt Marge," she said, with a wry twist to her lips. "Made me sound like an old lady." She pulled out a cigarette and fixed it to her holder. "Do you think EJ will ever come back?"

"She might when she sees my pictures," I said. "If she's well enough to travel, that is." First Jeannie and now Marjorie seemed to truly miss the Adairs' niece. I hoped my pictures would make her want to come back to Sugarland, or at least remember it more fondly. "EJ told me how much she loved her summers here."

"You should take a picture of the grand staircase," she said, walking me back to the foyer. "She used to like to slide down the banister. Nearly gave Graham a heart attack." Her laugh sounded like bells. "He's always been the overprotective sort."

I took several pictures while Marjorie told me stories about EJ sneaking baby ducks from the pond into her bath; EJ naming an entire litter of kittens "Marge," even the boys; EJ sneaking into the guest rooms during parties and eating the bedtime chocolates off the pillows.

I stopped taking pictures. "You mean guests stayed here?"

Marjorie took a drag of her cigarette. "Naturally, dear. This is a house party. Not everyone could fit, of course, but—"

"Was Larry staying here?"

The inspector hadn't mentioned it, but then again, he didn't tell me much. I wondered if I could learn anything from the belongings Larry left behind.

Marjorie frowned at something over my shoulder, and I turned to find Inspector De Clercq and a very bored looking Frankie. De Clercq heaved a put-upon sigh. "I have already pursued this line of questioning."

"Exhaustively," Frankie muttered. De Clercq ignored him.

The inspector straightened his tie. "Larry Knowles was not staying in the Adair mansion. He lived less than four miles away. We swept his home and found nothing. You're wasting your time."

"Larry came here with my buddy Fern," Marjorie said, speaking to De Clercq but looking at me, her eyes full of mischief. "They were sharing a room here the night he died."

Inspector De Clercq flipped open his notebook with a vengeance. "You failed to mention this before, Mrs. Phillips."

"I don't like you," she said pointedly. "Besides, you didn't ask me about Fern," she added. "She went to the light a dozen years ago, and nobody's seen her since."

De Clercq stiffened. "I talked to her before she ascended."

"Apparently not enough," Marjorie mused. "Oh, it's probably not your fault," she assured him. "Who'd want to volunteer anything to a stuffed shirt like you?"

De Clercq frowned at me. I simply shrugged.

"Trick is," Marjorie continued, "it's hard to go up there during this party. Whoever's got a hold of this place, they don't want us messing around up there."

"That's true." De Clercq frowned. "I've not been able to go upstairs."

So maybe he needed a live girl after all.

"Do you know who the dominant ghost is?" I asked Marjorie.

"No clue, sugar," she said. "But whoever it is, they're not playing games. They don't want the living *or* the dead anywhere near that room. I don't think I'd even make it past the landing." She glanced toward the grand staircase. "That's as far as anyone ever gets, from what I've seen."

"I made it to the hall," De Clercq said, "before I was forced to turn back."

"It's bad." Marjorie shivered. "It's the closest thing to Hell I've ever experienced. Makes you feel like you're dying all over again, trying to move around up there. It sucks at you…*eats* at you." She stared at me, her face pinched and humorless. "You don't want to go up there, Verity. Trust me."

"Believe me, I trust you," I assured her. At least on that.

But it didn't seem like I had a choice.

CHAPTER 12

J stepped away from the group, and De Clercq seemed glad to see me go. Good. I doubted he'd approve of the live girl going off on her own to investigate, and I didn't need any trouble from him.

No doubt, I'd find enough of it upstairs.

"Frankie," I said, ushering him over, thankful for once that the gangster was easily distracted. "I'm going to check out the second floor."

His eyes widened. "Are you nuts?" he hissed, trying to keep it down. He didn't have to. The room was plenty loud on its own. He grinned at a passing wood nymph. The gangster had a sixth sense when it came to keeping up appearances while attempting something nefarious. "I'm not going up there," he said, eyes hard, the smile still pasted on his face. "You heard what the lady said. It's bad news."

"I get what you're saying. I do," I insisted when it appeared he didn't believe me. It wasn't like I wanted to test the temper of a murdering dominant ghost who had kept his or her crime hidden for almost a century. But if I was the only one capable of getting past the dominant ghost's barrier, I didn't have a choice. "It might be different for me as a living person." I hoped. "You don't have to go," I added, much to his relief. He covered an outward whoosh of air and a sagging of the shoulders by straightening his tie and assuming his resting ticked-off gangster face. "You stay down here and create a distraction."

He cocked his chin. "I have been known to take part in such pursuits from time to time," he offered casually, as if he hadn't pulled half the bank jobs from here to Chicago in his day. If there was anything Frankie loved, it was a treacherous, ill-planned plot. The corner of his mouth ticked up. "What do you need me to do?"

"You decide," I said, hoping I wouldn't regret those words. "As long as everyone, including the dominant ghost, is looking at you and not me while I climb those stairs and sneak up to the second floor."

"It'll have to be creative," he said, by way of warning. Frankie gestured around us at the laughing ladies, drunk men, and increasingly indecent-looking costumes. The band played louder than ever, and through the front door, I could see the flare of Graham's lightning bolts bright against the dark sky.

"I leave it to your good judgment," I told him.

He merely grinned. He was going to remember I said that. "Let's get cracking." He clapped his hands together. "I'll take this party up a notch or three."

He glided away, and I sank back against the wall, trying to make myself as unobtrusive as possible. It wasn't as hard as I'd imagined. I was the only live person in here, and as a matter of habit, ghosts tended to overlook the living. It wasn't as though most people could see *them*, after all, so usually the ignorance was mutual.

I had to admit, a part of me felt a bit jealous. I had never been to a party like this in my entire life. The ritz, the glamour, the bawdy fun of it all—it was all Greek to me, literally. The closest I'd ever come to such a big, extravagant event would have been my wedding reception if I'd gone through with it.

I wasn't sorry I hadn't. I'd never be sorry for that, not when I was with Ellis now. But I had to admit seeing the ladies in special dresses and heirloom jewelry, their hair done up and holding fancy drinks, I'd like to try that sometime. Although I could do without the men in togas and the tittering wood nymphs.

"You're going to make a go for it, aren't you?" Marjorie appeared next to me, scaring me half to death. "Yikes. Babe." She held a hand up, her drink sloshing, her heart earrings swaying. "I thought you were used to seeing ghosts by now."

I was. "I am." I cleared my throat. "I just wasn't expecting you."

She flattened her back on the wall next to me. "You're going to get a bigger shock once you get past that landing," she said, looking out over the party.

"How do you know?" I asked.

"I hear things," she mused.

I hoped she wasn't the dominant ghost. It was too late to hide my plan to investigate upstairs. She already knew.

She sipped her drink and took her time swallowing. "Okay," she said, as if coming to terms with something in her mind. "When you get up to the top landing, take a right. Go down until you see an alcove with a stone statue of a sphinx. It's enormous, and it's real—a gift from a big-time archaeologist named Treadwell. You might have heard of the guy."

"Yes." I'd met him.

"It's on the left after that," she said, her brows rising as the diamond dealer caught her eye from across the room. "See ya," she said, pushing off the wall. "Shaney!" she crowed, dodging a gathering of sirens and a band of harpies to join him.

"I can do this," I reminded myself.

Unless Marjorie was leading me into a trap.

Or, if Shane Jordan was the dominant ghost, maybe she was giving me a distraction.

But why? She had no reason to help me. At least none that I knew of.

The staircase grew dark and shadowed near the top. Ghosts crowded the lower landing, but it seemed nobody would go farther. Except for me.

Lucky me.

"Ha-*ha!*" Frankie's laugh floated over the crowded foyer.

I looked up just in time to see him sweep an arrangement of rose vines and poppies from one of the stone columns near the door and jump up to take its place. The gangster held a lighter in one hand and a bucket of what appeared to be bottle rockets in the other. He'd lost his Panama hat and replaced it with a hastily made crown of grape leaves and parsley that, if I wasn't mistaken, had recently garnished the buffet table. He'd also tied a tablecloth around his shoulders like a cape.

"You think Zeus is the only guy who can shoot lightning from his hands?" Frankie called, working the crowd like a carnival barker. "Think again!" He brandished the lighter high and grabbed one of the bottle rockets. "Ladies and gents, may I present the *indoor* light show!"

Graham stood at the front door, his eyes wide, jaw dropping. "We've never done that before."

"It's not like he can burn the place down," Marjorie countered.

"King of the gods, baby!" Frankie roared, getting a little too into his role. He lit the bottle rocket. It shot straight toward the ceiling, tangled in the chandelier, and a moment later—

Boom! The sound echoed in the closed space. Sparks shot off the crystal. Guests gasped and shrieked as hot embers showered them. Some partygoers dove for the door. Others—the more inebriated ones, from the look of things—laughed and shouted for more.

And Frankie had a lot more.

His eyes met mine from across the room.

Go! His voice sounded in my ear.

Right.

I turned and began climbing the staircase, past the gawking

guests, ignoring the *fffzzzt* as another rocket shot from Frankie's hand.

Bang.

I felt the reverberation down to my toes.

Faster. His voice sounded again in my ear.

Dang, he was pushy. I stuck close to the wall and avoided eye contact with any of the ghosts. I was up near the top in less than half a minute. I could do this. I could make it. Then I stepped on the landing, and my entire foot sank down into the carpet.

"Holy smokes!" I dodged backward to the step below, my heart catching as the ground fell out from beneath me and I tripped.

I went down to my knees, hitting hard, but I managed to stop myself from tumbling down the staircase. As I knelt, staring up into the darkness on the landing, I realized I might need more than Frankie's fireworks to make this work.

At the bottom, the gangster waved another rocket while Mr. Adair yanked his cape off and Mrs. Adair tried to talk him down. Marcus stepped inside, drink in hand, looking horrified. He didn't even notice when Marjorie took his hand.

Shane Jordan merely laughed.

Nobody cared about me.

I looked back up to the landing. The threadbare carpet lumped over uneven floorboards in my world. It appeared Hollywood perfect on the ghostly side.

Gripping the top stair, I reached my other hand up and over and felt it sink. It wasn't a ghostly illusion. This was a loose board in the real world, probably rotting away underfoot.

Great.

So now I had to worry about the integrity of the second floor. Worse, there was no mistaking the dark, heavy presence of something lurking beyond the landing.

Go, Frankie urged, sounding more panicked this time.

He wasn't going to be able to keep it up much longer, even if the Adairs had to drag him out of there kicking and screaming.

Now or never. I forced myself to stand. To take the next step, to walk up and onto the landing.

Maybe the foreboding presence was merely a ghostly illusion. Maybe there was nothing to fear.

And maybe it was a trap

Either way, I was committed. I stepped up onto the landing.

It felt like stepping into another world.

I'd entered a soundless place, bathed in shadows. At the top of the stairs stood a pedestal with a white marble statue of a weeping woman. She seemed to be staring directly at me.

I could barely hear the party downstairs, and that scared me most of all.

I ventured past the weeping woman into the upstairs hall. The shadowy passageway stretched out far in either direction. I watched it pulse.

Oh, heck no.

The hallway appeared to bulge and shrink at the same time, the walls threatening to split open on one side of the hall while on the other side, they pulled back so fast and so tight that I felt like I'd be drawn toward them if I kept watching. Couple that with the feeling of wet, sucking sand underfoot, and it was almost like being on the world's worst cruise ship during a terrible storm. With every wave, the landing around me threatened to spill me right back down the stairs where I belonged.

The dominant ghost definitely didn't want anyone up here, and I certainly didn't want to be here. Even though I knew to go to the right, it was going to feel like an awfully long walk to find the creepy sphinx stolen from a tomb in Egypt. At least I knew the sphinx was harmless. I'd solved the case involving the Treadwell curse.

You can do this, I thought hard to myself. *You have to do this.* I might not get another shot. I groped for the wall, which quivered like a living thing under my hand.

I yanked my hand back. Wiped it on my dress.

As if that would help.

Bang-bang-bang!

A fresh infusion of fireworks stilled the walls.

"Thank you, Frankie." He'd distracted the dominant ghost enough to give me a bit of peace. Ha. As if anything could make a darkened hallway possessed by a murderous entity a bit more peaceful.

Still, I was glad to see the floor firm up to something only slightly sticky, and it became light enough that I could see more than five feet in front of me. I didn't have any time to waste if I wanted to get into Greasy Larry's room—and make it back out.

I hurried down the corridor.

The hallway was long, which shouldn't have surprised me. It was a big house. But it felt like the farther I stepped, the more distant the rooms became. *More tricks.* I gritted my teeth and pressed ahead. I would make it. Just ten more steps. Ten more little steps, I could do that.

I waded forward against the clinging darkness, thick one moment and nearly gone the next as a distant *bang* sounded.

There. To my right, a sphinx statue rose out of the shadows of an alcove. The sculpture had the sleek body of a lion with a face like the *Mona Lisa*. It sat tall on a pedestal, its eyes on a level with my head as I approached. It didn't speak any riddles, but those eyes glowed menacingly, and I was sure I saw its claws scratch at the marble beneath it.

It had better not be getting ready to jump me.

I'd never seen a statue attack, but then again, I'd never seen a ghost snake until last night.

I braced myself and hurried past. Glancing back at the statue, I found it had turned its head to watch me.

I was shaking by the time I reached the first room past the sphinx, but at least I'd made it.

I took a deep breath and opened the door.

"Oh my lord!" A hairy man dressed as cupid had found a stray siren and—

I slammed the door. Apparently, not *all* ghosts were scared off of this floor.

How could they stand it up here? Unless they weren't real.

Maybe they were memories, remnants from the past. Or perhaps they were nothing more than images the dominant ghost wanted me to see.

I glanced back toward the sphinx, thankfully still on its perch. Marjorie had said the first room past the sphinx, and this was it. I pressed my ear to the door and heard no sound.

Bracing myself, I opened the door once more.

There were no frolicking ghosts this time.

The ornate bedroom was breathtaking. I took in the wide window with the night sky twinkling beyond, and a heavy, expensive dresser and wardrobe. A canopy with a pleated fabric top and tousled bedding. The mound of sheets stirred, and I stifled a whimper as a huge feline head shook itself free of the blankets and twisted my way.

Ahhh...hah. There was a lion in the room now.

Not a slender mountain lion, either. This was a full-on African lion, complete with a bushy mane, long, twitching tail, and paws that were bigger than both my hands put together. It yawned, displaying huge razor-sharp teeth.

I froze.

The lion might not even be real, but I wasn't about to take a chance. A ghost lion could still cut me to ribbons.

It hopped down from the bed, and I realized that I was still standing in the open doorway, too shocked to do the smart thing and close the heavy door before the lion made a meal out of me.

And if the way its tongue swiped across its enormous lips was any indication, it was ready for a taste.

Shut the door. Shut the door. The lion took two more long steps, close enough that I could see my own reflection in its huge hunter's eyes. Holy wow. I slammed the door closed.

Wham! Ghostly paws connected with the other side, rattling the hinges.

I sincerely hoped Marjorie had been right about Larry's room, that she had been looking out for me and trying to help. Because the dominant ghost clearly knew I was up here, and I didn't want to open that door again.

A riotous boom sounded from downstairs, and I knew I didn't have a choice. Praying that Frankie had just distracted the dominant ghost, I whipped open the door.

Silence greeted me.

No lion. No lovers.

The room before me appeared ordinary. For now.

A rumpled bed stood near the left wall, but at least this one appeared empty. It was flanked by a pair of bedside tables strewn with jewelry, half-full cocktail glasses, and, oh my—a ghostly revolver. Perhaps Larry knew someone was after him.

Opposite the bed stood a wooden wardrobe and a vanity with a big mirror and a lacy, ruffled stool. A tube of lipstick, a pair of earrings, and tangled silk stockings littered the top.

I stepped inside the room and felt the air whoosh out of my lungs so fast it was like being stuck inside a vacuum chamber. I couldn't breathe, I realized, panicking. Stars floated in front of my eyes. The air pressed in on me, thick and smothering like a poisonous fog.

Eyes shut, arms flailing, I threw myself forward as hard as I could. The air pressed closer, tighter, and then—

Pop. The smothering sensation burst, and I staggered into the room.

Sweet heaven!

I rested my hands on my knees and gasped for a few seconds, struggling to catch my breath. The dominant ghost *really* didn't want me in here. At least that confirmed that I'd found the right room.

I made my way to the bedside table.

The ghostly door banged open behind me. I turned and let out an inadvertent shout, ready for—I didn't know what.

Frankie burst through the opening.

I wanted to both strangle him and hug him. "What are you doing here?" He needed to be downstairs keeping the distraction going.

"Bad news," he said, staggering into the room. He'd lost his hat and his crown of leaves. Wisps of smoke trailed from his hair. "The dominant ghost is onto me."

"Yes, well, the ghost is onto me, too." I'd just gotten in here. "I need more time."

"There ain't none." Frankie stiffened as a low groan sounded from the hall. "Yikes," he said to himself, then to me, "Look, I used up all the fireworks. Not to mention the number I did on the ceiling down there. Graham is ready to gut me. It's time to go."

No. I couldn't get this far and then give up before I got to see anything. "You need to distract the ghost again."

He looked at me like I'd told him to dance the cha-cha backwards. In heels.

"Frankie," I pleaded.

"Jesus, Mary, and Joseph... *all right*." He zipped away.

I hurried to the vanity table. Not much to see here: lipstick, a half-pack of Lucky Strikes, and a letter opener under the nylons. I took a closer look at the earrings and realized I was seeing a set of cufflinks instead. They were square, solid silver, and engraved with the initials LK.

All right.

Larry had definitely been staying in here. Now to search for any evidence that might explain his untimely death.

Through the open wardrobe doors, I could see a few dresses hanging up, as well as a man's dress shirt and tie, along with gray pants and a matching jacket. It wasn't a party suit, like so many of the gentlemen attending the Adairs' Red Hot Ritz had worn yesterday, but business attire. Something a judge might wear.

I hurried to the wardrobe, startling when a sudden chorus of "Ooooooh!" from dozens of voices rose up from the front lawn.

"Go, Frankie," I said under my breath.

I studied the wardrobe, careful not to touch the clothes with my hands. If I handled ghostly objects for too long, they would vanish, and we might need them as evidence. Yet from a cursory inspection, I didn't see anything unusual about the items in the wardrobe.

Through the ghostly images from the past, I could see glimpses of the room as it appeared in my time, the bed sagging, one table missing, the other ready to topple. A rusted letter opener lay forgotten under a lurching old vanity.

"Dang it all." I stepped back, surveying the room. I thought I'd find something. I didn't have time to be wrong.

What else, what else... Should I be knocking on the walls, listening for hollow spots? Moving pictures to check for hidden safes? That was what they did in the movies, but...no. This wasn't Larry's house. Technically, this wasn't even his room. If he *had* stashed something here, it would need to be easily accessible.

I tried to think where that might be.

I slid open the ghostly drawer in the bedside table, feeling the chill as it creaked open.

Empty.

I bent and looked on the floor of the wardrobe, then stood tall and jumped so I could see over the edge of the shelf above the clothes. Nothing.

Hurry. Frankie's voice sounded in my ear. *I'm running out of material!*

Where else was there to check?

There had to be something in this room to give me a clue as to the murderer or the motive. If not, I might as well join De Clercq on square one.

I took a deep breath, or tried at least. I wheezed. The air in the room was starting to feel heavy. Noxious.

My head swam a little.

Okay, *think*. There was one more classic hiding place in the room. I hastened to the bed, dug my fingers under the edge of the mattress, and lifted.

On the far edge of the frame lay an old briefcase bound in scarred leather.

"Ow!" I gasped as a sudden chilling pain seared my right toe. A wet chill shot through my body as if my bones had iced over. I yanked my foot back to see what I'd touched. What I saw almost made my heart stop.

Thick black ooze, like a malevolent tide of tar, pooled at my feet. It hadn't been there a minute ago. It shouldn't be there at all. It had seeped in from the hallway, under the door. And it had angled straight for me.

It smelled caustic, acidic. I hadn't even touched it. It was still six inches away and I'd felt it down to my soul.

Lord have mercy.

I could taste the metallic tang of it in the air, feel it in the heaviness in my chest.

Frankie's head shot through the floor, barely missing the goo. "Get out!"

I wanted to. My stars, did I want to. I heaved out a breath. "I found something I think might be important."

I scrambled to the other side of the bed, very much aware that I'd need to exit the way I'd come.

"You're out of time." The gangster rose out of the floor. "This," he said, pointing to the ooze on the floor, the ooze that had begun trailing from the corner of the ceiling to the right of the windows, "this is a badass angry ghost."

"I have one shot." He knew it, and I knew it. I shoved the

mattress off the bed, letting it splat into the goo on the other side. "Now. This is my chance."

"You don't get it, Verity," he said, stalking toward me as the floor around us began to fill. "I pulled my last trick. I put all the high-octane hooch into one of them shells out front and lit it on fire. Good booze! Gone." He nodded fast. "They thought it was a real great show, but they're going to figure out soon that they're out of liquor." He ran a hand through his disheveled hair as if he couldn't quite believe he'd done that. "The worst thing is, it only distracted that crazy dominant ghost for a minute." He looked at me, eyes pleading. "What kind of sicko can ignore a river of burning booze?"

But it had worked long enough. Almost. "You're doing great," I said, grabbing the freezing cold ghostly briefcase. "Look."

"Drop it!" he ordered. "It's part of the dominant ghost's memory of the room." He stared openly at the advancing tar. "The memory he's trying to erase."

I flicked it open and dumped it. Photographs and documents tumbled to the floor. I recognized the Adairs, Shane, Marjorie.

His jaw dropped. "What are you doing?" he demanded.

"I can't actually touch the contents, or they'll disappear. If I scatter them, at least I can get a closer look." This part of the floor was clear.

"That's not what I meant," he pleaded. "What are we still doing here?"

"You can keep distracting the ghost," I assured him. "You can top the river of booze. If I know you, you're just getting warmed up."

He had to be. Otherwise, I'd end up engulfed in goo, and Ellis would come in here to find me dead for reasons unknown. I needed Frankie to focus.

"This is the last time," I said. "I promise."

"Eyah!" He danced sideways as the ooze neared his feet. It was coming in faster now. It seeped over the edge of the windows and slunk down the wall. It started bubbling through the wallpaper right next to me, obscuring the classy vertical stripes with dark, spreading stains.

"Unless you want to look at the contents of the secret briefcase and I'll distract them." At least he could touch the papers without them disappearing.

Frankie looked at me, as serious as I'd ever seen him. "I wouldn't take odds on you getting out of this room."

"Don't say that." We were too close to let this one go. "Think of what it will be like to solve this case," I told him. "De Clercq off your back forever. No more kowtowing to him. No more forced investigations."

He threw his head back. "You're killing me."

"We can do this, Frank," I said. "But we have to do it now."

He dropped straight through the floor with a tortured groan.

I felt for him. I did. But we all had issues here.

I dropped to my knees to check out the contents of the hidden case.

Right away, I knew it had been worth it to stay.

CHAPTER 13

I crouched down and saw the photograph of a familiar face right on top.

It was Marjorie Phillips, my friend from downstairs, the one who had told me about this place. Had she known I'd find this?

She appeared several years younger in the photo. Her hair was shorter, and she wasn't wearing makeup or jewelry. Gone was the saucy girl from downstairs. She held a white placard with black lettering that read *Marjorie Gershowitz*. The young Marjorie stared straight into the camera, terrified. It took a moment to hit me, and when it did, I gasped. It was a mug shot from when she had been arrested and booked in Chicago in—I checked the date—1921.

Interesting that a judge in Sugarland would have Marjorie's Chicago arrest record. I'd have to ask my sister, Melody, to do a library search on her.

I studied the youthful roundness of her cheeks, the fear in her eyes. I hoped she hadn't done anything too terrible. I could imagine her being a wild child. The first time I'd seen her, she'd been dancing on a table. She had a husband and a lover and seemed to handle both them and the party crowd with ease.

Below Marjorie's picture, I could make out a faded scrawl.

ANGIE FOX

Bootlegging, resisting arrest, public indecency.

Okay. She liked to flirt with danger. That didn't seem too bad. Or perhaps I was hanging around Frankie too much.

A handwritten letter was clipped underneath the photo and appeared to tell the same story.

Just last Friday night, Marjorie was seen drinking bootleg gin with not one, but two unsavory gentlemen, one of whom she accompanied home that night.

I sat back on my heels. If this was the situation that Marcus had gotten her out of, it hardly seemed worth marrying him after, even if he was an old friend. Unless he lent her some respectability in the eyes of...who? Family? Society? She didn't seem to care what people thought.

I coughed a little. The air in the room felt heavy and I had trouble drawing a deep breath.

It still didn't make sense why Larry would care about any of this, or about Marjorie.

I spotted a photo of a glowering Shane Jordan near my foot. A slight sneer curled his lip. It wasn't a mug shot, but he certainly hadn't been happy to have his picture taken. The jaded diamond dealer appeared even sharper when captured on film, like a man made of knives with a skin mask thrown over the top. I shivered and turned my attention to the paper clipped to the photo.

The ink lettering had faded more than the scrawl on Marjorie's page, but the crowded, stiff handwriting was the same.

Machine Gun Riley...30,000...Square Deal Laundry
O'Flannery Gang...20,000...Happy Housewife Laundry
The South Town Boys...20,000...Sugarland Laundry

That was Frankie's old gang.

It seemed Shane didn't just deal in diamonds. According to the judge's notes, it appeared as if old Shaney had an extensive money-laundering operation going. I mean, that was what they did in the past. Laundromats dealt in cash, and it was the perfect way to turn dirty money clean.

Heaven knew how Larry figured into this. Was he taking bribes to look the other way? But that didn't make sense. Shane would have to be charged before he was even brought up in front of the crooked judge. A man like that didn't pay blackmail for no reason.

From the notes, it was unclear if Shane was laundering money for the mob or hiring the mob to do the work for him. I huffed under my breath. Frankie would know.

No wonder Shane never relaxed. It had to be nerve-racking to deal with the mob on a daily basis. I wondered if he handled Greasy Larry's dirty finances too.

A ledger page protruded from underneath, one with columns and columns of numbers. Perhaps my answer lay there.

I hoped so. The acrid air stung and thickened my throat. I didn't know how much longer I was going to be able to breathe.

A sudden crackle made me jump. The ooze had drawn closer while I was reading. It was eating up the edges of the room, burning down into the carpet with ghostly smoke tendrils rising as it made its advance.

I turned back to the jumble of evidence.

The tar would engulf it soon. I wondered if that would be the end of it. The dominant ghost obviously wanted it hidden. Although maybe he didn't have enough power to block it out completely, not if he wanted to also hide the murder. Perhaps that was why he had to keep people out. Why I might not make it out.

The black ooze sliced its way across the floor, forming and reforming like frozen waves pushed by an invisible wind.

A glob dripped down from the ceiling. I dodged. It landed with a hiss on the photo of Marjorie, sizzling a hole in her forehead.

Sweet mother.

I stared up at the ceiling now black with goo.

This evidence was toast. Might as well touch it.

An enormous *boom* shook the house. The lights flickered,

dimming to nothing for a long moment before reluctantly flaring to life again.

Goose bumps shot up my arms as I grabbed a chilly handful and started sorting and tossing car thieves, cheating husbands, small-time bookies. My fingers stung. I lost feeling in them, but I kept going until a new face greeted me, a smiling one. *Graham Adair.*

I nearly dropped it.

Was every one of our murder suspects in this briefcase of sins?

"Oh, Larry, what were you doing?"

Under it, I found an icy ledger page, similar to the one I'd seen earlier, with the columns and columns of numbers. Only this one was more personal.

Marjorie

Shane

Graham

Marcus

They'd all had money dealings with Greasy Larry. They were the only ones on this ledger.

Marjorie had paid or received a thousand dollars a year. That was a lot of money back in the twenties.

Shane was in it for five thousand a year in addition to the sums I'd seen on his page. Why not keep all the money on one page? I didn't see the Laundromats on this sheet.

And Graham? Ten thousand a year.

That one surprised me most of all. He seemed so carefree, so full of life. What was he doing dealing with Greasy Larry?

Yet a rich, powerful man like him was bound to have a few secrets.

Like Marjorie's, Graham's page had a folded piece of paper clipped to the backside. I pulled it off and opened it.

It was a birth certificate from the state of New York. For Eliza Jean Adair, born June 12, 1916.

Only the Adairs didn't have any children, did they?

Father: Graham Adair.

Mother: Marjorie Adair. Maiden name: Gershowitz.

I clapped my chilly hand over my mouth.

Marjorie was not only Graham's old friend, but she was also his ex-wife and the mother of his baby. EJ wasn't Graham Adair's niece, she was his daughter. I was willing to bet she'd been born well before Graham married Jeannie, and obviously Graham and Marjorie had parted ways before that as well.

Unless their relationship was still going on?

No.

Graham Adair was very much in love with his wife. I didn't see him having an affair. Jeannie didn't even forgive a stolen tiara. There would be no way she'd forgive a straying man. The whole thing had to be in the past, before they met.

Did EJ know the truth? If she did, she didn't let on. She'd had fond memories of her relatives here, but maybe the truth had driven her from this place.

And what was Greasy Larry doing with the birth certificate?

I set it aside and, underneath, I found my answer: adoption papers signed by Rose and Henry Adair in New York, and by Graham and Marjorie Adair in Sugarland, witnessed by Judge Larry Knowles. EJ Adair had stayed in New York and become Graham's "niece." No one would ever know. A crooked judge like Larry could make paperwork disappear. In this case, right into his briefcase.

"Run!" Frankie's voice sounded in my ear.

"Just a minute," I shot back.

I had to see if there was more before the contents of the briefcase disappeared, but as I looked up, I realized the clock had run out.

The ooze had built, swelling like a tsunami ready to break over the shore, and *I* was the only island around. Only it seemed the ghost had a limited amount of goo. While it closed in on me, it had left the door clear. I pushed to my feet, leapt over a three-foot-wide arm of ooze and made a run for it.

That was when the dam broke.

Cracking, snapping maliciousness poured toward me from all sides. My lungs seized. My bones iced over from the inside.

"You stayed too long!" Frankie's voice hollered.

I knew that.

I did the only thing I still could do. I ran like the wind.

CHAPTER 14

I charged down the darkened hall at full speed, not stopping for anything. A heavy, freezing presence lashed at my back.

"Shut off your power!" I yelled to Frankie. I didn't want to see the ghosts or the haunted house or any of it anymore.

I can't! His voice sounded in my ear. *The dominant ghost is in control!*

The sphinx leaned forward out of its alcove, eyes glowing red. It raised a paw and took a swipe at me. I dodged and kept running.

I made it to where the landing should be and saw only a wall of filmy gray, like a twisted spiderweb. I flung myself into it, crashing through the wet, sticky haze, tripping over the broken board on the landing. Thank goodness. The landing!

The brightness on the other side threw me for a second, and I stumbled, my heart lurching as I lost my balance at the top of the staircase. I grabbed hold of the banister and stumbled down. I had to keep going.

The partygoers toasted and laughed as if nothing had changed, but I felt the ice at my back. A brutal, clawing force surged like an angry freight train bent on running me down.

Halfway down the staircase, I dodged a pair of overweight men dressed like two freaky, full-grown cherubs.

"You feel that?" The first guy turned to his buddy. "It feels like an earthquake!"

The other gaped up at the landing behind me. "Holy mother!"

"Run!" I shouted as I kept going. A woman below screamed.

But it only wanted me. It only chased me.

I reached the bottom of the stairs and chanced a look over my shoulder, immediately wishing I hadn't.

The dominant ghost burst out from the upstairs hall as a dark, thundery cloud churning with malevolence and rage. It reached toward me, forming large grasping hands.

"Help me, Jesus," I whispered.

I'd thought the dominant ghost might stop at the landing. That was where it was strongest, where it had concentrated its energy. Instead, the entity shot out over me into the chandelier. The crystals rattled with dark energy as the spirit churned, ready to unleash holy terror.

"Wow! Would you look at that?" a woman carrying a sheaf of wheat in one hand exclaimed, pointing at the dark cloud above. "That's better than the flaming booze!"

"Live girl coming through!" I hollered, catching a stalk of wheat to the ear. It stung like a mother and I spun, narrowly missing a Hephaestus who swung his hammer for a pair of admiring muses. And I literally jumped right over a prostrate Hermes who'd passed out in front of the door.

"Frankie!" I called, landing hard on the stone patio.

"Way ahead of you!" He rocketed past my left shoulder, nothing but a ball of light. The gangster knocked over two papier-mâché trees out in the yard and buzzed past a waiter so fast the startled ghost dropped his canapés and fell straight into the champagne fountain.

It seemed our gangster hadn't blown up *all* the booze.

Frankie kept straight on going, and I was right with him, lungs heaving as we raced for Ellis's car.

Up ahead, past the lawn party, I could see Ellis in the light cast by the open driver's side door, still on his phone.

"Ellis!" I shouted. He looked up in surprise. I waved my arms. "Start the car!"

I saw his lips shape my name, the question in his face. There was no time to answer questions right now. "Just do it!"

He didn't hesitate after that. He stuffed his phone in his pocket, revved up the engine, and had the car turned around by the time I flung myself into the passenger side. "Go, go, go!"

He hit the gas and my back smacked against the seat.

When it came to narrow escapes, Ellis didn't kid around.

I slammed the door closed, Frankie's urn rattling at my feet. If the gangster weren't already with us, he would be as soon as we hit the property line.

"What's the emergency?" Ellis demanded, launching us over a bump in the road. My gut dropped as the car went airborne, and my teeth rattled when we hit the dirt on the other side.

"Angry ghost," I said, bracing my hand on the dashboard, daring a glance behind us. No Frankie. Just a churning black shadow blocking out everything we'd left behind. I watched in horror as it reached *through* the back window of the car.

The police cruiser shook wildly.

Ellis cursed.

I heard a scratch like fingernails on a chalkboard. *Inside the car.*

Ellis heard it too. He went a little white.

"Hold on." He steered a hard left, over an embankment. I tumbled sideways and nearly into his lap.

"Where are you going?" I demanded. The exit was straight ahead. A long, long way ahead.

"Shortcut," he gritted out, both hands on the wheel.

A metallic scratch rattled the top of the car.

"I got it!" Frankie hollered from the backseat.

I peeled myself off Ellis. "You made it." I turned to see the gangster draw a revolver out of his shoulder holster and fire three shots straight up.

Bang.

Bang.

Bang.

I clapped my hands over my ears. The noise was deafening in such a small space.

Click.

Frankie cursed and tossed the gun onto the seat next to him. "How many times has Suds said, 'Always check your bullets. Never leave home without six bullets!'"

The car lurched wildly as Ellis shot across the side yard, aiming straight for a small arched gate that should have been locked, but stood wide open and ready.

"How did you—?" I began.

"Keys," he said, shooting through the gate, barreling down a narrow road and away from the house in less time than I would have imagined possible. He clenched his jaw, both hands clutching the wheel. "It always pays to have an escape plan."

"We're not out of it yet," I warned.

"It's trying to take control of the car," Frankie warned.

The darkness pressed in closer, making my ears feel like they needed to pop. Clawlike tendrils of smoke sank through the roof.

"How much energy does it have?" I hollered, cringing. It used up a lot on me.

"Too much," Frankie gasped, sinking down into his seat.

We weren't going to make it. The ghost was too strong.

Ellis gunned down the side road, the car bouncing wildly.

"We need to get off the property," I pleaded. With any luck, that would weaken the dominant ghost.

"Fastest way," Ellis said, turning hard onto another side road, the car sliding, tires spinning.

I wasn't cut out for this. I held onto the dash with all I had.

"Buckle up," Ellis insisted, not taking his eyes off the road.

I wasn't about to tie myself to this car with claws coming through the ceiling and leaving scratches down the side. This was a big property and we had made a giant mistake.

"Verity," Ellis barked.

The car had stopped shaking.

"Belt. On. Now."

The cloud behind us appeared lighter.

"Holy heck!" Frankie pounded on the back of my seat. "We're losing him!"

The air felt lighter. I could breathe a little easier. In fact, I couldn't stop drawing short, quick breaths. I reached for the seatbelt, my fingers numb as I yanked it around me and fiddled with the clasp.

The tendrils above me withdrew. The weight on top of the car lifted.

"Way to go, fuzz!" Frankie barked.

Ellis kept going. He turned onto the rural route by the peach orchard.

"We lose him?" Ellis asked, zipping over the blacktop.

Smooth road. At last. I tried to take a deep, slow breath. It didn't work. My heart was still jumping all over the place, and my lungs demanded more air than deep and slow would give them.

"Let me check." I swiveled to look behind us and saw only the darkened road, the trees rising up on both sides. "Yes." I closed my eyes for a moment. "I think we're okay."

I couldn't believe it.

The gangster laid his head back, his arms stretched out over the backseat, like he was sleeping, or shot.

"Frankie, are you okay?"

He raised his head. "That was...fantastic!"

He had to be kidding me.

"Did you see that?" He popped up off the seat, leaning forward with bright eyes. "Did you see me back that bastard off with a gut full of lead?" He slapped the now-solid ceiling. Now *that's* what I call a getaway!" He leaned back. "Ahh..." he mused. "Why don't we do this more often?"

"Because it's terrifying," I snapped, more in control of my body but not quite there with my emotions yet. I felt like a bunny rabbit who had gotten an unexpected reprieve from a fox by falling down a hole. The fox was still there, but at least it couldn't reach me right now.

"I always make it." Frankie grinned. "Except for the time I got shot," he added with a frown. "I ever tell you about my first getaway?" He leaned forward again. "You never forget your first time. We hit up a bank right before they were gonna move their money. That's always the best time," he added, as if I were looking for tips. "Suds dressed as an armored car driver, only he loaded the money in my Packard. That car was a beauty—a twin six model with the souped-up engine. We had three cop cars on our tail before we cleared the block." He threw his hands up. "Bullets flying everywhere. I drove. Icepick Charlie had the tommy gun, and when it jammed, I thought we were done for. We ended up having to drive our car into a river to shake 'em, but we made it, and the money dried just fine."

"That's great," I said. My ears were listening, but my brain didn't want to process what he was saying. We had a problem now —a big one. The dominant ghost, whoever it was, was onto me. He or she knew I'd been snooping around in that room, and whether it was up on what I'd found or not, pursuing me out of the building was a clear sign that it wasn't willing to forgive and forget. How could I continue to investigate if I couldn't even enter the house? What would Inspector De Clercq say?

I sank back against the headrest and groaned. "The inspector's not going to be happy."

"He wanted us to find something and we did," Frankie said.

"That's gotta make up for him canning me after I lit the booze on fire."

Wait. "He fired you?"

"To be fair, it was a big fire," Frankie said. "Trouble is, I think he might arrest me now." The gangster cringed. "He said something about a warrant and imprisonment at your place."

I closed my eyes. "No." This was precisely what we didn't want to happen.

"But now we figured out something important," he insisted. "The guy's been after a new lead for almost a century. It took us one night."

"Two," I corrected.

"He's gotta hire me back on now," Frankie continued.

Maybe. I'd cling to that.

"We make a good team," I told him.

The gangster nodded. "I gotta say, we ain't so bad. De Clercq needs to be more creative in his investigating. Like I told him: When I say I can do something, I *do* it. No pussyfooting around."

That was the truth.

Ellis let up on the gas once we turned onto the highway. "Tell me what happened back there," he said, running a hand through his short dark hair, making a ruffled mess of it.

I laid my hand on his forearm, squeezing gently. "It was dangerous," I admitted. "I didn't realize how dangerous it would be when I started. But it was worth it." I was alive and mostly unhurt, apart from a few bruises, and the ghost hadn't caught Ellis or Frankie either. And De Clercq, well, he'd have to work with us now. With me. "I think I might have discovered something big."

Ellis's shoulders relaxed at that. "Well, that's good," he huffed lightly. "No sense getting in trouble over nothing."

Now he sounded like Frankie.

"I'm sorry if I pulled you out of an important conversation when I came running at you," I added.

Highway lights flickered over us, illuminating his drawn

features. "It's fine. Duranja and I were just repeating ourselves at that point." He paused for a minute, then said, "We uncovered the dead girl's identity. Her name was Maya Ramirez. She was from California. Her family lives in Los Angeles."

"Poor thing." I thought back to the family I'd seen in that picture. At least they'd have closure.

Ellis gave a quick nod. "Duranja talked to them. None of them have any idea what Maya Ramirez was doing in Sugarland. According to her parents, she had no friends here, no family." He glanced at me. "There's no obvious reason for her to be here, so why? How?" He shook his head. "I'm missing a big piece of this puzzle, and I'm not sure how to find it."

"I don't know." I wished I could think of a way to help. I could tell from the tension in his shoulders and the fatigue in his face that this was weighing on him. He didn't have the answers he needed, but he wouldn't let it go until he did. "I'm sure you'll figure it out."

"I will," he vowed. "Eventually." He blew out a breath. "Tell me more about your case. What happened tonight?"

Hoo-boy. What didn't happen? "Well…" I didn't want to go into too much detail when it came to what had happened upstairs. There was nothing Ellis could do to make it any easier, and he'd already seen enough to worry him. Still, I wanted to be honest. "It turns out the victim was staying in a room inside the mansion, so I went to check it out while Frankie kept the rest of the party distracted."

"I was brilliant." Frankie planted his elbows on the seat between Ellis and me and leaned straight through the metal police screen so that his head was in between us. "Go on, tell him I was brilliant."

"He did a great job."

"*Great job* is not brilliant," the gangster informed me.

"Pushy, pushy," I mused.

"Then tell it right." He eased back against the backseat, spreading his arms over the top once more.

Fine. I'd throw him a bone. "Frankie brilliantly distracted the partiers while I slipped upstairs into the victim's room. I found a hidden briefcase with pictures and information on three of our main suspects. The only ones I didn't see were Jeannie Adair and Marcus Phillips. Either one of them might have been in there, though. I didn't get a look at the whole collection."

"Not for lack of trying," Frankie mused.

He had that right.

Ellis glanced at me. "What, *all* of them are criminals?"

"Not exactly. Still, at least three of them had something to hide. And Marcus was paying out as well." I told him about the piece of paper I found in the back of the ledger, and how I hadn't been able to dig deeper into what it meant before the ghost got too close.

"I had to run," I finished. "The ghost chased us out, you manned the getaway car, and now here we are."

"Hmm." Ellis looked thoughtful. "You said the victim, Greasy Larry, was a judge."

"Known for taking bribes." What else could the numbers be? "But if you've already bribed him, why kill him? The money is gone. And I'm not even sure how an uncontested adoption case can go to court, so why was Graham Adair paying the biggest bribe?"

"He had the most money," Frankie said, ever practical. At least when it came to shaking people down. "You also need to tell your friend about the conversation I overheard at the tables last night."

"That's right. Frankie also heard that Marjorie was paying off the judge." I sat back. "That matches what I saw in the ledger tonight."

"All right," Ellis said, thinking. "But the only one that you're sure was in business with him was the diamond dealer," he concluded. "Nobody else was actually working with him."

"It's possible that Marjorie helped Shane with his business in some way. I doubt Graham would work with Larry, other than using him for the adoption back in 1916. Or if he did, it wouldn't have been for long. Jeannie came into the picture a few years after and she couldn't stand the judge. He let her tiara thief off with a slap on the wrist."

Ellis turned onto the rural road that led to my house. "Maybe the numbers he recorded weren't bribes. Maybe it was blackmail."

I sat up straighter.

Ellis tapped on the steering wheel with a fingertip as he thought. "As a judge, he'd have access to all sorts of police records. If he wanted to dig up dirt on someone and threaten them with it, it wouldn't be hard."

It made sense. In fact, it explained the whole briefcase. I would have kissed Ellis right there if I hadn't been worried about keeping the car on the road.

"Larry was collecting dirty secrets," I marveled. "Things that people didn't want to get out. Marjorie's married to a society guy now. She wouldn't want to be known as a former criminal. She'd hidden her child as well." No wonder she'd been so interested in my ties to EJ. "Graham probably paid to keep EJ's identity as his niece intact." I wondered if Jeannie knew.

"You'd need a judge to sign the adoption papers," Ellis added.

"I saw it with my own eyes," I said, nodding. I couldn't stop nodding. "And lastly, Shane wouldn't want anyone to know about his under-the-table deal with the mafia."

"I knew I recognized that guy from somewhere." Frankie slapped the seat as if it were a victory. "He ran the Sugarland Laundry for us, didn't he?"

"He certainly did." I turned around. "Is there anything illegal you haven't tried?"

Frankie lazily stretched over the backseat, shrugging a shoulder. "I ask myself that every day."

Oh brother.

I turned back to Ellis. "This is good, but we need to know more," I said, thinking out loud. "I mean, not everyone could have killed Larry." There was one dominant ghost. And even if we figured out who did it, we'd need evidence. "Problem is, I doubt I'll be getting another look at Larry's dirty laundry."

If the dominant ghost had any idea what I'd been doing, and it seemed like it had, that briefcase would be long gone by now, hidden from me and anyone else.

"You know who to call," Ellis teased, turning onto the long driveway that led to my house.

"Ghostbusters?" I teased him back.

Yes, I knew. "I'll call Melody." My sister was a whiz at research, and she had access to the best library in three counties. "She's researching the menagerie for me. I'll ask her to help me look deeper into our suspects."

Between Marjorie's criminal activities, Shane's shady business deals, and the hidden circumstances surrounding EJ's birth and the inheritance of the Adair estate, there was plenty to look into.

"We'll figure this out." I think I was saying it as much to reassure myself as to inform the guys. "We will."

As soon as we crossed my property line, Frankie vanished. Maybe he was as exhausted from tonight as I was. That left me blessedly alone with Ellis. Although by the time we pulled up in front of my house, I was only a few minutes away from falling asleep against the window.

He parked out back near my roses. We both got out and walked arm in arm up my steps. The porch light was surrounded by a swarm of amorous moths that cast fast, flitting shadows across Ellis's handsome face. "Do you want me to stay tonight?" he asked, sliding one hand up to the base of my neck and massaging gently. I groaned and leaned my forehead against his chest. Ellis knew precisely where I carried my tension.

"Mmm." I was about to say yes before I remembered—it was Friday. Ellis always worked the early shift on the weekends, which meant he'd have to be back at work in less than eight hours. I'd already eaten up his free evening. I picked my head up to look at him. "You're sweet to offer, but I'm fine now. Go home and get some rest." Or, knowing Ellis, he'd stop by the station first in case something new had come in about the dead girl. Maya. Poor soul.

He touched his forehead to mine. "I don't mind."

I smiled at him. "I know you don't. But you already saved me once tonight."

"The offer's always open." Ellis cupped the back of my head, leaned in, and placed a slow, tender kiss on my lips. I felt a little light-headed as we parted. "I love you. I'm always going to be there when you need me."

"Just like I will for you," I said, tracing my fingers over his jaw. "That was some fancy driving tonight."

"I do my best." Ellis winced and looked back at his patrol car. "I think it might have dented the roof. Not sure how I'm going to explain that one."

"I'm sorry," I said. I'd put him in another bad spot. "I had no idea we'd run into such a powerful ghost."

He smiled, but it looked a little grim. "I'd rather be a part of it than lose you to it." We kissed again, and again. "All right, if I'm going, I need to go," he said at last. "Sleep well. We'll talk tomorrow, okay?"

"Okay." I ran a hand down his muscular arm as he drew away. "Drive safe."

He chuckled ruefully. "You don't have to tell me twice."

I leaned against the door frame and watched him drive away, enjoying the warm evening air, still feeling the gentle pressure of his hand on my neck. They didn't come any better than Ellis Wydell.

I was lucky to have him by my side, not to mention *on* my side.

"Goodnight," I murmured as his taillights disappeared, then opened my door and walked inside.

I hadn't turned the air on, and it was stuffy in the house. That alone should have brought Lucy to the door. The outside light cast a yellow circle onto the porch. My little skunk was always ready to zip out the door and claim a breezy spot near the rail, or a cozy nook between two flowerpots. But I didn't see her.

I frowned. This wasn't right. Lucy should have been scratching at the door, trying to get my attention while Ellis and I said our goodbyes.

I placed Frankie's urn on the kitchen island.

"Lucy?" I called. I'd let her out while I had the door open. "Lucy, honey?"

Nothing.

I had a second to register the *tap-tap-tap* of running paws before Lucy barreled into my calf, squirming between my legs and hiding like she'd done when she was a little kit. "Aw, baby." I crouched down to pet her head and got a palmful of quivering snout. "What's wrong? Did you see a ghost?"

I checked my kitchen for any wayward spirits. Frankie had forgotten to turn his power off. Again. But I didn't see anyone lurking in the shadows or up by the ceiling.

Frankie was the only ghost that drove her crazy, and I was starting to see her point on that one.

"Come here, sweetie," I said, cuddling her to me, stroking her soft back. I cradled her in my arms as I walked over to the sink to get a glass of water. My throat was dry after all that running. "Mamma's home now." I poured myself a glass, flipped on the light, then turned and stopped dead in my tracks.

A pie sat on the kitchen island, exactly where the other one had been before Lucy knocked it to the floor. It was pecan, like the first, and it was still warm. The scent of buttery crust, nuts, and cinnamon once again tinged the air. A chill went down my spine.

Someone was trying to send me a message. And whoever it was had been inside my house tonight.

CHAPTER 15

*S*omeone had been *in my house*. That wasn't normal, or nice.

This wasn't a polite social call. They'd even scared my skunk.

Sugarland was a safe place where you were supposed to be able to leave your doors open and not worry about anyone taking advantage.

My entire body stiffened as I stepped closer to the pie. Perhaps there was something else with it—a note, just a word or two, maybe Lauralee saying, "I made an extra and thought of you."

But there was nothing.

Just a pristine, flaky-crusted invasion of space on the edge of my counter.

I put my free hand over my nose, the scent of roasted pecans and brown sugar suddenly noxious.

Giving other people food was a way of life in the South. Birthday? Food! Someone got married? Food! Someone died? Lots of food! It was a perfect mechanism for gossip, too. "Hey there, I made you a casserole! By the way, have you heard..."

But to enter my house while I was gone, to invade my privacy like that and leave behind a pie, tempting though it might be...no.

This was beyond normal decency. Something was wrong here, and there was no way I was eating this thing. I needed to report it.

Lucy wriggled in my arms, her eyes intent on the pie. Oh, heck no. She'd almost gotten the last pie. There was no way I was letting her anywhere near this one.

"We're going to take care of this," I told her, putting her on the ground. I rummaged in the drawer by the sink until I found the aluminum foil. I faced the pie, unwilling to let it out of my sight as I pulled off a long sheet of foil and wrapped the pie up, careful not to touch it myself. There might be fingerprints on the pan.

Are you actually going to report a suspicious pie *to Ellis? Really?*

It sounded kind of crazy when I thought about it like that, but if anyone would understand, it was Ellis. He trusted his gut and so would I. I'd bring the pie to him at the station tomorrow and see what could be done.

Lucy touched a cold snout to my calf and I reached down for her. "You know something's wrong," I said, cuddling my skunk, letting the feel of her warm little body and soft, silky hair comfort me.

It was too late to call Ellis. He'd turn around and come right back if I asked him to, without a word of complaint, but he had his own case to tackle. I was fine. Freaked out, but breathing. And skunk cuddling.

While still carrying Lucy, I placed the pie on top of the refrigerator, well out of her reach. "You'd need a fire ladder to get this one, baby," I murmured against her fur before placing a kiss on her head. Then I methodically locked my back door, front door, and all of the windows. It made the house a bit stifling inside, but I'd take a little extra heat over an uninvited guest any day.

Unless the intruder was still in my home.

I jolted, and Lucy let out a cry of protest.

"I know, you were just getting comfortable," I murmured, trying to sound natural in case anybody was listening.

I retreated to the counter by the door and lifted my cell phone from my bag. I dialed 9-1-1 but didn't hit send. I kept my finger on the button.

"Come on, Lucy," I murmured. We'd check out the house together.

I turned on every light as I explored the parlor, the front room, and then the hallway back to the kitchen. I wished my foyer chandelier wasn't missing—sold—as I stood at the bottom of the darkened staircase that led to the second floor.

I cradled my skunk close, keeping my finger on the button of the phone as I crept upstairs, the boards creaking under my weight. I stopped at the top, listening.

The floor did creak a lot when you walked on the second floor. It was the one advantage I had. When I didn't hear a sound, I crept into my old bedroom and turned on the light. The lone wardrobe stood open, empty except for the ungodly ugly Technicolor winter coat I'd bought at the thrift store.

I braced myself for the small upstairs bathroom. It appeared undisturbed, so I locked the stained-glass window over the monstrous claw-foot tub and retreated to the hallway.

Back in the master bedroom, I locked all the windows and kept the lights on as I ventured into the second bedroom that faced the front of the house. I took a deep breath as I flipped on the overhead light, simply a bare bulb in a socket. There, I found an empty room with lovely green vine wallpaper.

"Goodness," I said, feeling my heart in my chest.

Lucy shifted in my arms.

"One left," I told her, hoping we were alone.

I was ready to run, all set to hit the button on my phone as I flipped on the lights to the final, small bedroom that faced the front of the house.

It lay empty as well, the brighter spots on the blue-painted wall making it clear where furniture had once stood. Relieved, I flipped off the lights, and what I saw then made my blood run cold.

"Oh, baby." I kissed Lucy on the head as I crept forward toward the front windows.

Down at the far end of my driveway, close to where our property ended and the 1960s bungalows and tract houses began, I saw a car parked under a large oak tree. From a distance, I could almost make out the shadow of a person inside.

Maybe it was only the front seat.

It could be my imagination.

There was no reason for anyone to be watching me. Nobody alive, anyway.

Lucy's fur tickled my chin, but I remained still. I needed to watch until I could detect some kind of movement, any sign that there was a person in that car and not a figment of my paranoid mind.

If it was a person, they'd seen me turn on every light in my house. They'd watched me lock the front windows. They knew I was onto them.

One wrong move and I'd press the button and have the police here.

Then again, I had to think that if there were truly a stranger sitting in a car under the big oak, one of the neighbors down the road would have called already. It was the benefit—and the curse —of small-town Southern living: most people were on the lookout for anything unusual.

I stood and watched until my eyes grew tired and my arm went numb under Lucy's weight. She let out a soft snore. The little skunk had fallen asleep.

At least one of us could relax.

I locked all the windows in the room and kept the lights out. I might need to come back up and observe. But for the time being, I needed to sit down before I fell down. With Lucy snuggled in my arms, I carried her down to our bed in the parlor.

The rest of the lights in the house remained blazing, the doors and windows locked as I moved my phone charger next to the futon. I eased Lucy to sleep beside my pillow and erased the 9-1-1 from my cell phone.

Fifteen new messages. I hadn't noticed them before, focused as I was on the mystery pie and my sweep of the house.

"Since when have I become so popular?" I asked the sleeping skunk.

Hopefully, one of the messages would be from a friend or a neighbor, someone friendly who'd dropped off the pecan pie.

I sat cross-legged next to her and took a listen.

There was one message from Melody, asking me to call her when I could, because she'd found some old pictures of the Adair estate. I'd go and see her at the library tomorrow. There was a lot more research to be done now, and I'd need her help.

Next up was a thank-you from a nervous-sounding Beau. Odd. I'd be ignoring that one, thank you very much. I saw the next number and felt my back stiffen.

My body still recognized the caller, even if it took my brain a moment to catch up. With shaking hands, I pressed "play" to listen to the voicemail. "Hello, Verity." It sounded like more of an accusation than a greeting.

Virginia Wydell hadn't called me on the phone since I broke up with Beau. Before that, we'd talked daily, consumed with the intensity of wedding planning.

I clicked out of my messages. Tonight had been rough enough without listening to whatever Virginia Wydell had to say. I knew all about her problem. I still didn't know what she expected me to do about it. I sat back and plugged the phone into the charger. For heaven's sake, the man was in his thirties. He could make his own choices, even if those choices happened to be mistakes.

I recalled his latest "masterpiece," the three-headed snake thing, and shook my head. Those choices might even be *bad* mistakes, but again, they were his to make. At least he was reaching, growing. Even if it was like a weed.

I sighed. The air in the house was growing stale with the windows closed, and it would only get worse.

Rather than worry about it, I changed into my summer nightgown, a pretty white eyelet one, and joined Lucy in bed.

I'd be useless tomorrow if I didn't put down a few of my worries and get some sleep. Yet I didn't feel quite comfortable enough to turn the lights off.

"I need to be more like you, babe," I said to the sleeping skunk, who had curled into a comfortable ball next to my pillow.

I lay down next to her and folded my hands under my head.

Let it go.

Don't think about Virginia or Beau or who might be waiting under the old oak tree outside.

Don't think about who might have left that pie on the kitchen island.

Don't think about how much easier it would be if it were only an angry ghost after you.

I rolled over, trying to find a more comfortable position.

My back hurt from bending over that spilled briefcase inside the Adair mansion. My toe throbbed from where that black ooze had drawn too close.

And what was that stuff? It was gross and wrong and oh-my-word the sphinx statue had taken a swipe at me and the dominant ghost had nearly run us down.

I'd never been this unsettled by a ghost before, and I'd had some pretty scary interactions. I'd almost been shot—more than once. I'd been shoved off cliffs and hurtled toward certain death on trains, but this felt different. It felt ferocious and angry and *mean*.

I had no doubt the dominant spirit at the Adair place would have hurt me, possibly even killed me tonight. Thank goodness for my ability to sprint from danger, and for Ellis and his mad driving skills.

I rolled onto my back and stared at the tangled cords on the ceiling, where my great-great-grandmother's chandelier had hung for generations. Until the wrath of Virginia.

And now my worries had come full circle. I sat up.

I sighed and grabbed my phone. I might as well see what my almost-mother-in-law had to say. Virginia was intimidating, but she couldn't be any worse than what I'd survived today already.

Beep. "Verity, this has got to stop."

"I agree," I said to the phone.

"You must see that," the message continued. "I'm sure all it would take from you is a few words and Beau would snap out of this phase he's going through."

Hmm… I wasn't sure what those words would be, since Beau liked to do what he wanted despite anything I said.

Beep. "Are you encouraging Beau? Is this some sort of twisted revenge against me? I assure you, I will *not* be bullied by the likes of a penniless waif with no good reputation to speak of. You'll make Beau see reason or you'll answer to me."

I lay down flat on my back. These messages were making me tired.

Beep. "Is this all a game to you? Have you even seen the…the eyesores he's concocting? Does it amuse you to watch my son throw his life away for Southern eclectic garbage collecting?"

I listened to messages four through twelve with a sinking stomach. They were all variations on the same theme, an overestimation of my power—and hers—to change the heart of a man who might have been a mamma's boy at one point, but who seemed to be coming into his own.

For better or worse.

The messages were blunter than I'd expect from Virginia. Beau's budding art career must really have her rattled.

Message thirteen made me sit up and take pause.

ANGIE FOX

"Verity, listen to me." Her voice this time sounded on edge, desperate. "I'll make you a deal. If you fix this situation—fix Beau, get him back into his law practice where he belongs..." She paused as if she had to force herself to say the rest. "I'll give your grandmother's necklace back." She sniffed. "It's never suited my taste anyway."

Click.

I stared at the phone. My grandmother's necklace—it had been the hardest thing for me to part with when I was trying to save the house. It had been my grandfather's gift to her on their wedding night. She'd cherished it and had passed it on to me because she knew I loved it as well. But when it came down to the end, I had to give it up or lose the family property. It would be cruel of Virginia to give me hope if she had no intention of ever returning it.

But if she was serious...

I wrapped my arms around my knees and pulled them against my chest. I took in the parlor where I now slept, my memory filling in the blank spaces where familiar, beloved furnishings used to reside. All the pictures, all the keepsakes, even the chandelier that had once filled the gaping hole above me—I missed them all, but none of them carried the same personal importance that the necklace did. Every time I thought of my grandmother, I saw her wearing that cross.

I touched the base of my neck, imagining the feel of the delicate gold and silver filigree beneath my fingertips. This could be the only chance I'd ever have at getting it back. If I failed at this, Virginia would keep it out of spite.

Knowing her taste for revenge, she might even sell it.

I'd call Beau first thing in the morning.

FIRST THING in the morning ended up coming early, just after

180

sunrise. Then again, I hadn't expected to sleep well after the night I'd had.

Lucy watched me with big black eyes, nudging me and shifting on her paws in the way I knew meant, 'Move it or I lose it!'

"I hear you, girl." I scooted out of bed and unlocked the back door for her, half-afraid I'd find another mystery pie on my porch. When I saw nothing but early morning sunshine, I leaned against the door frame, glad to start a new day as Lucy bounded into the bright backyard to do her business.

My spirits lifted with the light of day. Last night had been terrifying, but I couldn't deny it had also been productive. We'd made real progress in Greasy Larry's murder case, and with Melody's help, I hoped to do even more before Frankie and I met with Inspector De Clercq again. I was going to take the pie to Ellis to get some answers, and miracle of miracles, I even had a shot at getting my grandmother's necklace back.

I set out a bowl of blueberries and Vita-Skunk for Lucy, made myself a blueberry parfait for breakfast, and sat down on the back steps to call Beau. I could have done it inside, but I felt like I needed the touch of sunlight on my skin right now. I closed my eyes and soaked up the rays for a few minutes—I needed all the brightness I could get—then pulled up Beau's number.

It had been a while since I'd reached out to my ex-fiancé on the phone—even longer than I'd gone without talking to his mother. Hopefully, things wouldn't get...weird.

Beau answered on the second ring. "Verity?"

"Good morning." I said it as cheerfully as I could manage, given the situation.

"Hey!" You'd think I'd called to tell him he'd won the lottery. "What a surprise, this is great! You're—hey, Zoey! It's Verity on the phone!"

If she replied, I couldn't hear it. Beau was back on a moment later. "I knew it," he said smugly. "I knew you were impressed with me now."

"Now don't get yourself in a fever." That wasn't what this was about. "Your mother left about a dozen messages on my phone last night. She's worried about you."

"I can't help that," Beau said. "Besides, Mom's not talking to me now that I've officially quit the law firm."

"Officially?" Virginia hadn't said a word about that in her messages, and believe me, she'd said plenty. "When did you find time for that?"

"I left my resignation letter on my dad's desk late last night. I'm going to burn all my suits." He sounded thrilled by the prospect.

"No." This was quickly heading the wrong way. "A bunch of burned suits is not art." I didn't want to date Beau again—ever— but I had to admit he had some nice suits. He could donate them at the very least, but we weren't even going there because he needed to rethink this whole decision.

There was a moment's pause, then a little gasp. "Verity, you're brilliant."

"I hardly think—"

"I need to *create* art with my burned suits! It won't happen on its own." He let out a whoop to match my groan. "It will make such a statement about the illusion of wealth's connection to true joy, help me tap into the millennial zeitgeist."

"Zeitgeist?" I repeated. I didn't even know what that was.

He laughed. "See? We're on the same wavelength. Finally," he mused. "I think that was our issue all along. I didn't get it before, but I do now. I truly do."

Oh lord, what had I done? "I think you're moving a little fast."

"Come out to my studio and see for yourself," Beau challenged. "Once you're here, once you get a good look at what I'm doing and absorb the *feel* of it, you'll see what I'm after—what you helped me create."

If there was anything I didn't want credit for, it was that.

"Beau," I began. The last thing I wanted to do was to encourage him, or this strange connection that he thought existed between us. On the other hand, if I didn't try to change his mind, Beau could wreck his career. What if he did some crazy, criminal, public suit-burning that got him disbarred? At the rate he was going, I'd never get my necklace back. My heart throbbed with longing for it.

"I'll help you," I said at last. After I handled the ghost case and my pecan-pie stalker. "I'll stop by sometime this afternoon."

"Great," Beau said as if our get-together was a foregone conclusion. "I'll text you the address."

I clicked off my phone and tried to focus on happy things—the bees buzzing around the blooming hydrangeas that flanked the bottom of the porch steps, Lucy sniffing a path through the sinfully green grass. The sky was blue. The sun was bright. It was a perfect Southern summer's day.

It was the perfect day for a Southern girl like me to take charge.

I let Lucy inside, cleaned up, and slipped on my favorite yellow sundress. I eased the pie from the top of the refrigerator and headed out. I'd handled plenty of trouble before, and today would be no different.

I prided myself on my brains and my focus. There would be no more cringing from my own shadow, no more putting up with anonymous pie-bearing stalkers. I'd tackle Beau's pipe dream and Virginia's veiled threat. Come hell or high water, today the people of Sugarland were going to start answering to me.

CHAPTER 16

First, I'd take the creepy pie to Ellis, who would already be at work by now.

The Sugarland Police Department was housed in the same quaint two-story brick building it had occupied for the last fifty years at least. It stood south of Main Street, across from Roan's Hardware, which had been there about as long. There was plenty of street parking. I found a spot just down from the hardware store, in front of Collin's, the shoe store my mom used to take me to visit every year before the start of school.

Things had been a lot simpler then.

I shut off the car and retrieved the pie from the floor of the passenger side, where I usually stashed Frankie's urn. The aluminum-foil-covered threat appeared innocent enough, but then again, so did Frankie's urn.

I nodded to Mrs. Humphreys from my grandma's old sewing circle and waved through the window to the gray-haired men playing chess in the window of Roan's, before crossing the street and pushing through the front door of the Sugarland PD.

The place smelled like old bricks and coffee.

I made my way to a big wooden desk that had to have been

there since the '50s. Cammi Stapleton, who used to be a crossing guard at my old school, sat on a tall chair behind it and waved me over with two fingers.

"Hey, sugar." She wore a tan uniform shirt and a badge that said Cammilla Jane.

"Cammi, is that you?" My sandals felt slick against the smooth, polished marble floor. It was a good thing they had some tread left on them. "You look so official."

She did. This was a nice step up to a desk job.

The long wooden desk looked ancient, scarred and sanded and scarred again so many times the surface had a permanent tilt in places. The tablet computer Cammi held seemed totally incongruous by comparison. "I need to speak to Detective Wydell," I said, placing the pie on top of the desk. "Official police business," I added, lest she think this was a social call.

She glanced between me and the pie, her mouth forming a knowing smirk. "That's a sweet thought, dear, but Gertie brought a dozen homemade chocolate donuts in this morning, and your man dug in like he'd never seen a glazed goodie before."

Heavens, no. "This pie isn't for eating," I hurried to clarify. "Definitely not for eating. I found this pie on my counter last night."

Cammi placed her tablet on the desk and gave me a good hard stare. "Forgive me, sugar, but that sounds like a decent place for a pie to be."

"Oh, you see, I didn't put it there," I informed her. "Someone broke into my home and left me a pie."

"Uh-huh," she said, which is Southern for, 'You've gone crazy.'

Duranja walked in from the back room, papers in hand. His mouth tightened when he saw me. "Ellis is busy."

"I'm here reporting a suspicious pie," I corrected, refusing to back down when he openly stared at me. "It was left inside my home. I was just telling Cammi. Nobody should eat it. This is evidence."

Duranja looked down his nose at me. "Were your doors locked?"

"No," I admitted. "Nobody forced their way in. But it was rude and strange."

Duranja shot Cammi a look as if to say, 'This is what I'm dealing with.'

"I've got to go work on a murder case," he said, leaving me to it.

Cammi's wrists went limp as she leaned over the desk on her elbows. "Are you seriously complaining about one of your neighbors bringing you a pie? Because, you know, that's just friendly." Her eyes narrowed slightly. "Or do you think maybe one of your spooks left it?"

"That's not how it works." I refused to be embarrassed by my reputation. Or my suspicions about mystery baked goods. "Look, it doesn't matter what you think of the pie. Or what I think of the pie," I added, going for generous, but instead making her lean back like I was contagious. "I need to talk to Ellis."

"Your boyfriend's out," she said, no doubt wondering what he saw in me. "Working on a murder investigation."

Of course. "Okay, when he gets back, you give this to him and tell him it's covered up so he can pull prints from it if necessary."

"Right," she said, looking down her glasses.

She passed me a bright pink sticky note. "You write him a message, and I'll see he gets it. And I'll leave your pie wrapped up." Her expression clearly said, '*Because you're crazy, and* that's *what's really wrong with this pie*,' but at least she didn't voice it out loud.

"Thank you." I wrote out a quick note and handed it back. She stuck it to the foil and placed the pie on top of the polished metal filing cabinet behind her, right beside the printer.

"You have a nice day now, Miss Long." *Crazy girl.* Again, she didn't say it outright, but I spoke enough Southern to know.

"You take care," I said, adding a friendly wave.

I left with my dignity slightly dinged, but I supposed that was all right. At least I'd made it clear that no one should be eating that pie.

Crazy did have its advantages.

I was back in the land yacht and halfway to the library when I began to worry. They hadn't taken me seriously. And baked-goods deliveries were common enough in the South that if Cammi didn't stick the note on well enough...

I slowed at the crosswalk and waited for a couple of teenagers to make their way over Main. Maybe I shouldn't have dropped it off with anyone but Ellis.

I should at least let him know what I'd done. I found a parking spot in front of Sheer Haircare and pulled out my cell phone. Ellis's voicemail picked up and I repeated my concerns and my warning. "Make sure nobody eats that pie."

With that warning in place—yet again—I pulled into the town square.

There were only three cars outside the library this morning, and one of them was a red and orange food truck. It might not have been a fixture like Roan's Hardware or the old shoe store, but somehow, it looked right.

I parked, walked over, and knocked on the cashier's window. To my surprise, Lauralee was the one who slid the plexiglass open. "Hey, Verity!"

"Well, hey yourself." I grinned up at my best friend. She'd pulled her hair back into a messy bun tied under a bright green kerchief, and she wore a white apron over her pale pink shirt. "I figured you'd be at the diner."

"They cut my hours again." She cringed, leaning her elbows on the counter. "Thank goodness for the truck. Zoey has me doing all the prep work, and she just called and said I'm in charge of the whole truck again today."

"Wow." Zoey sure delegated fast.

Lauralee read my mind. "Shoot," she said, with a wave. "The

only thing that girl cares about is Beau Wydell and his budding art career."

"Good thing she has you to mind the store." Not everyone would be as dedicated as Lauralee, or as trustworthy.

She fiddled with her wedding ring. "This job is so much better, I can't even tell you. No more waiting on six tables at a time and putting up with complaints about food I know I could have made better." She pursed her lips in a conspiratorial grin. "Don't tell Zoey, but I've been tinkering with the menu."

"You're kidding." That might not be the best idea.

Lauralee bent down closer to me. "Thai-barbecue fusion is great, don't get me wrong, but yesterday I did a little test run of cheesy jalapeno grits, just to gauge interest. And, girl, people ate. It. Up!" She bounced up and down a little. The truck shook with her. I couldn't remember the last time she'd been so excited about something other than her family. "Pair it with some crispy fried chicken, or maybe one of my hot biscuit sandwiches that I make right here..."

"Do you have any now?" All this talk about food was making me hungry.

"Come back for lunch and I'll have it all. With ham and redeye gravy."

"You're a tease." My breakfast parfait had been good, but a fresh biscuit covered in gravy with grits on the side... "That sounds amazing."

"Doesn't it? I don't know why I never thought of this before. Sugarland is ripe for a food truck." Lauralee's smile dimmed a little. "Not that I can afford to buy one, but hey—maybe someday."

"You will," I promised. I wished I could poof one into existence right here for her.

"It would be amazing," she said, staring out past me, toward the large statue in the center of the square, the one that honored our founder. But I knew she wasn't seeing Colonel Ramsey Larimore on his horse. She was imagining what could be.

"I'd be good at it, I really would," she said. "I could drop my other work and make this my one full-time job. I could be home at night for the boys instead of catering people's parties and make them breakfast before school instead of running in to work the early shift at the diner."

It did sound perfect for her. "In the meantime, I'm glad you have this," I told her.

"That's right. Be thankful for what you have," she vowed. "I've got to get back to prep, but if you get a chance, stop by later and I'll feed you for free."

"Ooh, tempting," I teased before I grew serious. "I'll see where I'm at after I talk to Melody. I'm working on a big ghost-hunting case."

"Be safe," she cautioned.

I smiled and nodded. I wished people would stop saying that.

At least Lauralee was safe and happy. And hopefully on a good path. I walked up the wide stone steps of the library, cool air settling around me like a veil as soon as I entered the high-ceilinged lobby. Air-conditioning was a way of life in the South, but the library was one of the few places that kept it going all the time.

I searched for Melody in the large main reading room that opened off the lobby. Rows of neat wooden desks lined up like soldiers before a long, curved librarians' counter that spanned the entire back of the cavernous space. I finally spotted her helping a customer at the reference area. She caught my eye, and I nodded toward the town history bookshelves on the left side of the room. I practically had them memorized and didn't recall anything on the Adair estate. But I could do something else. What time was it in New York, anyway?

"Full house," a familiar, throaty voice crowed. "Read 'em and weep, boys."

I ducked into an alcove at the end of the row and glanced around the corner. It seemed the Civil War soldiers I'd met here on Cannonball in the Wall Day still had the poker game going. They were just a little harder to see now that the bookshelves were back in place after the festival exhibit.

Three confederate infantrymen sat in a circle on the polished wood floor, playing five-card stud from the look of it. Corporal Owens laid down his cards to the groans of his fellow soldiers.

The baby-faced corporal caught my eye as he gathered his confederate money. "Hiya, Verity."

"Good to see you, buddy," I replied.

Frankie really needed to keep his power off.

I leaned against the end of the bookshelf and pulled out my phone. One detail from last night bothered me as much as the murder case itself.

EJ, the woman who had been so kind to me, who had been so willing to believe me when I talked about historic preservation and my need to be on her land—I wondered if she knew she was Graham and Marjorie's child. It would have been a big secret to keep, but people were funny about family reputations in those days. She might not know.

Although if she didn't, I wasn't sure it was my place to tell, not without proof.

Hopefully, Melody would be able to help me with that.

I dialed up EJ's number and hit *send*. There was no good way to bring it up, but there was also nothing wrong with making conversation. Plus, it would only be polite to give her an update on the property.

"Hello," she said warmly.

"Good morning, Ms. Adair. This is Verity Long, with the—"

"The heritage society, yes." I heard a faint *clunk*, like she'd set down a mug. "I've had my aunt and uncle on my mind all morning," she confided. "I found some old photos of Aunt Jeannie flirting with Sir Charles, the snake. And there's one of Uncle Graham with his new electric razor. It looks like a medieval torture device, and I remember my mother saying he'd burn his whiskers straight off, but he sure loved that thing."

"That sounds like Graham," I mused.

"Excuse me?"

"I've done some research on my own," I said quickly. "I learned he owned a Tesla coil."

"We didn't tell my mother about that one." She laughed. "Did you get the key and the photos? I overnighted them. They should be at your home by noon today."

"I haven't seen them yet, but I'll keep an eye out." In fact, I'd have to make sure I stopped by to grab them before someone else could. "Thank you," I added.

I'd never worried about someone stealing my mail before, but after the problem of the pies, I couldn't be sure of anything.

"It was my pleasure, dear. I hadn't looked at those old pictures in such a long time, I'd almost forgotten what my aunt and uncle looked like." Her voice softened. "They were so good to me. They always told me to dream big. When I was eight, I decided I wanted to have a tea party with all the animals in the menagerie. Obviously, they couldn't let them out. They kept a cougar, for goodness' sake. But one evening they had the staff prepare all our meals on fancy china, people and animals alike. We dined in the garden, and then we wheeled a take-out cart into the menagerie and fed each of the animals. Them in their fancy dinner clothes and jewels, me in my party dress, with a teacup in one hand and a cookie in the other."

I could practically see Graham and Jeannie trailing a little girl in a pink taffeta dress, watching her sip sweet tea and love on their animals. Did she honestly not know she belonged to them? To one of them at least. "That's such a wonderful memory," I said. "They must have loved you like you were their own."

"I know they always regretted not being able to have children, so they made do with me and my siblings." EJ paused. "Eventually they made do with just me. My brothers and sister lost interest, but for me visiting the estate was like going home. I visited every year until I was about twelve. Then, Uncle Graham and Aunt Jeannie visited us in New York. I saw them at least once a year until they grew older. Uncle Graham went first, and then Aunt Jeannie not a month later. They were too close to be parted for long, I think."

"And they left the estate to you." Of course they did.

It not only seemed fair but right that EJ know who her birth parents were. I couldn't be the one to tell her, though—not without any proof to show her.

She sniffed and then firmed up her voice. "My siblings weren't happy to learn I was the only beneficiary, but my parents were fine with it. None of them had such fond memories of the property like I did. Besides, they would only have broken up the estate and sold it, and I could never imagine doing that."

"It still is a beautiful place," I assured her, "even after all these years." I walked toward the lobby as the card-playing ghosts started talking smack. "I have some wonderful pictures of the old telephone, as well as some downstairs shots of that gorgeous foyer and chandelier. I'll send them over."

"It's gotten to you, too, hasn't it?" she asked, pleasure warming her voice.

"It has." It was a beautiful place. Despite the murderous ghost who controlled it. "You should come back and visit." I couldn't see how she'd allowed herself to forget the estate and her heritage for so long.

"I'm too old to travel much anymore," she said, dismissing the thought. "Besides, I have everything I need in New York."

Maybe, but she'd left a lot behind.

I ended the call and stared at nothing for a moment, wondering how to tell EJ about her family and her legacy.

Perhaps the pictures I'd taken last night would help bring her back home. I emailed them to her and added a quick note of thanks. She didn't have to share her inherited property—or even her memories—with me, but I was grateful that she did.

"Verity?"

My sister had walked up without me even noticing. Her hair was braided around her head in a circlet. I didn't know how she did it. I'd probably tie my fingers together if I tried. She looked cute and professional in her knee-length pleated skirt and a sunny yellow blouse.

I pointed a finger at her. "I have a question for you."

I gave her a quick rundown on what I'd learned about EJ and how much it would mean to her to know the truth.

Melody tilted her head, thinking. "I'm not promising anything," she began.

"But," I prodded.

"I'll do some digging. I'm getting pretty good at genealogical research. We do a lot of it here. The only trick with the birth certificate is that there may be a different, official copy filed with the state."

"The one EJ has," I said, the one listing her New York relatives as her parents.

"We'll see if we can find the adoption papers," she assured me. "This way," she said, ushering me to one of the private rooms on the side.

"The briefcase contained more than the documents surrounding EJ's birth and adoption," I said, following. "I'm thinking the old judge, Larry Knowles, was a blackmailer." We slipped into a private room with a wood desk and tall windows. "He had photos and information on several of our murder suspects." Melody helped the door close all the way. "Marjorie Phillips had been arrested in Chicago for bootlegging, and Shane Jordan was laundering money for the mob."

She nodded, her back to the door. "That lines up with what I learned about Mr. Jordan. Come look at this." The microfiche machine on the far table displayed the front page of the *Sugarland*

Gazette, dated February 12, 1930. The headline read *Diamond Dealer In Deep!*

"That's our guy," I said, leaning in to look at the photograph below it. There was Shane Jordan, a familiar scowl on his face as officers led him away in handcuffs. "I knew he was shady."

"It turns out Jordan used the Adairs' parties as a cover to meet his mob contacts," Melody said, leaning close to turn the knob. A second photo showed Jordan and a man I didn't recognize at one of the Adairs' parties, taken just as they retreated through the glass door of the menagerie. Jeannie had been right in her suspicions. "They'd slip into the animal house for secret meetings. No one ever noticed, with so many people there." She turned the dial to another photo of Jordan ushering another man in through the glass door. "I know you said he was in with some of the gangsters, but this guy did a lot more than clean the mob's money. When he was finally arrested, it was for putting a hit out on a prosecutor threatening some of his connections."

"If he was willing to kill a prosecutor," I began.

"He'd off a dirty judge," Melody finished.

"Not necessarily." I leaned against the machine to get a closer look at the grainy photo of Shane Jordan with those cold, steely eyes. "A dirty judge would be useful for a guy like that. If anything, Shane's shady dealings would be a prime motive for keeping Greasy Larry alive."

"Even if Larry was blackmailing him?" Melody countered.

Possibly. "He could afford it."

She didn't appear convinced, and I wasn't, either. But it was worth considering both sides before jumping to conclusions.

"Can I get copies of that article and those photos?" I asked. I needed positive proof if I was going to bring this information to Inspector De Clercq.

"Sure. I also got you a transcript of the trial," Melody said. "Plus, I pulled a bunch of photographs of the 1928 Red Hot Ritz from the society section of the paper and found something interesting." She led me to the wood table and opened the file folder. "Here. Look at this," she said, handing me the top photo. It was a big panoramic shot from last night's lawn party. A group of laughing women holding shell drinks posed in the foreground. I didn't recognize any of them. "Check out what's going on in the background," Melody said. "In this one, you can see Bruno Scalieri entering the menagerie. He was a notorious hit man for the Canova family."

"Darn it, Frankie," I muttered. He should have caught this.

"I doubt Scalieri was mingling at the main bash," Melody said. "Maybe he snuck in the back."

"Or in the side," I said. We'd used a side exit on the edge of the property to make our escape last night.

"Look," she prodded.

Melody held out another picture from last night's toga party. It had faded with time and featured a society couple toasting with their fruity shell drinks, the menagerie in the background. And in the shadows, a horse-faced man with a patch over his eye—identifiable with the magnifying glass Melody handed me—slipped furtively through the side door. "Scalieri?"

She was right. "Scalieri would be hard to miss."

"See the scar down the cheek? And the patch over his right eye," she added before producing another photo, this one a mug shot, of the same man. Underneath read *Bruno Scalieri, inmate number 27360.*

"You are amazing," I told her. "Truly gifted."

Melody shrugged modestly, but she was grinning. "I'm good at research, and I like it. "It's easier than what you do."

I shared her grin. "I about gave Ellis a heart attack last night."

"Are we still talking about ghost hunting?" she teased.

I shook my head. Right now, my focus was on solving this murder. If we could catch Shane in the act of laundering money or covering a crime, De Clercq could arrest him. Maybe that would satisfy the inspector until we could suss out who killed Larry Knowles.

I hoped Shane hadn't completed his illicit meetings. We needed to catch him red-handed.

"I had a gut feeling from the start there was something wrong with that guy," I told Melody as she ran off the microfiche article. "I should have watched him more closely." I leaned against the table. "This is the final night of the Adairs' party. Last chance to figure out what happened."

"The last night is probably the biggest," Melody mused. "This is the time everyone will be there, making the most of it," she added ominously. "It'll be Jordan's last chance to conduct this kind of clandestine business meeting for a while. He won't appreciate you interfering."

Heavens. A chill went through me. "You could be right."

"Please be careful," she warned.

There it was again. "I'll do my best."

"Be sure to take Ellis with you," she added. "A cornered killer is a dangerous one."

Ellis would most likely be pulling a double shift, what with the murder investigation, but I didn't bother to pass that along. It would only worry her. Besides, it wasn't as if he could do much to protect me from a ghostly killer, and I'd have Frankie and the inspector with me.

Speaking of De Clercq, I needed to find the inspector as soon as possible. This information could be the key to his entire case. He wouldn't be happy with Frankie and me after we'd dashed out of the investigation early last night—again—but this would more than make up for it.

I left the library filled with a renewed sense of well-being. I was contributing to the case now, finding out things that neither Inspector De Clercq nor Frankie could. Maybe I'd even earn some appreciation from the stoic policeman.

I hurried down the library steps with the file from Melody. I'd run by home, grab EJ's package from my porch, and hopefully find Frankie in his shed, ready to help me hunt down De Clercq.

My phone rang. I saw who was calling and almost didn't answer. But if I ignored it, he'd keep calling, and at least right now I wasn't in the middle of anything. "Hey, Beau," I said, heading toward my car. I'd parked down from the food truck, which was a good thing. Lauralee was already starting to get a line.

"Zoey said Lauralee said you're at the library," he informed me.

Oh, to be from a town where nobody knew your business. "I'm working on a case," I said, waving at one of my neighbors, who carried a large brown paper bag from the food truck.

Go, Lauralee.

"I've been waiting at the studio all morning," Beau said as if I'd asked him to do it. I very clearly recalled telling him I'd drop by in the afternoon.

I reached my car and tossed the file folder into the passenger seat. "I'm in the middle of something," I said, slipping behind the wheel, "but I'll be there as soon as I can."

"Try not to take too long," he urged as I fired up the engine. "If you're not here by the time the paint dries, you won't have a chance to leave your handprint on the chicken's back."

I plopped my head onto the steering wheel and fought the urge to ask questions that I probably didn't want the answers to. "I'll do my best," I said, lifting my head and fluffing my bangs. "I'll see you soon, Beau."

Heaven help us both.

In the meantime, I drove home as fast as I dared, hoping nobody had disturbed the key and pictures EJ had sent to my house. I wouldn't know how to explain it to her if someone had stolen them, then left a pie in their place.

I was so worried about EJ's things I barely stopped in time to avoid running my car—and worse, myself—into a filmy gray barrier that cut right across my road.

"Stars!" I cried, hitting the brakes. By the time I stopped, the ghostly gray chain-link fence sat halfway through my engine block. That was all right, I supposed. My car was part of the living world. But that fence would have cut me in half.

The ghostly barricade circled my entire property. It had to be twenty feet tall, with barbed wire at the top.

It looked like a prison.

A thick chain secured the gate and a sign over it read *Sugarland Federal Penitentiary: Maximum Security.*

CHAPTER 17

"*L*ucy!" My little skunk darted straight through the ghostly gate and into my arms. "Are you okay?" I held her up, her back legs wriggling in excitement. "You're fine," I said, snuggling her to my chest. She might not be able to see how her entire backyard play area had been turned into a prison, but no doubt she could sense something was wrong. "You're a strong girl," I said, stroking her. "I'm proud of you."

"Hey! You want to back your car out of our gate?"

I looked up and saw a ghostly gray-uniformed guard approaching, a glower creasing his forehead. His mustache reminded me of a janitor's broom, but other than that, he appeared quite neat and official: jacket buttoned from the base of his neck to below his waist, shoes so shiny they could have doubled as mirrors, and flat-topped hat on perfectly straight.

"Just a second," I said, hurrying to place Lucy into the backseat of the land yacht. I tucked her into her favorite car blanket, an afghan I'd inherited from my grandmother, and gently closed the door.

The guard stopped inches from my front fender, which was

indeed poking straight through the prison fence. My car wasn't on the ghostly plane. It could go where it wanted.

The guard held a clipboard in one hand and used it to tap the shield-shaped badge on his chest. "You see this? I'm in charge of this entrance. You can't leave your vehicle like this. It's against regulations."

"It's not like there's a parking lot," I pointed out, regretting my words almost immediately. I didn't want to give these ghosts any more ideas.

My ancestral home, the place I'd fought so hard to protect, had been turned into a prison. Well, I wouldn't stand for it. I refused.

I kept my back straight and my head held high. "Let me inside this instant," I said to the guard, my voice sweet and calm—with an edge of steel. "This is my property and my house, and you're the one who has no business here."

His mustache quirked. "The inspector warned me about you," he drawled, more indulgent than threatened. He leaned closer, like a parent to a child. "Maybe it would be best if you found a new place to live, eh? This place isn't fit for a lady."

"We'll see about that," I said, stepping around him to look for a gate, a break in the fence, any place I could use to walk onto my property, to go home.

I about cried when I took a good hard look at the front yard. Once upon a time, a ghost who had known my great-great-grandmother had shown me the old peach orchard that used to stretch for acres across the front lawn, back before my family had to sell off all that land. I'd recently planted saplings in the hope of starting fresh. I could hardly see the young, tender trees now.

Instead, I saw bare dirt. Rough-looking men gathered in small groups, some in heated discussion as they openly stared at me. They wore gray chambray shirts and rough-hewn pants with thick black-and-white stripes. One particularly sketchy fellow with an eye patch and a nasty scar blatantly checked out my legs.

"Trust me, miss. You're safer out here," the guard said, reading my fear. I despised that he could see it so easily and that I had a good reason to worry. "Best for everyone if you move on."

I closed my eyes. "I can't." I wouldn't. I'd sacrificed too much for my home to have it end like this. "You wouldn't understand," I told him, not unless he had a family legacy to protect. I didn't need to explain myself anyway. "I need to see the inspector. Now."

"All righty," he said as if it were my funeral. "I'll need proof of residence before I can give you a visitor's badge."

I dug into my purse for my driver's license and held it out to him. He gave it a good hard look, glanced over the top of it at me, and then checked out the picture again. As if anyone in their right mind would want to be on my property now. Well, except for me.

The guard gave a satisfied grunt and then spent the next long minute filling out things on his clipboard. Lord save us from bureaucracy. When he'd finished, he handed me a piece of paper. "This is your visitor's pass. Don't lose it."

"Believe me, I've been trusted with bigger things." The ghostly slip of paper chilled my fingers as I took it.

"It's only good for one day," he instructed.

It wouldn't last five minutes in my mortal hands.

"Thanks," I said, heading for the gate.

"You'll have to renew it tomorrow morning."

This prison wouldn't be standing tomorrow. Not if I had anything to do with it.

"Now back your car out of the fence," he added as if I were the one creating problems around here.

"Right," I said, turning back to my car. "I'll move it right now, sir." He was just doing his job. It wouldn't keep me from doing mine.

I slid into the old Cadillac. "You doing okay, Lucy?" I looked in the backseat to see her curled up, asleep. At least one of us wasn't worried how this would turn out.

I pulled my car back and parked it about twenty yards down the road from the prison.

The *prison.*

The ominous gray fence contained my entire property. Guard towers loomed at the corners. It disturbed me on a level I didn't even know I could feel. Even if I wasn't tuned in, even if I never again borrowed Frankie's power to see ghosts, I would know this was here. I'd feel it. And it would make my home unlivable.

What I had to figure out was how it got here and why. I could understand why De Clercq would be upset about last night. Frankie and I hadn't exactly been subtle in our investigation. It wasn't a quality either one of us possessed in spades, but we'd gotten the job done. And the party wasn't over yet.

Not until tonight.

I grabbed the folder Melody had given me at the library, the one with the articles about Shane Jordan. With any luck, the FedEx envelope with EJ's photos and keys would still be on my porch. It wasn't like the dead would disturb it, but the living were another matter. And judging from the strange pies, it seemed someone with a pulse had taken an unhealthy interest in me.

The guard stood at the gate, observing my parking job.

"Your husband know you're driving?" he asked as I walked up the drive. "He know you're here?"

I held up my visitor's pass. "Let me in, please." I smiled politely, fighting the urge to flex my hands from the chill of the ghostly paper.

The guard tutted under his breath, then slowly unlocked the chain and pulled the gate open. "Bet you're a suffragette, too."

"Women got the right to vote in 1920," I informed him, breezing past.

He looked gobsmacked. "Glad I missed it. He shook his head. The gate groaned and rattled as he closed it behind me. "I can't tell you how many of those suffragette harridans I arrested in my day."

"Good for them," I murmured, tucking my pass in my folder. The pass might not last longer in there than it would in my hand, but at least I didn't have to touch it.

That was when I realized all eyes in the yard had turned to me.

I notched my chin up and strolled for my front porch, refusing to give them my attention or let them know how fast my heart had started to hammer. There were no more warm summer breezes in my front yard. Goose bumps prickled up my arms from the chill of so many ghosts in one place.

Never mind.

I could do this.

I needed to secure EJ's envelope before anything else, then find Frankie and Inspector De Clercq.

Straight ahead was the awful ghostly prison barracks that took up the left half of my house. Over the bright white paint and blue hydrangeas my grandmother had planted with her own hands, I saw rough gray walls and narrow barred windows. A group of dangerous-looking men with handlebar mustaches and dirty faces stood outside near a darkened doorway, watching me.

This should be interesting.

Over on the other side of the yard, a shouting match between two men was escalating to a fight. Other prisoners ran to join in, cursing and hollering, with guards on their heels to break it up.

"Jeez, Capone and Moran are at it again," one of the guards groaned as he jogged past me, pulling out his nightstick and blocking a punch from a prisoner. "Get them separated!" he yelled to his colleagues as he wrestled his attacker to his knees and slapped a pair of cuffs on him.

Lordy. I'd seen enough gangster movies to know that it was bad to have Al Capone and Bugs Moran in the same prison. If those two stayed, I would never be able to fall asleep here again.

I hurried up my front steps, careful to avoid the wall of the barracks that took up most of them, and found the envelope from EJ on my porch.

Okay. I breathed a sigh of relief as I stacked it on top of Melody's folder. I'd accomplished the first thing I'd set out to do. Not everything was bad.

"Hiya, sugar."

I turned. A prisoner stood at the bottom of the steps, blocking my way. It was Bruno Scalieri. I'd have bet my life on it.

His scar crinkled and the toothpick between his rotten teeth tipped up as he treated me to a predatory smile. "Why don't you come on down here and greet a fellow proper?"

My breath caught, and I looked for someone, anyone, to help, but the guards were all busy with the fight.

"I know you. I saw you at the Red Hot Ritz party last night," I fibbed.

He stared at me.

"What were you doing in the menagerie with Shane Jordan?" I asked.

His expression darkened. "I wish you hadn't witnessed that," he said, climbing the stairs to come get me.

"Stop," I ordered. "I mean it. Not another step." I clutched the envelope and my folder to my chest. I'd never make it past this guy.

"Hey now." Suds materialized at the bottom of the stairs, next to the creepy guy. Frankie's old bank-robber friend wore a visitor's badge and a wary expression. Suds placed an arm between the prisoner and me. "Lay off it, Lefty. She's with the South Town Boys."

Scalieri's leer intensified. "I saw her first." He blatantly checked out my body. "I didn't know the live girl could see me back."

"Come on down, Verity," Suds ordered, his voice casual, his body tense. He kept his focus on the sleazy ghost and his arm up. "I'm gonna have a talk here with Mr. Scalieri." He cocked his chin and stared me down as if to say *hurry*. "Frankie's out back."

"Gotcha." I clambered down the stairs, skirted the ghosts, and shamelessly dashed away from the barracks and around the side of the house.

"See you soon, sugar," Scalieri called.

No, he wouldn't. I'd make sure of it.

Just as I neared the rose garden near the back porch, I spotted Frankie and De Clercq out by the shed.

I kept my head down, rushing past the pond, where a half-dozen rickety tables were crowded with prisoners shouting and playing cards.

Frankie lifted his cuffed hands, arguing with the inspector.

Somehow, I didn't think that was going to work out for him.

"You gotta believe me," Frankie pleaded with the inspector, who was having none of it.

De Clercq always appeared somewhat severe, but today his expression bordered on outright loathing. "You are a crook and a liar, Mr. Winkelmann, and I am done giving you chances."

Frankie's cuffs rattled as he held up a finger. "Just one more."

"You abandoned our investigation early both nights." The inspector's mustache quivered, and he was as close to an outburst as I'd ever seen him. "You've provided no new leads or evidence. And worst of all, your juvenile antics nearly destroyed the mansion last night."

"You can't burn it down forever," Frankie pointed out.

Veins were popping out on the inspector's forehead. "I will not have this blatant disrespect taint my investigation. You, sir, have failed. I will press on alone. I will not stop. I will not surrender, or our murderer will escape justice forever."

"We have leads," Frankie insisted. He pointed to me. "She found a briefcase with pictures and ledgers—"

"That you can't produce," De Clercq said flatly.

Frankie held his hands up in supplication, as far as they would go. "It's not my fault our evidence got eaten by black tar."

We had that problem a lot on ghost-hunting investigations. Tons of evidence, no proof.

I was finally close enough to add my two cents. "Inspector," I called.

"She'll tell you," Frankie insisted. "Let it rip, Verity."

I flung a hand back toward my house. "You're destroying my home!"

"That's not the point," Frankie said.

"It is to me," I said, slightly out of breath as I reached them.

De Clercq frowned. "Your ghost is grounded here. Therefore, the prison must be here."

"Absolutely not." I stopped directly in front of him. "You don't have my permission to do this."

He smiled thinly. "Then it is a good thing that I don't need it."

"I can break him out," I said, "take his urn off the property." I didn't want to threaten the inspector, but he'd given me no choice.

"Not a chance. You take that urn and I take over your entire house," De Clercq ground out. "Every inch of it filled with the worst criminals you can imagine. Even if you turn off his power, I'll make sure you feel them."

My entire body numbed with the threat. "You're an awful person," I managed.

"I get the job done," he countered.

So did I, but this was not the way. "You know what, you're an officer of the law," I said, trying a different tactic. "It can't be legal for you to take over my land. Or invade half of my home. Or force me to host criminals."

The man lived for logic, I'd give him logic.

De Clercq appeared unmoved. "The laws of the living and the dead rarely intersect cleanly, as you can see." He waved a hand at the prison yard and the guard towers posted at my property line beyond the pond. De Clercq returned his attention to me. "You should not be able to interact with us at all, yet you do so on a regular basis. If I may be blunt, your own inappropriate behavior in a world that doesn't concern you, not to mention your partnership with a criminal, has brought this on you. So yes, Miss Long, as a matter of fact, I can indeed turn your property into a prison. Here it is, and here it shall stay as long as Frankie the German is bound here."

Lord in heaven. "That could be forever."

"You said you were working on it," Frankie countered.

We were. It was just that we hadn't come up with anything that worked yet.

"This is a nightmare," I said. Worse than a nightmare—at least I could wake up from one of those.

My home, my heritage, had been overrun by the ghosts of some of the worst criminals in American history. I couldn't live like this. Even if Frankie took away his energy, I would still know they were here, moving around me and through me, invading every corner of my life. And poor Lucy! She would never be comfortable here again.

I had to fix this. For me, for Frankie and Lucy, for the sake of my future and my sanity. Not to mention my ancestors. My grandmother had trusted me with this property. It was mine to preserve and give to my children someday.

"No," I said. I had given up everything to keep my house. I wasn't about to lose it now. My fingers tightened on Melody's folder, and I exhaled slowly.

I had to do this right.

"Inspector De Clercq," I began, civil, logical—even though he had been anything but. "I understand that you're upset with how we gathered our information last night. I know you believe that we don't even have anything real to go on. But tell me this, did you ever search the dead judge's room?"

His mouth tightened. "You know quite well I was never informed that Mr. Knowles stayed at the mansion."

"No, you weren't," I agreed. "I discovered that."

He huffed. "By treating murder suspects as cocktail-party acquaintances."

"It worked," I reminded him. "Sometimes it's better to treat people like people."

He stared at me long and hard. "They are suspects and it's dangerous to forget that. It can also lead to compromised behavior." He nodded pointedly at Frankie. "Case in point, Mr. Winkelmann's ostentatious fireworks display."

"That worked too," Frankie said.

The inspector looked Frankie up and down yet remained unmoved. "I warned you not to trust the word of a living girl, a silly thing desperate to make herself useful in a world she doesn't understand." He turned his cold gaze on me. "I need solid proof, not wild theories from a criminal and his dubious assistant."

"I have proof," I said.

I opened my folder and drew out the first article that Melody had found. "Proof at least that Jordan was involved in some shady activities at the mansion during the Red Hot Ritz parties." I turned the paper toward him, the wide black headline shouting it to the world. "Along with your prisoner, 'Lefty' Scalieri."

The inspector scanned the article.

"Did you know that was going on?" I asked.

His mouth tightened. "I've never seen that before." He tried to take it, and his hand passed straight through. He drew it back in disgust. "Where did you find this?"

"The library," I said simply. His eyes darted over the page as he read, his eyebrows rising with every line. "This all came out in 1930," I explained, "a year after you died."

He'd been killed in the wreck of the Sugarland Express and had remained at the accident site for years after. That was how we'd met him, and right now I wished he had stayed with the train instead of following us home.

He withdrew his attention from the page and turned to the nearest guard. "Johnson," he called, "find me someone who was alive in 1930."

"Well—" the guard took a gander at the yard "—there's George Miller over there."

"Fine," De Clercq snapped, his eyes on the paper.

"I'll go get him, then," the guard said. "Hang on." He jogged over to the ghost in question.

A moment later we were joined by George Miller, a pockmarked young man who wore an earnest expression. "You called for me, sir?" he asked the inspector.

De Clercq pointed to the page in my folder. "I need you to look at this article and tell me if this is true." He glanced at me, and I held the paper out toward the newcomer.

It took Miller a few minutes, his lips moving as he read. He obviously wasn't the most practiced reader, but eventually he nodded. "Yeah, this is right. I remember when the news broke. It was a big deal around here. This Jordan guy was sent to prison." He looked out over the yard. "He might be here."

"He is not." De Clercq nodded once. "Thank you, that will be all." He turned back toward Frankie and me, and for the first time in a while, he appeared pensive.

"You see?" Frankie wheedled. "He just confirmed what the papers in the briefcase told us. Jordan had a side gig. He was laundering money for Greasy Larry. They probably had meetings during those shindig parties, and Jordan killed him. Question Scalieri. He might even admit it. Our intel was good. We can still make this happen."

The inspector appeared uncharacteristically torn. "Your investigative methods are nontraditional and dangerous." He treated me to a withering look. "You don't rely on observation and procedure, but on gossip and hearsay."

"That's because it works," Frankie said, a bit too saucily for my taste.

"Our methods might be different," I said quickly, "but you can't argue with results. After all," I reasoned, "you brought us on board because you wanted a fresh perspective."

De Clercq twisted the end of his mustache, thinking.

"We can do things you can't," I added.

"Or won't," Frankie said.

De Clercq dropped the hand from his mustache. "It's too risky. You stay here."

Oh, heavens, no.

Frankie smiled his friendliest con-artist smile. "Risky caught your killer on the Sugarland Express."

The inspector clenched his jaw. "You realize tonight is the final night of the party." He trained a steely-eyed glare on Frankie and then on me. "I cannot afford for either of you to do any more damage—to the property or the investigation."

"We'll be good," I said, hoping I wasn't promising the impossible. "I swear it on my grandmother's grave."

"That won't be necessary," De Clercq huffed as I fanned the articles out for his perusal. The inspector looked every piece of paper over, some of them twice. I kept still and held my breath. It was good, solid evidence, and I had faith that De Clercq would see that. He had to. He might be mad at us, but his first priority was always going to be the case.

"It must be solved tonight," he said, almost to himself.

"It can be," I assured him, praying I was right.

His eyes flicked up to me. "We will solve it tonight, or this prison stays here for eternity."

My stomach knotted, and my palms grew damp. Forever was a long time. We'd better be right about Shane Jordan and his covert meetings. And hope that he had one coming up.

"Tonight," I said, my voice shaking, betraying my fear.

"And throw in a full pardon," Frankie chimed in.

Good lord, did he ever know when to quit? I opened my mouth, ready to jump in and smooth things over, but to my surprise, De Clercq nodded.

"If you can come through on the murder of the judge, I'll see you are granted a full pardon from the state of Tennessee."

PECAN PIES AND DEAD GUYS

"And you'll get rid of the prison," I added.

I didn't get a genial nod like Frankie had, but after a moment De Clercq said, "If we don't need the prison for Mr. Winkelmann, we will relocate it. You have my word on that."

It would have to do.

"Tonight, then." I resisted the urge to press a hand to my chest to ease the knot of tension that had been building there ever since I saw what had become of my home. "We can do this," I added, for myself more than anyone else.

"We're real close," Frankie said. "I've got an inside track, don't you worry."

De Clercq reached into his pocket and withdrew a set of keys. He unlocked the cuffs around Frankie's wrists, but didn't pull back immediately. "One last chance." He caught our gazes and collected his cuffs.

As he turned and walked away, I realized we had another problem. I eyed Frankie. "Now we just have to figure out how to get back into the party tonight with the owners angry at us and the dominant ghost ready to chase us off the property."

The gangster rubbed his wrists. "We have to be sneaky."

"That's your plan? Be sneaky?" We'd need more than that. "Were you serious when you said that you had an inside track?"

"Heck no," he snorted, "I'm as terrified as you are."

"Great." The prison loomed large in my vision. Everything I owned was on the line.

Frankie stood next to me, so close our shoulders nearly touched. "At least we got one thing going for us."

"A reckless willingness to do whatever it takes?" I asked.

"Tonight's party is a masquerade. It'll be harder to spot us. The invitation says the theme is Crowned and Bejeweled, so you're gonna have to get glitzy. And wear a mask."

"I'll still be the only live girl there," I reminded him.

"And I'm still the only devastatingly handsome mobster." He grew serious. "Look, there's nothing we can do about you being

213

alive. We'll have to make the best of it. Keep you in costume so you don't stick out. Try to hide in the crowd. We're going to have to stay on the down-low, keep an eye on our suspects without them knowing. It all starts at sundown."

"Let's do it, then," I said, my mind forming a plan. "Sundown it is."

CHAPTER 18

"At least Molly made it out before the gates went up," Frankie said, fingers drumming against my dashboard. "She's back home."

At the heritage society house where we'd met her. "We'll fix this," I promised him.

First things first. I needed a costume. There were two stores in Sugarland where you could buy used clothes. The first was a consignment store off Main Street that carried higher-end items, brand names and business casual. Melody shopped there for a lot of her outfits. It was a tad out of my price range and not likely to have anything glitzy enough for a "Crowned and Bejeweled" masquerade, so instead I drove to Dani's Bargain Market.

Dani's was a combination dollar store and flea market on a quiet corner a few blocks south of downtown, near the laundromat and the beauty outlet. It was the hottest store in Sugarland during Halloween, since it carried a wide variety of cheap costumes kids loved, but right now it was July. I had to hope that there were a few things in there that would suit me for tonight. It didn't have to look like high couture, it just had to get me through the door.

We'd dropped off Lucy with Lauralee's kids. She'd been very understanding when I'd mentioned a pest problem in the house that I needed to handle, and the kids were ecstatic to spend more time with their "practice pet."

"Ha, you're lucky," Frankie grumbled from the backseat as we pulled up outside Dani's Market, its red and white awning fluttering a bit in the breeze. "Most people are going to ignore you anyway. Me, though? It's hard to hide charisma like I got."

"Then I guess you'll need a good costume," I said as I headed for the front door. Too bad he'd never find anything here. Poor Frankie had to source his disguise from the ghostly plane.

A bell rang gently as I entered, and I had to resist the urge to sneeze as my nose registered the scents of worn cotton, old leather, and other people's sweat. Dani waved from where she'd camped out behind the register, reading a magazine. Her wild blond hair fought to escape the vintage bandana tied around her head, and she wore more friendship bracelets than I could count.

"Welcome," she called, chewing her gum. "Let me know if you need help with anything."

"Thanks." I headed straight for the formalwear area in the back near the dressing rooms. There had to be a used bridesmaid's dress or something that would make do for one evening. I found my size and started sifting through the rack. No, no—orange, gosh no—too much cleavage for this one, not nearly enough for that one...

"Did I show you what Suds put together for me?" Frankie asked, clearly not able to resist interrupting me when I was concentrating. "Take a look at my brilliant disguise."

He held the spade end of a rusted shovel over his face. Two eyeholes and a slit for a mouth had been cut out of the metal. "The man in the iron mask," he said proudly. "It's not like Suds needs his shovel to do any more work."

No. He'd died using it to tunnel under the First Bank of Sugarland. Frankie could mess with Suds's shovel all he wanted.

The holes wouldn't stay for longer than an evening because they weren't there when Suds died.

"Are you going to get a medieval costume to go with it?" I asked.

Frankie lowered the mask. "Like I'm going to find someone around here who died in a doublet and pantyhose. I got something better anyhow. Icepick Charlie's friend died in a casino shooting. He's letting me borrow his tux for the night. Only one bullet hole through the chest and I can put a flower over that."

"Lucky you," I murmured, returning to the clothes.

At least Frankie was fully on board with tonight's do-or-die mission. He had a lot personally riding on this one, which was more than I could say for most of our investigations.

Usually, he couldn't wait to strike out on his own when we traveled. The fact that he was sticking by my side showed he was as worried as I was, probably more. At least I wouldn't be imprisoned on my property for the rest of eternity.

"What do you think of this?" I selected a red sequined dress with a high waistline and held it in front of me.

Frankie shook his head immediately. "That's perfect if you're going for the frumpy showgirl look."

Okay then. I put it back and kept searching. "This looks better." It was teal, which I thought was a good color on me, and had slightly poufy sleeves.

"Sure. If you want to go as somebody's maid."

Ouch. "Frankie Winkelmann, fashion critic," I mused, moving to the next rack.

"I'm here to make you look good," he agreed.

He stood in the middle of the rack as I looked. I tried to ignore him.

"Nah...nope...no...na—wait, that one there."

I looked at the dress he indicated. "Are you sure?" It was a cream color, floor-length, with a lace bodice and long sleeves. It seemed plain to me.

"That's it," Frankie said, with the certainty of a man. "It looks old-timey, it covers most of you, and the skirt's got enough give so you can run if you need to."

"Good point." I clutched the hanger tighter. "I hadn't even considered that I might need to run."

He shrugged as if it was nothing. "You're not the first moll I've used to help with a job," he said with a smirk.

"I'm not your moll," I said, not even sure what that was. If Frankie hung with them, they weren't nice ladies. "I'll try it on. Now I need a mask."

"And some jewelry."

"If I can afford it," I said, closing the dressing room curtain behind me.

"You know the other girls will be wearing it," his voice warned.

"Fine. Some costume jewelry," I said, slipping my sundress over my head.

Some very cheap costume jewelry.

The dress fit. I wore it out of the dressing room and went to select accessories. There were masks in the back of the shop, leftovers from last Halloween. I found one that was a simple cat's-eye edged with metallic beads and a few peacock feathers, then stood in front of a long mirror at the back.

The effect was…not bad. I didn't look like anybody's idea of royalty, but I didn't look like myself either, which was the important thing.

Frankie hovered behind me, grinning. "I like when a plan starts coming together."

"It's a start," I agreed.

The front counter had a decent selection of costume jewelry in it. I counted my cash and ended up springing for a matching set of huge fake pearl earrings and a necklace. They were ridiculous, but they were cheap.

"This looks like fun," Dani said with a smile as she rang up my purchases. "Are you going to a party here in town?"

"That's right."

"Huh, you're the only person who's come in looking for a costume recently." She took my two twenties and slowly set about making some change. My phone buzzed in my purse, but I ignored it. "Where is it?"

"It's, um..." *It's a party for dead people only and I'm doing my best to sneak into it so the ghosts don't recognize me.* "It's not for a while yet, but I like to be prepared."

"Smart," she said with a nod. "You get the best pick of the clothes that way." She handed over my change and my receipt. "Thanks for visiting and come back soon!"

"Oh, I will." I'd try to sell back the dress and jewelry, assuming they survived the night. Dani paid twenty percent on all return merchandise in good condition. "Thanks."

I checked my phone in the car and groaned. Three new texts from Beau, each one progressively more demanding. He was more like his mother than he realized. *On my way,* I messaged before slipping my phone into my pocket.

Frankie stood on the curb, staring a hole in my back as I dug in my purse for my car keys.

"Seriously? We're working on a huge case at the Adair mansion and you're going to visit your ex-boyfriend? I don't get to see Molly."

And I didn't get to see Ellis. "Frankie," I began, opening the car door and slipping inside, "we have two hours until sundown when the party starts. We can do this and still be good for the Adairs.'"

He materialized in the passenger seat, frowning. "Just so long as you don't forget what's at stake here."

My home was not my home anymore. How could I forget?

"I'm aware of what we have to do," I said, pulling away from the curb, heading for the north side of town. "This is also something I said I'd do."

The ghost stuck his hand through the closed window to catch the breeze. "Some promises are made to be broken," he mused.

"Not by me," I reminded him.

Although, truthfully, I almost agreed with him on this one. Handling Beau was the last thing I wanted to be doing. But I had to keep the bigger picture in mind. Assuming everything came together at the masquerade tonight—and I desperately needed to believe that it would—then apart from the mystery pies, the only thing left hanging over my head would be Virginia's promise to return my grandmother's necklace. In order for that to happen, I had to convince Beau to go back to working at the law firm. I didn't want to throw that chance away just because I was stressed over keeping my house. I had the time. I had the opportunity. I'd follow through. I'd go and see Beau and do my best to get him to go about his artwork a little more...reasonably.

The barn he was renting was on a local soybean farmer's property, at the first turnoff beside a dirt road that ran the length of the farmer's fields. The barn itself was rather pretty. It had a timber frame and gambrel roof painted bright red with white trim. Beau's silver BMW coupe was parked outside it, and the double doors were thrown wide open.

By the time I'd turned my engine off, Beau was at my door. He appeared almost unrecognizable in a paint-splattered T-shirt and jeans, and were those Crocs on his feet? Yes, they were. Neon green ones at that. Zoey had clearly made an impact on him.

"Finally," he exclaimed as I got out of the car. "I've been waiting for you all day. Where have you been?"

"I'm sorry for making you wait, but I had a few important things come up." *Like a stalker pie and a ghost incursion.* "I'm here now, though," I added cheerfully. "Give me the grand tour."

"You're gonna regret asking for that," Frankie muttered from behind me as Beau reached out and took my hand. I immediately tried to pull it back, but he held on and turned toward the barn.

"Let me lead you inside. It's best if you close your eyes until you're in the middle of the exhibit," he said by way of explanation.

"I want you to get the full, visceral experience. I can't wait to see what you think of it."

I sighed quietly but allowed him to guide me in, carefully turning me in places until I finally came to a stop on a concrete floor. Beau let go of my hand, and I heard him take a few paces back. "Okay...open your eyes!"

I did. I blinked twice and stifled a gasp.

I stood in the middle of a bevy of sculptures as large as I was, all of them tall, bright, and hideous enough to give me nightmares. A metal lady—painted yellow except for oversized hot pink lips— rose out of a bucket filled with empty dish soap bottles. Then there was one that could have been a bird or perhaps even a spider, made from repurposed rebar with chunks of concrete still clinging to it. Beau could still be cleaning that one, or maybe the odd bits of concrete were part of the art. The one right in front of me was particularly confusing, and to be honest, it made me a bit uncomfortable. Beau's basic metal frame hung with multicolored rags twisted together and weighed down at the end with what appeared to decapitated doll heads.

I'd know. I'd seen a whole fountain full of them on one of my last adventures.

These heads were wearing dunce caps in midnight blue, painted with melting stars.

"Ahh..." I began, trying to take it all in.

"Ain't there a book out there that describes all the levels of Hell?" Frankie asked. "Do you think this is one of them?" He gave a visible shudder. "I'm outta here. I'll wait in the car."

Lucky.

Beau stared at me expectantly.

"Wow," I finally said. "It's so...gosh, I don't even know. I don't think I've ever seen anything like it before."

"I know! They're completely unique! I added a gothic flair to this one." He pointed to the questionable masterpiece directly in front of me, practically bursting with pride. "All the fabric comes from the Armani suit my mother bought me last Christmas. Zoey recorded me ripping it to shreds," he added, with relish. "She thinks it'll be great advertising, kind of like a multimedia piece. Me interacting with my art. The heads represent the poor office drones who are never strong enough to break free of the golden handcuffs that bind them to the humdrum life of money and expectation."

I still couldn't get over the first part of his explanation. "You ripped up your Armani suit?"

"It felt so good." Beau grinned at me. "I'm totally over my obsession with material things. So, you like it? I was thinking of setting my asking price at ten grand."

For someone who claimed not to care about material possessions, that was an incredibly high price for what amounted to a freaky scarecrow. "I think it's important to see what the market will bear," I extemporized, easing myself out of the circle of awfulness, careful not to catch my sundress on the tower of tin cans with arms. "It might be smart to start a little lower."

Beau crossed his arms as he stared at the sculpture. "You think? Because if I'm going to make as much with this as I did before, I figure that's already on the low end of the scale."

Oh my god. And people thought I was crazy.

Worse, I didn't know how I was going to talk him out of this. He was not only drinking the Kool-Aid, but he'd also bought the giant jug that busted through walls.

"When it comes down to practicalities, I think maybe—" A picture taped to the side of the barn caught my eye, and I walked over to get a closer look. "Oh." It was Zoey's food truck, in black and white, with Zoey at the counter and two of the library staff chatting and eating in front of it. "Wow." The picture had a liveliness to it, a composition that drew the eye and made me wish I could step into it and join them. "This is a great photograph." I looked back at Beau. "Did you take this?"

He stepped closer to me and shrugged. "Yeah. Just for

inspiration purposes. I mean, I've got to remember to put the Southern into my Southern eclectic style, right? So I took these to provide reminders."

These? There were more of them? I looked down the wall and, yes, there were, and they were all exceptional. Here was a shot of the diner teeming with customers and two servers with full trays. There was a picture of one of the benches in front of the ice cream shop, with a little girl in a ruffled dress sitting on it and barely hanging on to her enormous waffle cone. There was even one of the exterior of his parents' house, and he'd somehow managed to make it look both elegant *and* inviting.

"These are fantastic," I said, one hundred percent honest this time. They were gorgeous. Inspired, even. I waved a hand at the nearest one, a shot of the barn before he'd moved his stuff in, if the tractor sitting inside it was any indication. "Beau, these should be your art!"

"These?" He appeared dumbfounded for a second, then shook his head. "No, these are just—they're photographs. Anybody can snap a picture with a camera. What I'm doing with my sculptures is a unique expression of my inner self."

He'd been hanging out with Zoey too much.

"This look at Sugarland is unique too," I insisted. "These pictures capture the reality of living in a small Southern town, and they do it beautifully. I think people would jump all over prints of these."

Beau smiled softly. "You're so supportive of me. I can't tell you how much I appreciate that. But trust me—I've found my niche." His look became more calculating. "If you truly want to help out, you could call your dealer friend in New York for me and set up a meeting."

Of course, he knew I was talking to EJ. Who didn't know all my business in Sugarland? "I don't think I can do that."

I saw hints of the old lawyer flicker across his features. "You could do it if you wanted to."

"I don't have that kind of relationship with Ms. Adair," I said firmly.

"We'll see," he said. "Or maybe I'll make my own way like you did." He winked at me, like the Beau of old. "Admit it, you're impressed with me now."

I was, but for all the wrong reasons. "I'd be more impressed if you were a lawyer."

"No, you wouldn't."

He had me.

"You're right, I wouldn't," I admitted. "But I want you to think carefully about this and take the time to decide what's right for you. Part of taking your time is making sure you can take care of yourself before you jump headlong into something new. You could consider working at least part-time at the law firm until you've established yourself as an artist."

Beau shook his head. "You don't really believe that. You never take anything slow. Just—just trust me, Verity. Okay?" He stepped a little closer, and in the glowing light of the evening sun, his hair looked like it could have been spun out of gold. He gazed at me softly, affectionately, and I gulped. That was not a look I wanted to see on his face. "I can do this. I believe in myself. I want you to believe in me too. It would—it would mean a lot to me."

Oh no. "Beau, listen—"

"Beau?"

The unwelcome tension between us broke as Zoey entered the barn, a smile on her face that turned to a look of confusion. "Verity," she said, trying to summon up some enthusiasm and failing. "You finally made it."

I stepped back quickly, even though I had nothing to feel guilty about. "I was just leaving."

"Do you have to?" Beau sounded disappointed. "Because I was thinking the three of us could get dinner."

"I've got plans, sorry." I nodded at Zoey as I passed her. She looked cute today in a floral romper and strappy sandals, her long black hair in a loose, casual braid. "You guys have fun. It's nice to see you again."

"Let me walk you out." Zoey fell into step with me but kept a few feet of distance between us.

I welcomed the bright sunshine, and the sight of my car.

"Hey, Verity," Zoey said, keeping pace. "Um...sorry if this is a weird question, but I have to ask."

I stopped, and she turned to face me.

"I get the feeling that whatever happened with you and Beau, it isn't over."

"It is done," I assured her. "I'm sorry if that looked strange back there, but things are definitely over between Beau and me. I'm happy with Ellis." So much happier, I couldn't even describe it without offending her.

"Are you serious?" She sounded dubious. "Because that's not what I'm seeing."

Oh no. I could see why she thought that—it had been weird at the end there in the barn—but she was so wrong. "I promise you, I am not and will never be after Beau," I told her. "He's much better off with you, believe me."

"Okay." Zoey smiled, but it didn't seem like her heart was in it. "Drive safe."

"I will." I got into the car and suppressed a groan. Great, at this rate not only would I never get my necklace back, I was also messing up the only good thing Beau had going for him.

Zoey was a sweet girl. Maybe she should work more on her food truck and less on turning Beau into a bad artist, but she was a good person and she cared about him. I'd have to figure out a way to be kind to him and to her at the same time.

The sun hung low in the sky. We had maybe an hour left before sunset and the start of the final party at the Adairs'.

I was almost looking forward to it now. Playing hide-and-seek with an angry ghost was preferable to spending another second feeding Beau's artistic delusions and making Zoey worry. I buckled my seatbelt and turned to Frankie. "Are you ready to catch a killer?"

"I was born ready," he vowed. "Let's nab that wiseguy and show the inspector what we can do, right?"

"Right," I said, adjusting my grip on the wheel.

I admired his confidence. I felt good, ready.

I only hoped we could pull it off.

CHAPTER 19

The sun wasn't close enough to the horizon for me to head to the party yet. The last thing I wanted to do was arrive early and attract attention.

Frankie had vanished into the ether after he realized we had some time to burn. The ether was an in-between realm that seemed to relax him. The gangster didn't have to worry about preparing for our next move. I, on the other hand, needed a place to change into my dress and get ready for the night ahead.

To that end, I pulled into Judson's Last Stop near the old highway, about a mile off the new one. Lauralee joked that the place had stood there since the founding of Sugarland. And while her observation was good for a laugh, it didn't seem too far from the truth.

The well-worn, well-loved station had been owned by the Judsons going back to at least my great-grandparents' generation. They were a tradition in this town, and even though the highway had been rerouted twenty years ago, they never lacked for business. The newest patriarch, Josephus Judson, was in his seventies if he was a day, and he'd taken over from his daddy only about ten years ago.

I had a soft spot for him because he had loved my grandmother like a sister, and his station had a bathroom that didn't require you to make a purchase in order to use it.

I bundled my costume over my arm and headed inside. "Hi there, Mr. Judson," I said with a wave. The door chime gave a belated ding as I made my way past three rows of chips toward the corner with the restrooms.

"Good of you to stop in." He waved back but didn't look up from the little TV in the checkout stand, where he was watching a game, if the cheers were anything to go by.

The ladies' room was a single-stall affair, which was nice—more space for me to change. The fluorescent light flickered overhead. I locked the door and shimmied out of my sundress. I kept my sandals on and was pulling the gown up when my cell phone rang. I hitched the dress up over my shoulders and let it hang unzipped as I checked the caller ID. It was EJ.

"Hi," I said, glad to hear from her. "I just picked up your package and the key. Thanks again for sending them." In fact, the flat FedEx envelope was still in my bag. I hadn't even opened it in all the excitement.

"Oh, good." She paused. "I wanted to thank you for emailing those pictures of the house. I have them up on my computer right now. I..." she trailed off. "It's thrilling to see, and a little sad. Things have gotten a bit run-down, haven't they?"

"The years will do that," I agreed. "It's still a wonderful old place," I assured her, digging a finger under the seal of the envelope she'd sent.

She'd packed several photos, each in its own wax-paper folder. I pulled out one of a young girl in pigtails, Sir Charles draped over her lap, with a beaming Marjorie looking on. Then there was one of Jeannie and Marjorie and EJ blowing bubbles. Graham, Marjorie, and a smiling Marcus racing go-karts down the long drive. "I'm enjoying your pictures as well. I didn't realize you were so close to Marjorie and Marcus." They were in a surprising number of photos. But it made sense. The two of them had grown up as close friends to Graham.

"Ah, yes. Marjorie and Marcus Phillips," she said, her tone warm, but wary. "Mr. Phillips—Marcus—he didn't like me much. Or maybe it just seemed that way to a young girl. He ran hot and cold. But Marjorie was like a second mother to me."

No wonder she'd warmed up to me when she'd learned I was talking with EJ, trying to reconnect her with the house and her heritage.

"What's the story with Marcus Phillips?" I asked. "I've... researched him. He seems like an interesting fellow." It was a weak story, but more believable than *Marcus's ghost has some serious issues.*

"Uncle Graham always said Mr. Phillips should have been a great man. And Uncle Graham was usually right about people."

"A great man," I repeated, trying that on for size. "How so?" I asked when she failed to elaborate.

"I'm honestly not sure," she said. "I was just a child. But he did have a big personality."

"True," I said, thinking of the way Marcus had acted when I'd first met him: confident, understandably frustrated at his wife. I tried to reconcile that with the raw anger I'd seen in him when I'd overheard him in the hallway with Marjorie. Marcus could be a charmer if he wanted. But he definitely had a dark side.

"Looking back, I think he was simply unhappy and it showed. My aunt and uncle used to talk about how he'd changed, but they still considered him a very good friend. They still had faith that he'd put himself on the right path."

"I have a friend like that," I sympathized. Beau was frustrated, lost, and known for getting drunk and out of hand. But maybe with a little help, he could find a way to move forward and have a happier ending than Marcus did. "His wife, Marjorie, on the other hand—she lights up the room." I'd seen it in the photos EJ had sent, and in person.

"Auntie Marge was a force of nature," EJ said. "She taught me so much. And she didn't judge. I could tell her things I couldn't tell my own parents, or even my aunt and uncle. We used to write all the time when I was growing up. She helped me through a lot. Young girls can be cruel, and my mom was older. She didn't always understand."

I could see Marjorie jumping right in with advice. I'd experienced that firsthand. "It sounds like you were lucky to have Marjorie in your life."

EJ sighed. "I was, until my mother found letters where I told Marjorie about my first boyfriend and how I was getting close to him. Puppy love, nothing big. Of course, Marjorie wanted to hear all about it. But Mom was mad. She said Marjorie was a bad influence. She overreacted something terrible."

Perhaps she'd known about Marjorie's past. The mug shot had been a shock to me, but Graham Adair's sister might have known all about it.

"I was forbidden to write her again," EJ said, the pain in her voice clear. "Except one final letter where I had to say that I didn't think she was the type of person I should have in my life anymore. It hurts to even think about what I said in that letter."

"Your mother made you do it." EJ couldn't blame herself for that. She'd been a young, impressionable kid.

"That doesn't make it right. Marjorie did nothing but love me and help me." She cleared her throat and I could hear her on the line, regaining her composure. "My mom stopped sending me to my aunt and uncle's. They'd visit us in New York sometimes, but it was never the same."

"How awful. I'm so sorry." It had to hurt to be torn away from her happy memories and her Sugarland family. She needed closure at the very least. "I don't mean to pressure you, but I really wish you'd come back and see it now."

This time, I heard her hesitation. "I might…" she hedged. "I'd like to. But I'm not what you call a spring chicken."

"You have to do what you feel is right," I agreed. She must be amazingly spry for her age if she was still working at the gallery, but no doubt she had her health concerns and I had to remember Sugarland wasn't for everyone. Although, quite frankly, the idea that someone might not want to visit or live here was hard to get my head around sometimes. "In the meantime, I'll keep sending you pictures."

"I'm counting on it," she said before we ended our conversation.

I definitely needed to get a shot of the snake cage for her. It would also give me a chance to compare the ghostly murder scene with EJ's photos of the same place. Perhaps the killer had left a clue that hadn't been so obvious to us before.

I'd just placed the photographs back in their wax envelopes and the FedEx package in my bag when my phone rang again. Maybe EJ had reconsidered.

But it was Ellis.

I smiled to myself. Mr. Judson was going to wonder what I was doing for so long in his bathroom.

I clicked to answer. "Hey," I said, cradling the phone with my shoulder, hiking up my still-unzipped dress. "I left you a—"

"Verity, I need you to come down to the station," he said over me, which was very unlike Ellis. He sounded serious, almost grave.

"I'm changing into my costume for the ghost masquerade."

Well, that and turning the gas station bathroom into my private telephone booth.

I checked out my reflection in the cheap, slightly wavy mirror. "I might even look half-dead after doing my makeup in this light."

"Verity," he cut in. Again.

"I've got to be at the estate when the sun sets," I continued, balancing my purse on the tiny counter.

"That's going to have to wait." He spoke to me more like Frankie than my loving boyfriend. "Cammi is dead."

"What?" I gripped the edge of the sink. My purse slipped off the counter and spilled.

I stared at the mess on the floor as he explained, "She ate a slice of your pecan pie and keeled over. We got her to the ER as fast as we could, but it was too late."

"Oh, my God." I shuddered as my back smacked up against the cold tile wall next to the sink. I fought back a wave of guilt. If it weren't for me, that pie never would have been at the station in the first place. I should never have left it with her. "I warned her," I added, feeling a bit light-headed. "That was evidence. Good Lord. How could she eat it?"

"Duranja told me what you said to her." His voice lost its edge. "You tried. It's not your fault she didn't take you seriously."

I pushed off the wall. "Yes, but I should have kept the pie until I could give it to you directly." I never should have trusted Cammi to keep her hands off it.

"Ideally, a citizen, *any citizen*, should be able to make a police report without the police eating the evidence," Ellis countered. He sighed. "Anyhow, it's done." He paused. "Verity, you understand what this means."

The formal gown slipped off my shoulder. "I'm a terrible person?" I ventured, gripping the fabric, realizing I still hadn't zipped the back of the dress.

"Someone is trying to kill you," Ellis finished.

I almost dropped the phone. He was right. It was the only logical conclusion. Yet, I couldn't imagine who or why.

"I need you to come in so I can get an official statement."

"Of course," I answered automatically. This was important, as important as the investigation tonight. "I'll be right there." I'd make it work.

With shaking fingers, I zipped my dress and gathered my things. Well, at least my wallet. The lipstick that had landed by the toilet and the blush in the dirty corner could stay.

I couldn't believe I had been right about the pie. I mean, I could believe it. I wouldn't have made it a police matter if I thought it had been an innocent gesture, but part of me had still hoped to learn I'd been wrong and the whole thing was a misunderstanding. Instead, I'd been so right that someone had died from eating it.

Poor Cammi. She had a daughter about my age. Mary June had been in Melody's grade. She'd moved to Atlanta for an accounting job. She'd be devastated.

I hurried out of Judson's Last Stop with a halfhearted wave to Joe and headed straight for the police station.

Dusk had fallen by the time I arrived. We should have been heading for the mansion.

At least Frankie hadn't noticed. Yet.

The station was ablaze with lights, which made for a marked contrast with the darkened shops up and down the rest of the street.

I rushed inside and found Ellis waiting for me up front. He wore his official uniform, and rather than opening his arms to me for a hug like I'd expected, he held out a hand instead. "Miss Long, thanks for coming so quickly."

After a moment's hesitation, I got it. Ellis needed to be extra official right now. Everybody knew I was his girlfriend, but my kooky suspicions had now morphed into a homicide investigation. If he wanted to stay on the case, he'd have to prove he could be professional. I took a deep breath and shook his hand, conscious of a dozen eyes watching us. "Thank you. I'm so sorry this happened."

"It's not your fault," he said firmly, a tad louder than absolutely necessary. "I do need to question you about the pie and how it came into your possession. Let's talk in my office."

"All right." I followed him down a short hallway to the last door on the right. It opened to a room split into two offices separated by a tall gray partition. Ellis's was on the right and just big enough for two chairs, a desk, and a filing cabinet.

I'd been here before on much happier visits. Beside his computer, I spotted the familiar picture of me outside Southern Spirits, but apart from that, there were few personal touches.

Typical Ellis.

"We'll do a verbal statement for now," he said, pulling out a notepad as I took the seat opposite him. "I'll type it up later for you to sign." He wrote my name at the top of the page, jotted down a case number, and began. "Miss Long, where in your home did you find the pie?"

I'd included that in my original note, but I knew he had to be thorough. "On my kitchen counter."

He looked up from his notebook. "What time did you find this pie?"

"It was late last night." Gosh, what time had we escaped from the party? "A little after midnight, I believe."

Ellis nodded. "Were any of your doors unlocked before you arrived home last night?"

I stifled a nervous laugh. "All of them. All of the windows, too, except for the one that's been painted shut that leads to the storm cellar."

"Understood," Ellis said, his tone a bit sharp. Earlier this summer, he'd asked me to start locking my doors, and I had—for about a week. Old habits were hard to break. "We'll send someone out to fingerprint," he said, almost to himself.

"I won't be home tonight," I told him. "But the doors are unlocked."

His jaw tightened. "Of course they are," he said, writing.

He didn't have to get sarcastic. I leaned back in my chair.

"What did you do with the pie after you found it?" he asked.

"I wrapped it in foil." I'd thought I was being so clever. I should have sealed it with lead.

Ellis glanced at me over his notebook. "Was the foil tight?"

I shifted in my seat. "Tight enough to stay on. What does that have to do with anything?"

"It could be important, depending on how many prints we find on the pie plate. The tighter you wrapped it, the harder someone would have had to work to get their prints on it after the fact, which helps us narrow the field. Any detail could be useful when it comes to learning the identity of your would-be killer."

"That sounds so awful when you say it." I scooted to the edge of my seat. "I mean, think about it. Why would someone want to kill me?"

Ellis looked at me calmly, gently, the way a cop would treat any distressed victim. I hated being a victim. "I don't know, Verity. Not this time, at least," he said, slipping into a more familiar mode, a comfortable one. Then he squashed it by asking, "Can you think of any reason someone might want to kill you?"

"Not lately," I told him.

I wanted to have something to tell him, some insight or some new lead he could follow, but no one had threatened me recently, apart from the ghost at the Adair estate. Even the few spirits who could move objects in the real world wouldn't be able to bake a poisoned pie. Heck, I wasn't even working any live-people cases right now. I'd been useless when it came to the girl in the ravine. I hadn't crossed anyone in Sugarland except for Virginia, and if she were the murdering type, I'd be dead a dozen times over by now.

"Think," Ellis pressed. "Why would someone want you dead?"

The way his right hand tightened a little around the pen when he said "dead" made me feel like I was under interrogation myself.

"I don't know. I really don't." I needed a hug. "Ellis, I'm scared."

He reached across the desk and took my hand, letting his professional mask drop for just a moment. "We're going to get whoever did it," he promised. "But to figure it out, we need to pay attention to the details." He squeezed my hand, then let go. "Has anything else unusual or unexpected been left at your property?"

"I'm not sure," I said, my mind wandering back to who might want to hurt me.

"Anything you can think of," he pressed. "Don't worry about how it sounds."

"Well, there was the other pie," I said. "You know that." I'd told him about it and how Lucy had almost gotten it. "It looked exactly the same."

I wondered if that one had been poisoned too.

Ellis had plenty of questions after that. I answered them as best I could. The trick was, I didn't know anything. I was about to tell him that for the third time when an annoyed gangster cleared his throat behind me.

"We're supposed to be at the Adair mansion by sundown, getting my butt out of the eternal slammer, and you're getting cozy with your boyfriend," Frankie snipped. I turned to find him in a full tuxedo, arms crossed, glaring at me.

I didn't need reminding. "A woman died tonight, Frankie."

He leaned against the door frame. "I'll be worse than dead if we don't pull this off." He rested an elbow on the frame. "We're late for De Clercq. Again."

"I realize that." I didn't know what to say.

I turned to Ellis. "Tonight is our last night to find the killer at the Adair mansion." I explained our situation with the investigator, as well as the prison at my house.

It was hard to shock Ellis, but by the time I finished my story, I'd accomplished it. He ran a hand over his face. "That can't be legal," he managed after a moment.

I glanced back at Frankie. His tuxedo hung a bit long in the arms, and he wore a boutonniere on his lapel that could have registered for its own zip code. It wasn't a great look for him, but it sure beat a prison uniform.

"You and I both know the ghosts play by their own rules," I said to Ellis.

Ellis nodded, thinking. "I can't go with you tonight. I'm on duty and we have an officer down."

"I understand." I didn't expect him to abandon his post or his obligations. "I just need to leave sooner rather than later."

"As in an hour ago," Frankie added.

For once, I was glad Ellis couldn't hear him.

"Verity," Ellis began, tossing the notebook on his desk, "I have what I need for now, but as far as this ghost job—" He walked around the desk, clearly battling what he wanted to say. "I'm not going to tell you what to do—" he leaned against the desk and crossed his arms over his chest "—but I'll say it plain. I don't like you going there tonight."

I stood as well. "I get it." I truly did.

He took my hands in his. "Someone is trying to kill you. We don't know who or why. Now you want to head to an abandoned property by yourself, where you'll be distracted by ghosts that nobody else can see."

"I'm not thrilled by any of that, but if I don't go, I'll lose my home. Forever."

He nodded grimly.

"I realize it's a risk," I added. "But I don't have a choice."

"There's no good answer," he said, like a man headed to the gallows.

"I'll be okay," I assured him. "I've done this before."

"No, you haven't," he corrected. His eyes flicked up to mine, then back to where our hands were joined. "Every ghost is different. This never gets any easier."

He was right but saying it wouldn't make either of us feel any better.

So I did the only thing I could think to do. I kissed him.

Afterward, I leaned my forehead against his. "I'll call you as soon as I leave the estate." He'd still be on duty. He was already working a double today, and he'd be there longer with Cammi's death.

"Come on," Frankie groaned. "It's not like he's heading off to war."

If that wasn't enough to kill the mood, Duranja cursed from the hall. Ellis's cop buddy stood outside the door, visible through Frankie. As I pulled away from my boyfriend, the other officer glared at me like I was Cleopatra seducing Marc Antony.

"If you're done in here, we have work to do," Duranja said, walking straight through my ghost.

"Hey, hey!" Frankie stepped sideways, waving his arms like he'd just walked through a dozen spiderwebs.

At least Duranja wasn't open to the ghostly plane. That would have been worse. As it was, the officer didn't even notice.

"I'll show myself out," I said.

I'd done my duty. And now, well, I was going to do it again.

The rest of the staff went out of their way to avoid me as I left the station, and that was fine by me. Frankie was right. We were late. And De Clercq wasn't one to let that sort of thing slide.

CHAPTER 20

I walked down the front steps of the station and out into the dark. I wished the street wasn't so deserted. This was a safe part of town, but everything closed at seven on the dot. No one else was out, as far as I could tell. Closed shops with shuttered windows hunkered just beyond the pools of light cast by the lamps outside the police station.

It would have been nice to see someone, other than the person who wanted to kill me.

The skin on the back of my neck prickled.

It wasn't like he or she would be waiting outside the police station.

Although there were plenty of shadows to hide in and no one to see if anything were to happen to me. I had a fair distance to walk before I reached the safety of my car. I was parked in front of the hardware store again.

"You're being silly," I whispered as I hurried diagonally across the four-way stop. Why had I parked so far away?

Because this had been the closest space earlier.

I'd faced poltergeists and mobsters and one scary almost-mother-in-law. I could get to my car okay. But had I remembered to lock it?

No.

Someone could have gotten inside and hidden in the backseat or rolled beneath the car. I paused in front of the darkened entrance to the hardware store.

"Hey!"

"Aaaah!" I screamed and jumped half a foot into the air as I whirled around to face Frankie. "Please—" I placed a hand over my heart "—don't sneak up on me." He'd scared me half to death.

"You're fine. We're alone. Finally. And we need to go."

"You're sure there's nobody else?" I said, holding my car keys as a weapon as I advanced on my Cadillac.

"Just one nutty ghost hunter and me," he said.

I didn't even mind the insult. I was so relieved to be alive and finally at my car.

"Now drive like this thing is on fire," Frankie said, materializing next to me in the passenger seat.

I drove the speed limit.

"I don't want to be the fashion police, but it looks like you used a whole vase of flowers for that boutonniere." He'd stuffed a red rose in the middle of a spray of baby's breath, three carnations, and one, two, three, four...five daisies. "You might want to tone it down a bit if we're going to blend in."

"The bullet hole in the coat was bigger than I thought," he said, adjusting the greenhouse on his chest. "It looks fine. Festive. And, hey, at least I'm not alive. You're the one who's not going to blend."

I feared he could be right on that one.

When we reached the mansion, the party was going full swing. I could hear the music and the laughter from the other side of the gate.

We parked at the end of the drive, car facing out, keys left in the ignition. I wasn't taking any chances this time.

"Hurry up," Frankie hissed as I drew my mask out of the bag in my backseat.

I stiffened as a man wearing donkey's ears stumbled through the wall and down the walk toward us. He used one hand to hold his drink, the other to keep his crooked crown on his head.

Frankie and I exchanged a look.

"It's gold!" the man warbled as he stumbled past, laughing to himself. "Everything I-*hic*-touch is gold! Gold!" He fell into a bush and stayed there, his feet sticking out at odd angles.

"Maybe at least lay him on the ground," I suggested.

"He's fine," Frankie said, heading for the gate. "I've slept in worse places."

I shuddered to think.

He held the homemade "iron mask" over his face. "You ready?"

I placed my own mask over my face. "Ready as I'll ever be."

"All right, Lady X." He cocked an imaginary gun at me, mimed pulling the trigger, and grinned. "May every bullet miss."

"That's awful," I said, easing the key into the lock. He was assuming we'd get shot at.

"It's a good-luck thing," he said. "You know, so we don't get pinched."

"In that case, I'm all for it," I told him as the gate creaked open.

We eased inside, and what I saw next made me pause.

The exterior of the house was decorated this time, huge stretches of delicate silk panels hanging down from the roof to the hedges below. There were six two-story panels total, each one painted to look like we stood outside the castle of Versailles.

The lawn itself had erupted into formal gardens. I stuck to the edges, scanning the crowd as beautifully costumed people laughed and drank and danced. A full orchestra played on the lawn, next to a large fountain with frolicking cherubs. And the gems...

Diamond chokers glittered around necks. Hands drooped a bit, weighed down by solid gold rings and bracelets, and the crowns that most people wore were just as extravagant. I had no doubt that most of what they wore was real, too. Or at least it had been.

"That's it. I've died and gone to heaven," Frankie murmured as we eased over to an alcove near the far edge of the party, trying to escape notice. It held a small lovers bench. I heard a man's low voice and a woman's giggle.

"Let's keep moving," I said, narrowly avoiding the start of a hedge maze and directing him to a lily pond with a little footbridge. We crossed quickly. I felt exposed.

"You're doing good, kid," Frankie said, in a rare show of support. He must be more worried than I thought.

"I'm glad our costumes are plain." Even Frankie's obnoxious flower display paled in comparison. It gave people less reason to look too close as we made our way toward the house. We hung close to a series of tall topiaries and kept our eyes on the crowd. I didn't see any of our suspects. Yet.

"You're two hours late." The inspector nearly gave me a heart attack when he stepped out of the darkness directly ahead of us.

He looked exactly the same as he always did. No costume for him, apparently.

Frankie took it better than I did. "We've been here the whole time," he said. "Only we've been sneaking around, looking for clues."

"I saw you pull up," De Clercq said flatly.

Frankie looked at me and shrugged. "I tried."

"We're here now," I said, hoping to make it right.

De Clercq saw everything. He was like a dour version of Santa Claus. We just needed to use his power for good and get working on the case. "What's Jordan doing?" I asked.

The inspector's expression went from sour to calculating. "Mr. Jordan is on the other side of this hedgerow. He's been there the entire party, and I'm starting to have my doubts if his contact will materialize."

"Show us," I said.

He tilted his head, and I ventured a peek around the tall topiaries.

Jordan had removed his mask and stood staring at the fountain without seeing it.

"You'd think a money launderer who is about to meet his contact would be on guard and watching," De Clercq snapped as if Jordan's current mood were my fault.

"At least we know where he is," I said, looking at the bright side.

"Verity, watch out," Frankie hissed, disappearing into thin air. De Clercq did the same.

I turned. Marjorie strolled straight for me with murder in her eyes. "Hiya, doll."

My body stiffened. I prepared to run. If she was the dominant ghost, my cover was blown.

"So now you know," she said, trapping me against the topiary.

"I know, but I don't judge," I said, hoping to buy some time.

Only three ghosts knew for sure that I'd found Larry's notes: Frankie, De Clercq, and the killer.

Jordan spotted us. He shot me a dirty look and strode away toward the side of the house.

Her gaze traveled past me, toward her boyfriend.

"Trouble with Shane?" I asked.

"We broke up right before tonight's party," Marjorie said, her words icy. "I don't know why I bother getting my hopes up anymore."

"Don't say that," I countered, although come to think of it, I wasn't about to encourage her to date a dangerous man who ran with the mob, even if her husband could be a jerk. Still, I had to wonder... "Does this happen at the party every year?"

"This is a first," she said, backing off, "although people sure do like to leave me."

The pain in her voice made me wince. "I'm so sorry this happened," I told her. Even if Shane was bad news, it still had to hurt. And if this was a first, I wondered what had changed at this year's party—aside from my discovery of the suitcase.

Marjorie shrugged and took a sip of her martini. "I should be used to having my heart broken by now."

No, she shouldn't. "You deserve more." A man who loved and respected her. It would be awfully lonely partying for eternity without anyone who truly cared about you. "At least he knows what he's missing," I said, trying to cheer her up. "You look amazing tonight."

She blinked hard and stared into her drink.

She did look gorgeous. Her elaborate silk dress was fit for French royalty.

"Jeannie Adair is always Marie Antoinette, but I make a good handmaiden."

Ouch. I wished I had something to sip, anything to keep my hands busy. "I appreciate you telling me about Larry's room," I ventured.

She mock toasted me with her martini. "You made quite an exit."

"Yes, well, I'm trying to keep a low profile tonight," I said, taking in the Adairs' version of Versailles. "All things considered, it might not be too hard. I feel like I snuck into Cinderella's ball."

Marjorie's mouth twisted into a rueful grin. "You think this number is something, you should have seen me at this afternoon's Shake Your Sheikh party."

"I'm sorry I missed it." I'd have been glad to be on the case instead of dealing with De Clercq and his prison.

"I was a dancing girl," she added, and I saw her first real smile of the night. "I wore plenty of veils, but not a lot else."

Oh my. Just thinking of her social schedule exhausted me. "Don't you ever sleep?"

"Please," she scoffed. "I'll sleep when I'm dead." She paused. "Or at least that's what I used to say."

She'd steered me right last night. And now that it was clear her anger had come from her boyfriend troubles and not what I'd learned in the upstairs bedroom, I wondered if I should tell her about the suitcase. I'd be trusting her with a lot if I did. Still, we needed to solve this case tonight. I might need to take some big risks to make that happen.

"I talked to Eliza Jean today," I said, watching for Marjorie's reaction. "EJ told me how she liked to write to you, what great advice you gave."

Marjorie's party-girl expression fell away, and in its place, I saw a woman who longed for connection. I supposed it was a quality we all shared deep down. "She remembered me fondly?" Marjorie asked, with an abundance of hope that almost broke my heart.

"She looked forward to every trip to this place, every letter," I assured her. "She was so sad when her mother forbade her to write anymore."

Marjorie covered her mouth with her hand. "Of course. Her mother." She dropped her hand. "Graham said that was probably it. I just…figured it was something wrong with me."

Nothing could be further from the truth. "I hope I'm not overstepping my bounds, but I think you should know. Eliza Jean told me herself that she regrets having to write the letter that said she didn't value your advice and friendship. She loved you."

Marjorie nodded and hastily wiped away tears.

"I understand she's your daughter," I said gently.

Her watery eyes held shock and a heartbreak that took my breath away. "Larry Knowles was blackmailing me."

"I learned that as well," I told her. We'd find a way to make it right. "I'm trying to get EJ to come back to Sugarland. I think she needs to see this place again."

"After—" she sniffed "—after I died, I wanted to go see her, if only to watch over her. But the dominant ghost won't let me leave."

"And you have no idea who that is?" I asked, hoping for a break. "Any inkling? A feeling?" I'd take anything at this point.

She lowered her gaze. "I have no idea."

I nodded. "If your daughter comes back, I'll find a way to make sure you can see her."

"I—" she began, working to compose herself. "Thank you for that." She forced a smile. It was either that or she'd start full-out crying. I knew the expression well. "I always used to tell Eliza Jean that people will find their way back if it's meant to be." Her attention returned to the fountain, where we'd last seen Shane.

Yes, well, the farther she got from him, the better.

Hopefully, soon, she'd see that. Tonight was our last chance to nail him. It would be easier with her help.

I had to take a calculated risk here or we might not solve this in time.

"Marjorie." I urged her farther into the shadows. "I need to level with you about another thing."

She nodded and swallowed as if I were about to tell her something she didn't want to hear. That could be good…or very, very bad. Either way, I was doing this.

"I was chased out of that upstairs room after I found a hidden briefcase belonging to Judge Knowles. He kept notes on the people he blackmailed," I added, watching her expression fall.

She sniffed. "That's how you learned about Eliza Jean," she said stonily.

"Yes. And about your marriage to Graham," I said.

"Graham and I were never in love"—she blushed—"at least not that way. It was a mistake. A little adventure gone wrong." She wrung her hands and failed to meet my eyes. "We wrote his sister in New York," she said, her words coming fast. "Rose Adair was smart. Older. She and her husband had been married for seven years and hadn't had babies yet. She offered to take our baby and raise it as her own. I could be a favorite friend. My baby would have a great life."

"That does sound like a good plan," I assured her, at least for her time. I couldn't imagine the heartbreak that came with it.

She nodded and wiped her eyes. "We married for Eliza Jean. We didn't want her to be illegitimate in case it ever got out. We didn't tell anyone except Graham's sister and brother-in-law in New York. Until..." She gave a long sigh. "A few years later, when Graham met Jeannie, he told her everything before he proposed." She shook her head. "Jeannie was shocked at first, but she came around rather quickly. She couldn't have children and, if anything, I think sharing his secret brought them closer. Graham found a good one," she added longingly, before clearing her throat. "Anyhow, I had the baby out in New York. We needed Judge Knowles to handle the adoption quietly, as well as the divorce." She took a jagged, steadying breath. "He used both to blackmail me."

"You weren't trying to hide your arrest in Chicago?"

"No," she said, surprised. "I mean, it would have trashed my reputation, but I've never exactly been the shy and retiring type. Larry never hit me with that."

Interesting that Larry even brought it to the party.

"I admire how much you sacrificed for your daughter," I said. "She was lucky to have a mother like you."

"Maybe." She blinked hard, as if fighting fresh tears. "But I think Rose was right. I'm not the best influence. She was lucky to be a thousand miles away from me."

"Please don't say that." I wished I could fold her in my arms. "Eliza Jean told me herself how wonderful it was to have you in her life."

"As the crazy aunt," she chuffed. "I certainly wouldn't want her making the kinds of choices I did. I mean, look at me. I've been married twice and never for love. Graham felt sorry for me. Marcus wants to control me. Shane actually loved me, or so I thought, but now he's taking off without me after tonight."

"You're better off without him. He's laundering money for the mob," I said. "It was in the briefcase."

She closed her eyes briefly. "I should be surprised, but I'm not," she said. "You have to understand, Shaney isn't violent or mean. Marcus, on the other hand," she hedged, "did you see him in the briefcase?"

"I saw him on a ledger page. Was Greasy Larry blackmailing him as well?"

"Yes," she said quickly. "No," she hedged, toying with an earring. "Maybe. I always suspected they had some connection." She sighed and looked away. "I sure can pick 'em, huh? A lover who's in it with the mob and a husband who..." she trailed off. "I don't suppose it matters much anymore."

It did to me. "You can talk about it if you want."

She stared past me, toward the fountain and the darkened menagerie beyond. "A husband I don't want and a lover who doesn't want me. My life is a mess. You must not think much of me."

She'd shown me kindness and honesty. I'd judge her on that. "I don't think you can help who you fall in love with," I said. "Our hearts don't come with off switches."

"Yeah, maybe not." She took a long drink of her martini. "Sometimes, I wish they did." She looked to the fountain where he'd been. "I'm worried about Shane."

"Afraid he'll slip off to the menagerie alone?" I asked, keeping my tone casual. Pushing my luck.

Her expression fell. "How did you know?"

"I've been around," I told her. "I'm worried, too." Worried she was in love with a killer. "How does he manage to get in without anybody noticing?"

She hesitated for a moment, taking a sip of her martini. "He always creeps off when everybody else is distracted by the big show. He typically hangs by the fountain first." She glanced up toward the house. "But he left when he realized you were watching him. Maybe he won't go tonight."

I hoped he would. Justice would be waiting there for him this time.

While I was wishing for things, I hoped Frankie and De Clercq were tailing him now. I scanned the crowd and didn't spot them anywhere. Then again, we were all trying to stay incognito.

"We'll know in a few minutes," she added. "We're having the melee tonight." She fought to bring her grin back and failed. "It's a crowd favorite and the perfect chance to slip away."

"Oh boy." I hoped Frankie and De Clercq were around to hear this.

"The melee is a lot of fun," Marjorie continued. "You see these ribbons? Here." She directed my attention to a bright red ribbon tied to her upper arm as I casually searched the crowd for my partners. "All the ladies get them when we arrive at the party. They're favors. The men get swords—they're padded sticks, honey, don't look so worried—and when the signal goes off, they fight each other to win favors from us."

Holy smokes. It was a good thing these people were already dead, because this sounded like a recipe for disaster to me. On the one hand, perhaps it would distract the dominant ghost from seeing me and killing me. On the other hand, an enormous fight in the middle of the lawn would be the perfect cover for Shane to slip off and meet his contact. I only hoped De Clercq and Frankie were on it this year. De Clercq didn't have the best track record when it came to varying the investigation.

Bang!

A cannon went off right in front of the house. When the smoke cleared, I saw Graham Adair behind the big gun, decked out in an ermine-trimmed robe. He held aloft a bejeweled scepter. "Queens, bid your lovers good luck! Kings, draw your swords! The melee...has...begun!"

In under a minute, the charming, chatting crowd turned on each other and I was in the middle of *The Hunger Games*. I dodged an errant sword, spun, and almost tripped into a gaggle of wagering ladies.

I used the opportunity to step away from Marjorie.

"Frankie!" I risked calling his name as loudly as I dared. "Frank!"

He hated when I called him Frank. That would surely get a reaction.

A pair of men wielding champagne bottles as swords nearly ran me down. Worse, I saw no trace of Frankie or the inspector in the rollicking crowd.

This was awful. I would never find my partners in this mess.

"Look," Marjorie said. "There he goes now."

I whipped my head around to see Shane Jordan slip out the side door of the house, not twenty feet away from us. He had Greasy Larry's briefcase tucked under his arm.

"You see that?" I pointed at the brown leather case. "That's the briefcase I found in Fern and Larry's room."

Nobody but the dominant ghost would be able to get that briefcase back and just carry it around like that uncontested.

"I've never seen him with it before," Marjorie whooshed out as we watched her lover move swiftly through the darkness toward the menagerie.

Yeah, well I had a feeling he didn't exactly include her in his business dealings.

After one furtive glance behind, he snuck inside.

I exchanged a look with a wide-eyed Marjorie.

"What's he doing?" she demanded.

"I have no clue," I told her, but I had a feeling this was it. The meeting was going down right now.

"I'm going after him." She morphed into an orb of light and shot across the lawn toward Shane Jordan.

"Wait for me," I said, following as best I could, sticking to the shadows, heading straight for the haunted menagerie.

CHAPTER 21

Shane Jordan had to be the killer. He'd driven me out of the upstairs bedroom and taken the briefcase, which nobody else had known about and which he'd kept hidden until I found it in Larry's room. From the black tar he'd oozed and the horror he'd rained down on me, I didn't think he'd be giving that prize up anytime soon.

Fine. I'd figure out what to do. I just needed to learn why he was carrying the case into the menagerie.

And I'd be doing it alone if Frankie and De Clercq didn't show up soon.

The orb of light that was Marjorie hovered outside the wavy glass panes of the menagerie. "Hurry up," she urged.

I stopped at the door and gave one quick peek backward, past the darkened yard to the party beyond, desperate for one last chance to signal my backup. I spotted Frankie and De Clercq in the distance, lurking behind a tall oak, observing Marcus of all people.

Marjorie's husband towered over a small blond ghost who appeared as if she needed rescuing. I could see how the young woman's plight had caught the attention of both Frankie and

Inspector De Clercq, but I needed at least one of them right now, preferably De Clercq.

"Frankie," I called as loud as I dared, "Inspector De Clercq!"

They were too far away to hear, and I couldn't throw my voice like Frankie could. I waved frantically, but neither man glanced my way. They had their eyes on the blonde.

So much for the inspector and his ability to see everything.

"Shane's moving fast," Marjorie hissed.

Right.

I didn't have time to wait.

I edged the door open, its rusty hinges creaking loudly, announcing my presence to anyone within a twenty-foot radius. I prayed Shane Jordan was far enough ahead of me not to hear it. With any luck, he was as good as De Clercq at ignoring the living.

With a deep breath, I ducked inside the decrepit menagerie. The place was pitch-black, both in my world and on the ghostly plane.

In fact, the ghostly scene I'd witnessed the first time I'd been here had completely disappeared.

"Marjorie?" I whispered into the dark. No reply.

I stood, hoping my eyes would adjust and show me a glimpse of my surroundings. It was strange and unsettling. Shane had to be the dominant ghost. But if Shane had taken over this place, I should be seeing it as he did. Not as the darkened husk that it was in my world.

I spotted a flicker ahead, a glowing orb, and prayed it was Marjorie. I hurried to join her, then slowed.

For all I knew, she could be in this with Shane. I had only her word that they'd broken up, her word that she knew nothing about the briefcase he carried. She seemed eager enough to pursue him.

Marjorie could have been playing me all along.

The gritty floor crunched under my feet. I tried to keep my movements as quiet as the dead. I felt my way down the hallway, my fingers feathering over rusted cage bars. The only other time I'd been down this way, these pens had held monkeys and all sorts of creatures. Parrots had flocked overhead.

The silence now felt deafening.

Wrong.

The orb of light paused at the end of the corridor.

"There." Marjorie's soft whisper floated back to me.

I made it to the edge of the wall in just enough time to see Shane's back vanish down the left corridor. At the same time, I kept close track of Marjorie hovering above me.

I could see a little more of the left corridor by the light of the ghost. I hadn't been down that way the first night.

The floor seemed a little cleaner, the bars on the cages a little thicker. Perhaps the animals in this section had been bigger and stronger. The cage door to my right hung open, as did the one across from it.

All right. The animals were long gone. As far as I was concerned, that was a good thing. Trouble was, animal ghosts could still corner you when you least expected it.

"Let's go," Marjorie hissed, shooting down the darkened hall.

I followed as fast as I dared. My stomach sank when I saw ghostly light streaming from the cages ahead. At least those appeared locked. I kept going.

My toe caught on a broken pane of glass and I fell against a large heavily barred cage. A low growl erupted from it. I pushed away seconds before a frighteningly familiar lion crashed against the ghostly bars, swiping at me with its massive front paw. It might have snagged me, too, if not for Marjorie darting between us, her energy flaring bright enough to force the creature back. It seemed the dominant ghost had brought the lion home.

As soon as Marjorie's energy faded, the lion struck again, throwing itself against its cage. It roared loudly enough to alert our prey that he was being followed, and I saw the lion for what it was—an early warning system.

Shane Jordan was no dummy. No wonder he'd gotten away with murder for nearly a century.

"Let's keep moving," I said. But the damage had been done.

Marjorie hung back. "This feels like a trap," she whispered, the fear in her voice scaring me all over again.

"You think Shane planned this?" I asked.

"I don't know. He's scary smart." Her strained answer sounded in my ear.

Not what I wanted to hear.

But the fear in her voice seemed real, which meant she might be on my side after all. Either way, it wasn't like I could turn back now.

The lion hit the bars again, shaking its cage, rocking the supports, which were attached to the windowed ceiling, which —*crrrrack!*

A jagged line crawled across the ghostly glass above us.

The lion roared and slammed, and the glass ceiling shook and splintered. It was about to break.

"Run," I said, leading the way as the ghostly ceiling exploded and rained down shards of glass right where I'd stood. They joined the real-life shards on the floor.

I couldn't think about that right now. "We can't afford to lose him," I insisted, sprinting for all I was worth.

With Marjorie's help, I avoided a cluster of croaking poison dart frogs clinging to the rusted remains of a hanging wire cage. As we turned the corner, I almost ran into the ghost of an antelope—loose from its cage—whose horns looked sharp enough to skewer me.

I yelped. It darted. And there was no way Shane didn't know exactly where I stood.

Yet Marjorie stuck beside me, protecting me, or perhaps leading me to my demise.

I saw the distant glow of ghostly activity around the next bend. The short, tight hallway ahead held immense aquariums on both sides. I hoped that was a good sign. I liked fish. Moonlight shone down from the broken glass ceiling. I wasn't sure what kind of fish would be in the murky, low-lying tanks, but I should be able to handle...fish.

I barely repressed a shriek when the ghostly tank right in front of me exploded, gushing a flood of water onto the floor. A long, thick body slipped out with it, hitting the floor with a heavy thud. One look at its enormous jaws, bristling with teeth as long as my little finger, and I realized that the tank had held an alligator.

Oh, sweet Jesus.

An eight-foot-long alligator stood between the dominant ghost and me.

Marjorie was nowhere to be seen. Just as I'd suspected, just as I'd feared, she'd led me to danger and abandoned me.

She had been with Shane for decades, after all. Girl talk aside, it would be in her best interest to get rid of me, to keep the man she loved safe. Besides, I knew her secrets. I'd come too close. If she'd led such a hard life before she married Marcus, if she'd been rejected by the child she'd helped raise, if she'd craved love like it was air—she'd betray me for her man in a heartbeat.

Girls *didn't* always stick together. I'd been crazy to trust her.

A cage screeched open in the distance, and a moment later the triumphant roar of the newly freed lion echoed down the hall.

Cripes.

Stay calm.

Too late. Heart in my throat, I checked for anything I could climb to escape, or barring that, at least something I could use as a weapon. I ripped off my mask and used it to grab a piece of shattered glass, fighting off a shudder as the chill of the ghost version crawled through my hand.

Sure. A girl and a piece of glass against the Adairs' wild kingdom.

Worse, I had no backup and no quick exit unless I could learn how to climb walls and escape through the ceiling.

The rumbling lion began to move, big paws scuffling on the floor. I heard the glass I'd tripped over a minute ago crunch warningly.

I had a lion behind me and an alligator in front of me. Now was not the time for contemplation. I faced the alligator, which hissed. Maybe I could jump over it. I had to try. I grabbed my skirts, obscenely grateful Frankie had made sure my dress had the give for this sort of thing. I backed up a step, braced myself, and took a running leap.

I heard the snap of jaws as I landed on its tail, but I kept running. I didn't stop until I reached the end. I was alive. Whole. I looked back. The alligator hadn't followed.

Yet.

I pressed a hand to my chest. Hallelujah.

"Verity." Marjorie appeared in front of me, in human form once more, frantic.

"Where were you?" I demanded.

"Shh…" She brought a finger to her lips.

I kept my distance.

"The lion isn't your biggest problem back there," she hissed. "There's someone else following us."

I didn't even look back. I refused to take my eyes off her. "Who's following?" I pressed. "Alive or dead?"

She shook her head. "I'm not sure."

A dead person would have as much of a problem getting around those ghostly carnivores as I did. But a live killer would make it easily.

Cammi's death had made it clear. A living, breathing person was trying to kill me. I had no idea who or why, but that didn't matter. It only made my situation more dangerous.

I listened in the dark for any sign of my pursuer.

I was alone in a rickety, abandoned property far outside of town. If my stalker had followed me to the mansion, he or she could be hunting me where I stood. I'd been paying so much attention to the ghosts that I'd forgotten to guard against the living. Just as Ellis had been afraid I would do.

Or maybe it was all a lie—just Shane and Marjorie, looking for an advantage.

The crunch of the glass—had that happened in the ghost realm, or had a real person made that noise? With broken glass in both realms, there was no way to know.

My stalker could be watching me right now.

I held my ground, ready to stab with my shard of glass.

It was getting hard to separate the ghost realm from the real one. The alligator's hissing grew louder. The lion's claws scraped against broken glass.

"Come on," Marjorie pressed. "Shane has stopped."

"How do I know that?" The only thing I could count on was the glass in my hand and hopefully a wall at my back.

She stared at me.

My heart beat fast. My skin felt hot. "How can I believe anything you say?"

Her eyes grew hard, determined. "Because I want to see my daughter again, and I can't do that without you."

She'd turned her life upside down for EJ, she'd lied about who she was, loved her from afar. Lost her. I was the key to getting her back. Marjorie was right—either I trusted that or I didn't.

"Let's go." I pushed off the wall.

She gave a sharp nod and floated away down the hall. I hustled after her, using her pale gray light to avoid stepping on what looked like the world's biggest tarantula. It scuttled toward the darkness beneath the closest cages.

Marjorie paused up ahead. I joined her and peered around the corner.

Shane stood facing away from us, in the center of what appeared to be the home of every snake in this place save Sir Charles.

The snake house was built as a semicircle, with our hall and another intersecting there. It had at least a dozen cages and aquariums perched on elegant wooden shelves.

Shane strode to the middle row of cages and rapped a wire frame door with the edge of the briefcase. An angry rattle erupted from inside.

"Yeah, that's right. Get mad," he muttered, moving to the next cage. "You need to be hungry for this." He smacked the adjoining cage, then the next. The chorus of hisses and rattles began to grow.

"I don't know what he's doing. He's scared to death of snakes," Marjorie whispered harshly, hands over her mouth. She trembled. "I have to—I have to talk to him."

"No, you don't." Unless she really was on his side.

Shane seemed fine. He might be meeting someone. We had to keep watch.

She surged for her lover.

"No!" I tried to grab her.

It was pure instinct, and it hurt like a mother. My hand passed straight through her shoulder, the blazing chill nearly bringing me to my knees.

Marjorie cried out, stumbled from the impact, but kept going. "Shane!" She rushed to him. "What are you doing?"

Shane whirled at the sound of her voice, the case tight in his grip. "Marjorie?" Horror flooded his expression. "Oh, honey, no." He took a step forward and held a hand between them. "You can't be here right now."

"Tell me what you're doing with Larry's briefcase," she said as if he'd lost his mind.

"I stole it," he said, backing away from us.

"How?" she shot back, but he merely shook his head. "If something's going down, you need to tell me," she insisted. "I mean you set the animals free and everything. Why did you do that? The lion tried to take a bite out of Verity."

Shane gaped. "The live girl? I don't give a damn about her."

"Yes, well, an alligator could have eaten me," Marjorie said, advancing on him.

He took a step back, clutching the briefcase. "If you ever loved me, Marjorie, you need to get out now." His eyes darted from her to the exit. "The animals weren't me," he insisted, scanning the room as if he expected an attack any second. "None of what you see is me."

I stiffened, glancing behind me, to either side, to the cracked and broken glass ceiling. Shane was genuinely scared for Marjorie. That meant he wasn't the dominant ghost. But who was?

"Please." Shane looked into her eyes, the hardened man dead serious, just short of begging. "It would be a disaster if he found you here with me."

I could only think of one person who would be very unhappy to see Shane and his lover in the menagerie. "Marcus."

The ruined roof crackled as black ooze began to stream from empty panes of glass.

Shane's drawn face tightened even further. He swore. "You gotta go. Now."

I was starting to agree with him.

Tar edged up behind me, forcing me into the room.

"We're not leaving," Marjorie said, her eyes darting to the ooze. The air grew heavy. This was bad. "Not until you tell us what you're doing with the judge's case."

A long shadow fell over the room.

"He's hiding it." A sinister voice surrounded us. "From me."

Black tar ran freely down the walls and over doorways. Marcus passed through the burning ooze like it was nothing as he stepped from the darkened hallway across from us.

CHAPTER 22

*M*arjorie turned to Marcus, shocked. "You found Greasy Larry's papers." Black tar oozed down the paned glass wall behind her. "That's how you learned about the baby."

Shane gripped the case tighter. "Hold up. Baby?"

Her gaze darted from her husband to her lover. A stream of black tar bubbled up between her and Shane. "In 1916, before I ever met you, before Graham met Jeannie, before I married Marcus, I gave birth to a child, a little girl." Marjorie clenched her hands together in front of her. "I gave her up." She glanced at Marcus, frightened. "I had to. I couldn't raise her alone."

The brute's lip curled smugly. "What you mean to say is that Graham didn't want either of you." He ran a hand down his chin as he advanced on her. "What a mess, darling. You sleep with our best friend and he tosses you over, along with the brat. Seems I'm the only one who ever wanted you."

"It wasn't like that," she exclaimed, but I could tell his words had gotten to her. Marjorie backed away as far as she could go, up to the edge of the black sludge. "Graham and I were never in love.

We were never meant to be together. We were…experimenting. Learning. We made a mistake."

"A big one," Marcus countered, flashing her a smile that would have been charming coming from anyone else. "All those years neither one of you ever breathed a word about it. And here I thought Graham and I shared everything. Wait." He gave a dark laugh. "I suppose we did."

"You're disgusting," Marjorie declared, retreating from him. The heel of her shoe edged into the tar. "Oh!"

She darted forward, into Marcus's arms, and hastily shoved him away. Marcus let her go. For the moment, at least.

"You're a tease, baby," he smirked. "You like to play it sweet," Marcus rumbled, rattling the windows, sending ooze cascading down the walls. "But you left out the best part. The part where you married my best friend. *Our* best friend. In *secret*."

"I—" she began.

"Don't bother denying it," Marcus snapped. "I've already confirmed that you're damaged goods."

She swallowed hard. "We had to marry! Just for a little while. We wanted our baby to be legitimate. We wanted her to have a chance if the truth ever came out."

Marcus nodded to himself, turning to pace a few steps. "Just like you *had* to marry me a couple years later. Because I'm your *friend*."

"You were safe," she said, her voice small.

"Right. Good enough until you decided you wanted some excitement," he snapped, the glass crackling under his anger.

He cocked his head and strolled toward her. "I knew you were about to leave me for this bum. So I'm picking the sad little locks on your personal this and thats, trying to figure out how to get my *wife* to stay," he proclaimed to the room, his tone genial, his expression murderous, "when I find your letters to your secret daughter."

"You leave her out of this," Marjorie whispered.

Marcus grinned. "I hired Larry to check her out. Turns out he didn't have to look far."

"Larry told you everything," I said, horrified.

"For a price, like everyone else." Marcus shrugged. He whipped around to face his wife. "All this time, I thought I'd won! I'd gotten you, not Graham. Instead, I married a slut and a divorcée." He stopped in front of her. "Well, congrats to you," he said, once more crowding her dangerously close to the seeping tar. "You got the better end of the deal."

Her eyes were wide, her voice shaky. "Stop this. Please. I said I'd stay."

He smirked. "For now. Because *Shaney* dumped you," he said, pointing to the diamond dealer, who stood trapped in a circle of tar near the animal cages. "But what's to stop you from running off with the next guy who looks at you sideways?"

Shane looked ready to risk the oozing liquid. "You said you'd hurt her if I didn't end things. I held up my end. Now you need to leave her alone."

"Yeah, it would have gotten ugly," Marcus interrupted, "if you'd forced me to damage my own wife." He turned to her, his rough words taking on a soothing tone. "I wouldn't have enjoyed cutting you. I tried to make it easier for you to stay."

She gulped, afraid to move.

"You need to know," Shane said to Marjorie, the love he had for her clear in his expression, "I'd never hurt you or leave you if I had a choice."

She nodded, overwhelmed. I hoped she believed him.

Marcus brushed a lock of hair behind her ear in a gesture that could have been mistaken for affection if I hadn't known it was all about control. "I'm in charge here," Marcus stated. "I can make your afterlife a living hell." He rubbed a curl of hair between his fingers. "But we don't want that, do we? I wish you could learn to love me. We could be so happy."

This guy was sick, but I couldn't let it distract me. I had to make sense of what had happened. "You were meeting Larry by the snake cage to get the proof about EJ's parents," I said, hoping to draw his attention away from his poor wife.

Marcus huffed. "Larry wanted cash. Lots of it. It took a few days." He stroked Marjorie's cheek. "You were worth it to me."

"But you never got it," I said. Otherwise, EJ's adoption papers wouldn't have still been in Larry's briefcase.

Marcus's lip curled into a rueful smile. "It was going to be really simple. Until Larry met me in the snake cage to tell me I can't have the documents I need to keep my wife in line." His fists tightened. "I could have killed him for that."

"You did," I whispered, cringing as my voice carried in the old, high-ceilinged room.

"Not really," Marcus scoffed. "It wasn't my fault. Dumb bastard made some bad choices. Said he didn't want to hurt a kid. Damned crook picked the wrong time to grow a conscience."

He eyed his wife.

"Greasy Larry was my only link to the truth. When we met near the snake pit that night, I told him I'd choke it out of him." Marcus rested a hand on Marjorie's neck, and her eyes went wide as he gave a little squeeze. "I lost control. Just one hard squeeze." Her eyes widened as he tightened his grip. "Old buy-and-sell Larry let me kill him rather than ruin a kid's life. Ain't that pathetic? He didn't even know the brat."

So Greasy Larry did have his limits. He'd died for them.

"He deserved it," Marcus stated, his hand lingering on his wife's throat before he released her, leaving her breathless. "I'm tired of people thinking they can decide things for me."

Marcus strode past Marjorie, through the slime. He held out his hand to Shane. "Give me the briefcase."

"Why?" Marjorie croaked. "What else is in it?"

Marcus smiled at her. "Plenty on you. I'm doing you a favor."

Shane glared at him, ice cold. "Screw you."

Marcus chuckled. "What were you going to do with it in here?

Hide out and read all the dirt on your ex-lady love? Maybe try to tear up the evidence on your mob contacts? Why bother? You already got caught."

"I want to know why you wanted it so bad," Shane said through clenched teeth. "I've been watching you. You've had it on you since the live girl found it."

Larry must have had something on Marcus, something Marcus couldn't destroy.

Shane's plan hadn't been half bad. The menagerie would be a nice, quiet place to search the evidence—until Marcus arrived.

Shane backed toward the animal cages, cracking open the case as he went.

I had no idea what he planned to do, but I knew it would hack off Marcus. I braced myself, ready to create a distraction.

"Drop it," Marcus snapped, "or I'll get very angry."

A drop of black slime dripped from the ceiling, the chill of it grazing my cheek. I leapt back, and Marcus laughed as it sizzled on the floor beside me.

"You're out of time," the dominant ghost told his rival. "Or at least *she* is."

We all looked to Marjorie. While Shane had been talking, the slime had surrounded her until she stood in a pool of it. She cried out in horror as it climbed her legs.

"Take it." Shane shoved the case at Marcus. "Make this stop."

Marcus grabbed hold of the briefcase with a sneer. The lake of tar receded, and he let the other man rush to his injured lover. "You're pathetic," Marcus grunted. "I don't know what she ever saw in you."

Shane steadied Marjorie as the pool of slime retreated. He brushed at her legs where the tar had engulfed her. "I'm fine. Fine," she insisted, clinging to him. "He's hurt me worse."

"I'm trying to make our marriage work," Marcus insisted.

She released Shane and stood tall in front of her husband. "You don't want to love me. You want to own me."

"It doesn't have to be that way," Marcus said, running his hand down her arm. "None of it does. He directed his hard, cold gaze to me. All of this stayed hidden until the live girl stirred things up. If we kill her and agree to walk out of this together, no one has to know."

Heavens. I froze. It was the perfect solution.

For them, at least.

My heart squeezed. Marjorie's eyes widened as she looked from her husband to me.

"You're sick," she whispered.

Marcus was so focused on his wife, he didn't see Shane behind him. Shane's image glowed bright and clear. He rose up, powerful as I'd ever seen him, fueled by passion, love, anger, and I didn't know what else. "Get your hands off her!" He drove down onto Marcus with everything he had.

Marcus raised a hand and knocked him back, straight into a streaming wall of tar.

"Shane!" Marjorie broke free. Marcus let her. She ran a few steps then watched in horror as her lover screamed and disappeared into the muck.

The image of Marcus flickered slightly as if the energy had cost him, but then he glowed strong once more.

"If only that would get rid of him for good," Marcus said dryly.

But ghosts couldn't die. They could only hurt.

Poor Shane.

He loved Marjorie and she loved him, but a happy future for them seemed out of reach.

"You bastard!" Marjorie grabbed the briefcase from her husband.

"You wouldn't dare," he said, towering over her.

She threw the case at me. "Catch, Verity!"

"I can't!" If I touched it, it would disappear in minutes and go straight back to the upstairs bedroom that Marcus controlled. Besides, I needed to show it to Inspector De Clercq tonight.

I tried to duck, but the case caught me on the shoulder and landed hard on the floor. It skittered into the darkness behind me.

"No!" All our work. All of Marjorie's sacrifice. It was as good as gone.

I ran for the case. I needed to get it to De Clercq fast.

I charged into the darkened hallway. Toward the alligator and the lion and anybody else who wanted to kill me.

I could feel the chill of Marcus behind me, beside me, everywhere.

"Idiot girl," he ground out, grazing me as he surged past, the stinging cold force of his touch making me stumble over my feet. I fell hard on my knees.

He let out a victory yell and barreled ahead, straight into the grip of a half-dozen old-timey police officers and one smug investigator De Clercq.

"You are under arrest," he said as Marcus struggled against the two burly officers, "for the murder of Judge Larry Knowles." The hallway darkened to pitch-black. I could smell the tar bubbling up.

Then the cuffs clicked on and the shadows lifted.

De Clercq's mustache twitched. "I'd say that's the end of that."

"The case." I pointed to the ground where it lay.

"I've got it," De Clercq said crisply, very much in his element. "The briefcase is no longer your concern." For once, I was glad to have him leave me out of it.

Frankie stood several feet behind De Clercq. I gave the investigator a wide berth and sought out my friend.

"You're here," I said, coming as close as I ever had to hugging the gangster. "Thank heavens. How did you know I'd be here?"

"By the trail of destruction," the gangster said. "I mean, seriously. An alligator?"

"That wasn't mine," I told him, keeping an eye on the police while De Clercq read Marcus his rights.

The black tar smoked and evaporated from the walls of the

snake room. Marjorie cried out and rushed to a nearly transparent Shane slumped against the far wall.

"He's going to be hurting for a while," Frankie said, hands in his pockets, observing the situation as if he'd planned for it to go down this way all along. "That's some toxic rage old Marcus had going."

"Will Shane recover?" I asked, watching his eyes open as Marjorie fussed over him.

"It takes a lot of pent-up anger to produce tar like that," Frankie said, cringing. "When you get that on you, I won't lie, it can damage the spirit permanently. You just have to hope the guy is strong enough to recover."

With Marjorie's help, I had hope that he would.

Shane had been willing to risk everything for her. He'd stood by her no matter what. Perhaps they could be happy together.

Marjorie deserved someone who loved her, and perhaps crusty old Shane did as well.

A police photographer with an old-fashioned camera stopped to get a photo of the briefcase on the floor. The flash nearly blinded me.

"I'm glad you were here to back us up," I said to Frankie. "We would have been in real trouble without you."

The mobster tried to shrug me off, but I saw the tilt of his mouth and the pleasure behind his jaded eyes. "I had officers following Marcus," he said as the photographer took another shot.

"Truly?" It seemed like a very un-Frankie-like move, and I wouldn't put it past him to lie.

"It wasn't hard," Frankie said, straightening his tie as if this were par for the course. "De Clercq had a half-dozen plainclothes officers handy. He made me promise not to tell."

"Since when can you keep a secret?" I asked.

He ignored me. "The officers were observing, but they didn't know what they were looking for."

"And you did," I said, smelling the baloney.

Frankie drew the cigarette case out of his pocket. "I'm going to pretend you didn't just insult me." He selected a smoke and lit it. "Turns out I do know when a guy looks shady." He blew smoke out his nose. "We'd been observing Marcus for three days, and he never put down his drink once. Until he did." Frankie took another drag. "He ditched it like it was on fire and headed for the menagerie. That meant something big was going down."

"Like he'd caught a whiff of Shane in his territory." He was the dominant ghost, after all.

Frankie nodded. "We just had to stand back and let him incriminate himself." He waved a hand. "With your help."

Yeah, I did help a little bit.

But something was still bothering me. "The briefcase. Frankie, I touched it. It's going to be gone soon. There's something in there that Marcus doesn't want us to see."

Once it disappeared, it would return to Marcus, and there was no telling where he'd hide it. "I doubt Marcus is going to let it reappear in Larry's old room."

"Marcus isn't the dominant ghost anymore," De Clercq said. "Not since the cuffs went on." The investigator watched his men lead Marjorie's husband away. "I have an officer waiting upstairs for it to reappear."

"So ghosts can get into Larry's room now?" I said to the inspector.

He inclined his head. "Graham and Jennie Adair control their home once more, and I have no reason to believe they won't cooperate with our investigation."

"True," I said. The Adairs would be thrilled to have their house and their lives back, even if they would be saddened to learn the ghost who had caused their torment for so many years had also been an old friend.

De Clercq paused, toying with the end of his mustache. "I must admit I did not expect Larry Knowles to die because he tried to do good."

"People change sometimes," I said, eyeing Frankie.

I'd never pegged the gangster as one to actually buckle down and contribute to the investigation, either.

Frankie cleared his throat and became overly interested in blowing smoke out of his nose.

"What about Shane?" I asked, watching him embrace Marjorie. He'd regained his form, and it appeared the star-crossed lovers were well on their way to a reunion. Only Shane had done dirty work for the mob, and justice meant he and Marjorie would be separated again.

"Shane Jordan has served his time," De Clercq said.

"He has," I said, pleased to see justice prevail once more. According to the article, Shane Jordan had been sentenced to prison. He'd served that sentence during his lifetime, and as a dead man, he was free.

"We watched him steal the briefcase from Marcus," the investigator said. "Quite clever. He waited until Marcus stepped up to the bar. Marcus put the case down and it was gone before he could say, 'No olive.'"

"We weren't even sure Marcus was the dominant ghost," Frankie said. "I hadn't gotten a good look at the actual briefcase in the bedroom, you know, with all the slime and the yelling."

"What's in it?" asked Marjorie from behind him. She held Shane's hand. He appeared a bit unsteady still, but that was to be expected.

The investigator nodded to a colleague, and the man snapped the case open.

Marjorie knelt before it and lifted out her mug shot photo. A pained expression crossed her face as she unclipped the handwritten letter clipped to the photo. "It's from Rose Adair to Judge Knowles."

Shane knelt next to her and wrapped an arm around her shoulders as she read the letter. "She says she's disturbed by a letter from Marcus. With it, he sent this mug shot photo," she said weakly. "Marcus wrote her to warn her about me, that I was a bad influence on Eliza Jean." Her hands shook as she crumpled the letter in her fists. "Marcus was the reason she cut off contact."

"And Knowles had it in the case because he'd been using that to blackmail Marcus," I said. It made sense.

She nodded. "A betrayal like that would have been the one thing that would make me leave him." A tear fell onto the paper in front of her. "He took my daughter from me. All these years, I felt like I just wasn't a good enough person. I felt like I deserved it."

He'd cut her off from her child, her lover. All in the hopes that she'd love him if he took everyone else away. It was tragic, yet I couldn't seem to stir up much pity for Marcus, not after what he'd done.

Still, if Marjorie needed closure, I'd help her get it. "Would you like to talk to him?" I asked gently. The police still had him nearby somewhere.

"No." She raised her chin. "I'm done with him. I'm never speaking to Marcus again."

But Marjorie still seemed so lost.

"Come here, kid." Frankie urged me to the side. "I get that you want to make things right, but you can't fix everything."

I watched as Marjorie cried softly against Shane's shoulder. "She deserves a place in her daughter's life."

"Maybe," the roughened gangster admitted, "but there ain't nothing you can do."

We'd see about that. "Larry was willing to die to protect EJ and her family. The least we can do is make sure he didn't die in vain."

"What's this *we*?" Frankie balked.

"I may need your help," I informed him. "And if that happens, I expect to get it."

"This is becoming a bad habit," the gangster groused.

I saw De Clercq eyeing us. "You'd better not have another mystery for us," I told him.

The inspector smiled despite himself. "It's over," he said. "For me, at least."

I could hardly believe it. "So we're done?" I asked. We had to be. We'd caught his killer. We'd solved his case.

He pursed his lips and nodded. "I am at peace."

I had to smile. "Forgive me, but you don't sound too happy about it."

He wet his lips, searching for words, it seemed. "It's a strange feeling," he admitted. "To have this part of my life complete after so many years." He glanced at Frankie, who stood flicking the ash from his cigarette. "To have a man like that be the one who made it possible."

"Don't forget my partner," Frankie said, taking another drag.

The inspector gave a sharp nod, and I swear he looked at me—truly looked at me—for the first time. "Your methods are strange and unusual. I would never think to employ them. But they work."

"Thank you," I said. It was the closest I'd get to a compliment from the man. "I'm glad you can rest at last."

He turned to Frankie. "You will receive a full pardon from the governor of Tennessee. Luckily, we are in contact with one who died while in office," he mused. "I knew him. Good man. But I warn you, anything you've done anywhere else still stands."

"You can't win 'em all," Frankie said.

De Clercq pursed his lips but did not take Frankie's bait. He turned to me. "I'll remove the ghosts from your property immediately. And the prison itself."

"Hold up," Frankie said, raising a palm. "Can you give Lefty Scalieri an overnight pass? I need a word with him."

Yikes. "You know the creepy eye-patch ghost? The one who skulked after me in the yard?"

"He's an associate of mine," Frankie said noncommittally.

"I'll see that he stays there, under guard, until you get a chance to talk to him." De Clercq held out a hand to Frankie. "Goodbye."

The ghosts shook, and I watched the inspector smile, then slowly disappear.

"I'm glad he's found peace," I said to the gangster.

Frankie shrugged. "Peace is overrated." He looked around to make sure we were alone. Even then, he leaned in close. "Lefty and I used to work together. He was with me when I died."

"Did he shoot you?" I asked, a little too loud.

Frankie's eyes widened as he shushed me. "No. No. He didn't pull the trigger. But I think he knows who did."

CHAPTER 23

*I*t was well past two in the morning when we pulled onto my property. De Clercq had made good on his promise. The prison gates were gone. No barbed-wire-topped fence stood between me and my beloved home.

Just as the inspector promised, Lefty Scalieri stood vigil on my porch with a linebacker of a guard nearby. Scalieri hadn't looked right when I'd seen him in my yard earlier, and he still looked like a dose of evil. It wasn't only the scar, but the way he stared me down with his one good eye as if he wanted to cut me apart and eat me for dinner.

"I don't know about this guy," I said, slowing the car.

"That's what I said when they partnered me with him the night I died," Frankie muttered. "But what's done is done."

Lefty's fists curled when I stopped the car, and Frankie got out.

"I don't think you want to see this," Frankie said, taking back his power. I felt the energy drain from me slowly, like a shower of sparks passing down over my body and into the ground.

"Thanks," I said. "Let me know how it goes."

From the safety of my car, I watched him glide toward my

porch. Either it was my mind working overtime, or just knowing Scalieri was there, but I swore I could feel the heaviness of the evil that lingered beyond my potted geraniums.

I hoped they'd conclude their business fast and easy so that Lefty could get off my property and back to eternal lockup.

I drove around to the rear of the house and found Ellis's police cruiser parked near my rose garden. He flashed the lights once to let me know he'd seen me, then exited the car stiffly, as if he'd been waiting a while.

"To what do I owe the pleasure?" I asked, glad for the unexpected company.

He treated me to a tired, lazy grin. "Good to see you back." He kissed me. "It looks like your investigation went well."

"We solved the case," I said, resisting the urge to do a little twirl.

"That's great news. One down. One to go." He reached behind him and drew a tired, snuggly-looking Lucy out of his front passenger seat. "Lauralee called," he added, as Lucy nuzzled her nose against his uniform shirt. "One of her kids might be coming down with a stomach bug, so I told her I'd take this little girl."

"You're so sweet," I said to him, and to my skunk as he eased Lucy into my arms. She'd been sleeping on her tummy. It was nice and warm, and for a moment, I let myself enjoy the soft feel of her fur on my chin.

With the prisoners gone, she'd be glad to be back home.

Ellis walked us both to the house. "The fingerprint team was in your kitchen earlier this evening. I came by after and locked your doors."

And then he'd finished his shift, fetched my skunk, and waited outside in his car tonight, instead of in my more comfortable parlor. "You could have let yourself in again," I said, pleased to have him here. It felt good not to jump at every shadow.

"Didn't want to impose." He lingered close as I unlocked the back door. "But I will now. I'm not leaving you alone tonight."

His declaration warmed me to my toes. Yes, there was a live killer on the loose and I could use some protection, but I was also a girl who enjoyed having her boyfriend around.

"Have you learned anything more about Cammi's death?" I asked, easing Lucy down onto the porch. She nuzzled my shin, then Ellis's as I opened the door.

"The killer used cyanide," he said, bending to ruffle the fur on Lucy's head. "Not very elegant, but effective. Whoever doctored that pie wasn't concerned with this looking like anything but a cold-blooded poisoning."

So, someone wanted me dead and wasn't afraid to let me or anyone else know it.

"I don't understand this." It didn't make sense.

"We'll figure it out," he promised, walking ahead of me, turning on the lights to my kitchen. I half expected to find another pie on the counter. What I saw instead stopped me in my tracks.

Photographs littered the countertop, some two and three deep.

"Stop," Ellis said, inserting an arm between me and the photos.

Someone had been in my house. Ellis locked it, and someone had been in here anyway.

"Who else has a key?" he demanded.

"Just...Melody, Lauralee, my mom." Nobody that would hurt me. "I have to see," I said, skirting Ellis, pressing forward. "I won't touch it." I wouldn't even breathe on it, but I had to see.

What I found were dozens upon dozens of pictures of me, taken without my knowledge. I saw me walking up the steps to the library, talking to Zoey, laughing with Lauralee. All of them candid. And in every single one, somebody had torn my head from my body before replacing it neatly back where it belonged.

WE DIDN'T GET to bed until almost sunrise. The police came to take photographs of the photographs. They dusted for prints once more. And all along, I told everyone who would listen that my home had been locked.

Ellis tried to get me to go to his place for what remained of the night, but if my tormentor could get through a locked door, I didn't see the difference between his house and mine. At least here I had Frankie to keep an eye on things.

I hadn't seen him since his meeting with Lefty, but I knew that —unlike his shady partner in crime—my gangster wasn't going anywhere.

Ellis stayed. Another officer from the Sugarland PD remained parked outside the house.

And so I slept. Eventually.

Around mid-morning, I was awakened not by the persistent nudge of a wet skunk nose, but by my phone buzzing on the floor next to the futon.

"I've got it," I mumbled, fishing for it with my face still in the pillow. I vaguely recalled Ellis pressing a kiss to my cheek while I slept. He'd headed off to work, hoping to discover more about the killer plaguing Sugarland.

I didn't envy him in the slightest.

After a few tries, I located the phone. "Hello," I said, rolling onto my back, instinctively glancing at the kitchen just to make sure it was empty.

"Oh my god, Verity! Please, I need your help."

It was Zoey, and she sounded frantic. Please, not another emergency.

I propped myself up on my side. "What's wrong?"

"It's Beau. He's gone completely off the rails. He's just—it's crazy," she said, her words tripping over each other.

"Slow down," I instructed, sitting up, my head heavy. I checked my watch. It was past eleven in the morning, and whatever sleep I'd gotten hadn't been enough.

She hardly took a breath. "I think he might have been working in the barn all night, and when I got here this morning—" Her voice broke on a sob. "He's calling it his greatest artistic achievement yet. I don't know *what* it is, but I need you here. He listens to you."

"Not enough." She must be desperate if she was inviting me back into the picture.

"I can't handle this alone." Her voice warbled. "I'm *scared*."

I searched for my shoes. "I'm coming." I knew what it was like to be alone and afraid. "I'll call Ellis."

"No!" Zoey broke in. "You don't understand. Beau's been ranting about his family taking everything away from him. The last person he needs to see right now is his cop brother."

I didn't know who appointed me custodian of Beau's sanity, but I didn't want the job. "All right," I said, heading for the bathroom. "It's going to be fine. I'll be there in ten minutes."

Nine, I thought as I located a clean sundress on the banister.

"Please hurry." She ended the call while I dashed up to the bathroom.

I ran my free hand through my bed-messy hair. Beau Wydell needed to come back to this planet. I'd hoped his break from Virginia's expectations would cause him to mature, but it seemed as if he'd gone from one self-indulgent lifestyle to another. And he had no right to frighten Zoey like that.

I washed up, donned the new dress, and was ready to walk out the door in eight minutes.

Little Lucy lifted her head from the covers as I left.

She'd been up almost all night with us. "Sleep," I said, leaving her a plate of fruit before locking the door behind me. She'd be in bed for another few hours, as I would have been if Beau hadn't gone off his rocker.

I slid into the land yacht. It wasn't even noon and the thing already felt like an oven. I fired up the engine and backed out. I should call Ellis, and I would, no matter what Beau thought.

Ellis and Beau might not—ever—see eye to eye, but if his

ANGIE FOX

brother was in trouble, Ellis would want to be there for him. But first, I'd figure out what kind of trouble.

Truth be told, I'd hoped my own life would slow down a bit after last night.

At least I knew what to do about this.

The whole drive to the barn, I channeled my inner Zen. Whatever was happening with Beau, it couldn't be any worse than what I'd managed to live through last night. As long as he hadn't gone full-on van Gogh, Zoey and I could talk him down.

I squinted against the bright Southern sunshine. If only I'd stopped to grab my sunglasses.

My car's rear wheels kicked up a spray of dirt and gravel as I turned down the farmer's road.

The barn stood with its doors shuttered and Zoey's food truck parked outside. That made sense. She wouldn't be getting much business downtown on a Sunday. But as I parked my own car, I realized Zoey's engine was running and the back door lay open.

This could be worse than I thought.

I killed my engine and slipped out of the car.

"Zoey?" I asked, coming around the truck.

I peered into the back. The stove sat cold and the kitchen abandoned. All right. They must be in the barn. First, I'd calm Zoey down. Then we'd both work on Beau.

"Hello?" I eased open the large barn door and poked my head inside.

"Verity?" Zoey's voice quavered. None of the lights were on, but there were enough windows that I was still able to pick her out, crouched on the far side.

"It's me." I stepped inside. "How are you doing?"

She looked as if she were hiding from someone.

"Zoey." I took a few more steps inside, keeping my voice gentle. I was rewarded when she straightened up. "Where's Beau? Did he end up..." I trailed off as I registered the fact that Zoey held a gun.

Heavens. How badly had Beau scared this woman?

She raised the gun and pointed it at me.

"Whoa." I slowly raised my hands until they were level with my head. "It's okay. Calm down. I'm here to help."

Zoey strode toward me, the gun pointed squarely at my chest.

She wore her hair in a messy bun. Her colorful maxi dress swished around her legs, but her eyes were dead. Every hint of fear and sadness had vanished. And there was no sign of Beau anywhere.

"Looking for your old boyfriend?" she prodded. "He's not here. And you're going to be leaving, too." She drew a set of handcuffs from the back of her belt. "Put these on." She threw the cuffs and they landed at my feet.

CHAPTER 24

I stared at her, frozen. "What's going on, Zoey?" This was insane. She must have snapped. "Where's Beau?"

The bracelets on her wrist jingled as she tucked an errant lock of hair behind her ear. The other hand she held steady on the gun. "Beau's mother is staging another intervention at her house," Zoey snorted. "That should keep him busy for a while."

"All right," I said, trying to keep us both calm.

It wasn't working. At least not on my end.

I looked for some sign of the Zoey I knew, the one I'd liked. I tried to reconcile the laid-back California girl with the cold-blooded killer who held a gun on me. She believed in people like I did. She liked Beau, which seemed to be a positive thing for both of them. Sure, he'd been a little careless in telling her about his past relationship with me, but it was nothing to get homicidal over. I'd tried to stay out of their way. I'd been nothing but kind to her. I'd introduced her to Lauralee, for goodness' sake. "This is crazy," I said, refusing to show fear, but not about to pick up the cuffs she'd tossed at my feet.

I searched the shadows. Did she have Lauralee here as well?

"Your friend's working at the diner today," she said.

Zoey stood about five feet away—too far to jump, yet close enough to have a very, very good shot at me.

"Beau's moved beyond Virginia's petty interference," she said. "Soon he'll be beyond yours as well." She racked the slide of her handgun. "Put the cuffs on *now*."

"Fine." I held up my hands. "I'm doing it." I bent over and picked up the metal handcuffs. They were lighter than I'd expected and lined with fur. My fingers fumbled a bit as I threaded a wrist through one cuff.

"Tighten it," she ordered.

I nodded and complied.

She aimed the gun at my head. "Now the other one."

I really didn't want to do the other one. "Look," I said, holding my hands up, letting the cuffs dangle off my wrist, "I meant what I said. I'm done with Beau—"

Zoey's finger went white on the trigger, and for a second, I thought I was a goner.

"Put. The. Cuff. On. Now," she barked.

I did.

"Don't dig too hard into the skin," she added. Her lips curled into a predatory smile. "We don't want to leave any evidence."

Sweet Jesus. I tightened until she was satisfied. "Whatever you want, it's yours," I said quickly. Anything to keep her from shooting me before I could attempt an escape. Although my options were severely limited with my hands bound.

"Good." She nudged the gun at me. "I want you to turn around, walk to my truck, and get inside." The corner of her mouth ticked up. "We're going for a ride."

Oh, holy no. If I got into that truck, I'd be as good as dead.

We were out in the middle of nowhere, and if Virginia had Beau, it could take hours before he made it back. I hadn't told anyone where I was going, and I had no way to defend myself.

No ghost, either. I'd left Frankie back at the house. Not that he could do much to defend me against a living killer.

Think.

I needed to work out an escape plan, but until then, I had to stall. "I don't understand why you're doing this," I said, reeling a bit to the right, toward the yellow lady sculpture, the one with the ginormous lips.

"I don't know why I have to do this either," Zoey grated out. "Do you not like pie or something?"

It was her.

Of course, it was her.

"You left the pecan pies in my house," I said flatly.

"The first one wasn't poisoned," she said, defensive. "I was being kind."

Maybe, but the pie that poor Cammi had eaten was sure deadly. "You tried to poison me. Why?"

"It wasn't enough for you to break Beau's heart," she said, watching my every move. "You had to lead him on, even after he's with me."

Lord in heaven. If there was one thing I didn't want to die for, it was Beau Wydell. "I don't want him," I protested. "I thought you were good for him."

But she wasn't listening. "You don't believe in him. You don't support his dreams. You never deserved him." She aimed her gun at my head again, as if itching to pull the trigger. "You brought this on yourself, Verity."

I backed away, closer to the statue. I doubted it was thick enough to stop a bullet. I had to keep her talking.

"You were watching my house," I said. She must have been to know when I'd be gone.

"Hardly." She smirked. "Lauralee tells me all about where you go and what you do. She even keeps your house keys in her purse."

Oh no.

Zoey twisted her lips into a grin. "It was so easy to borrow her car to go buy some produce, then stop by the hardware store to make my own set of keys to your house. Sweet, trusting Lauralee." She tilted her head. "I think I'll keep her as a friend. She'll be so sad when she loses you."

There was no way I was letting this psycho anywhere near my friend or her boys. I had to figure out a way out of this.

The cuffs were light like they'd come from a commercial store rather than police supply. Maybe they wouldn't hold.

If I could get my hands free, I'd have options.

"Now come on out to the truck," she said. "You don't want to end it here. We'd leave a mess all over Beau's art."

Ha. The yellow lady sculpture with the huge pink lips was enough of a mess. But it was metal, and the skirt and lips were wide. It wouldn't be a great shield, but it was better than nothing.

I took another minuscule step to the right. "You don't want to do this, Zoey."

"I don't," she agreed. "I like you. If you hadn't messed things up with Beau, I'd be your best friend."

Yeah, I didn't think I needed her brand of friendship.

Still, as long as she was talking, she wasn't shooting. If I could keep the conversation going, I had a chance.

"My boyfriend's a cop," I said. "He'll put you in jail for the rest of your life."

She stared at me long and hard. "I don't think so. I got away with the girl in the ravine."

My mouth went dry.

She enjoyed my shock. "Ellis the Great won't solve that one, either."

"You're a serial killer." I regretted the words as soon as I said them.

If my accusation touched her, she didn't show it. "Maya was awful," Zoey said as if it were a fact. As if we were friends again, making small talk at Virginia's picnic. "Maya told Clint he'd never make it as a musician. I mean, who does something like that?" She notched her chin up. "Maya was completely wrong for him. I supported his dreams like she never could."

"Maybe they were a bad match," I suggested, scooting toward the statue a tiny bit more. Beau's art might be ugly, but if it could block a bullet, I would call it ten kinds of beautiful. "That doesn't mean Maya had to die."

"Are you kidding me?" Zoey lowered the gun a bit as she laughed. "No, she definitely had to go. Otherwise, he'd be carrying a torch for her forever. Why do the artistic ones always have to be so fragile? Like Beau, still thinking about what might have been if you'd stayed together. Do you know he had a file of pictures just of you?"

"I have an idea." She'd left them on my counter.

"That was the last straw," she vowed. "Once you're gone, I can stick with him long-term. Make a real go of it in Sugarland."

"You can be happy here without killing me," I said.

At least she could have been.

Zoey barked out a laugh. "I wish that were true." She raised the gun again. "He's still hung up on you. I'm going to fix that for him."

I moved a few more inches toward the statue. I was almost there.

"I know what you're trying to do." Something like compassion crossed Zoey's face. "Running won't solve anything. It'll just make you suffer."

We'd see about that.

I dove past the yellow lady and landed behind a sheet metal wall studded with old tires.

"Damn it, Verity," she said as if I were a stubborn cat refusing to get in the carrier.

She edged around the statue, trying to get a bead on me. "It'll be quick, I promise. Most of the girls don't even see it coming. I try to be gentle."

I backed up several feet and ducked behind the spider, the one made from repurposed rebar with chunks of concrete clinging to it.

"Come on," she coaxed. "Let's go to the ravine. It's pretty there."

She held the gun steady, stalking me.

The spider statue was top-heavy and didn't leave a lot of places to hide. I shoved it at her, sending loose concrete flying as it hit the floor.

"What the hell?" She jumped back, startled.

I'd missed, but at least I'd distracted her. I zigzagged sideways and ran past the three-headed snake sculpture. I looped the flimsy cuffs underneath a jagged coil and gave a quick, hard tug. One of the loops holding them together snapped apart. Point one to the snake!

With my hands free, I grabbed one of the hubcap heads and flung it at Zoey like a Frisbee.

She cried out. "You bitch!"

Good. It must have hit her.

I ran into a forest of spindly, screaming trees made from papier-mâché. Their bloodshot eyes glared at me, but I barely noticed. I was busy looking for a back door.

Zoey had the front covered. If I tried to escape that way, I was as good as dead. That left the rear. Only she knew this place and I didn't.

And she was closing in fast.

Too bad I'd left my bag—and my phone—in the car in my haste to rescue Zoey.

I crept through the fabricated forest, as fast and as silently as I could, until I reached the rear of the barn.

The double doors had been sealed, wired over with a trio of brightly colored planks of wood.

No!

"Veeeeeerity..." Zoey called from the other side of the forest.

I had a minute until she found me. Maybe less.

I grabbed for a hot pink wooden plank that had been wired over the largest section of door. Splinters dug into my skin. It didn't budge. I braced a foot on the door and pulled harder. It wobbled, then slid out.

One down, two to go.

I heard a gasp behind me and spun around.

Zoey stood at the edge of the papier-mâché trees, the gun at her side as she stared in dismay.

I chucked the board at her firing hand. It didn't even come close to hitting her—my aim was completely off, but she still shrieked with horror.

"That's the *Blocking of the Muse!*"

A sculpture? *The fricking barn door was a sculpture?*

I ripped the second board free in one swipe and tossed it at her. This one was lime green with wavy purple lines.

"Stop!" She tried to dodge, but it nailed her in the knee, and she stumbled.

I went for the last board. She raised her gun. I was wide open.

Bam!

She blew a hole in the door, right next to my head.

"Oh, my God!" she bellowed when she saw the damage. "Look what you made me do!"

Holy Jesus. There was no way I'd get the last board off before she shot me dead. If and when she got up the nerve to desecrate Beau's art again.

And there was nowhere left to run, no art that could stop a bullet.

I ran to the left, toward Beau's Armani suit nightmare.

Bam!

I had no idea where the next bullet went, but I swore I felt it whiz past my shoulder. I'd never make it to the door, and once she shot me, she'd have me. She could tie me up and toss me into the river or down an old mine shaft, and nobody would ever suspect her.

I had to take her out. I had to end this.

I screamed, falling down onto the floor behind the huge Armani mess. It stood in a thick wash bucket that I hoped was filled with rocks. "My leg!" I cried. She'd missed me, but my voice still edged on very real, acute panic. "Please, no. I can't take it anymore. I can't take the pain."

"Aw, Verity." Zoey's voice went from angry to sweet in a few terrifying heartbeats. "It's okay, baby." She said it like a Sugarland mamma as she stalked my hiding place, gun at the ready. "I won't leave you hurting."

I scrunched behind the statue as she drew closer.

Closer.

"It'll all be over soon," she coaxed. "Then there'll be no more pain ever again."

I cowered on my knees as if I wasn't a threat, as if I'd given in.

"All you have to do is relax and let me take care of you."

Blood pounded in my temples as she stalked me, and it took everything I had not to run.

I had one shot at this. I watched her every step as she came closer...closer...

I waited until she stood directly on the other side of the scarecrow of suits and doll heads.

Now.

I shot to my feet, kicking the sculpture hard right above the base. The top-heavy statue fell like a fighter hitting the canvas, right onto Zoey, whose bold talk and big gun didn't do much to help her handle a seven-foot-tall metal monstrosity.

Beau's monument to office drones and dead Armani suits took her down with a raucous clatter. Decapitated doll heads skittered across the barn floor, and so did Zoey's gun.

I ran for the gun like my life depended on it. Which it did.

It stopped just short of the back door. I grabbed it and spun around to train it on its owner, refusing to turn my back on Sugarland's first and only serial killer.

But I shouldn't have worried about Zoey.

She lay underneath the sculpture, knocked out cold. She'd need stitches and a dump truck full of Tylenol when she came to, but I was safe. And alive. And for once, I truly appreciated Beau's art.

CHAPTER 25

"*Verity's* right. Zoey is a serial killer," Ellis said. We stood outside the library the next day with his brother. Beau's girlfriend had been taken into custody, and as we spoke, the FBI team was investigating his barn. "She is suspected in at least one other California murder, another woman who dated her ex-boyfriend before her."

"I sure know how to pick them." Beau shook his head. "What's wrong with me?"

"Nothing," I assured him, ignoring the way Ellis almost choked. "You're making good changes in your life. You'll find someone."

Beau winced and shoved his hands into the pockets of his jeans. "I'm going back to the law firm on Monday."

"It's a good place to be until you know where you want to end up," Ellis said. "But I do have to tell you the guys at the station were impressed with your pictures of Sugarland."

Beau ducked his chin, embarrassed at the praise. That was a new one. He glanced at me. "Your sister has offered to display my pictures at the library," he said. "We're going to call the exhibit

Images of Sugarland. She thinks I can make a go of it as a photographer."

"You have real talent," I told him. He'd captured something special with his candid shots.

He cocked his head, and a bit of the old Beau surfaced. "I do have my moments."

Change was never easy, or fast. "I think you're on your way."

Lauralee stuck her head out of a trailer parked in front of the library. Zoey's food truck had been taken as evidence, but she'd scrounged a replacement. It was small, rusted at the edges, and only held a cooler and her serving supplies, but she made it work. She'd set up a barbeque grill outside and a cashier's table out front.

"Order up," she said, carrying a stack of paper plates. "Well, as soon as I get it off the grill."

She had barbequed pizzas going, and from the line out front of her trailer, I'd say she had a hit on her hands.

"Need some help?" I asked, strolling over to join her.

She pointed me toward the cashier's table. "Have at it."

Lauralee served, and I counted change until we'd made it a third of the way through the line and it was time to put more pizzas on the grill. They smelled amazing and looked even better, with crispy crusts flavored with smoke from the grill and Lauralee's signature sauce bubbling up through the cheese.

"You're a pro at this," I told her, watching her fuss over her creations.

"Big Jim traded his table saw for this trailer, and once I earn enough, I'm going to buy my own food truck." She gazed up at me, joyous. "I can do this, Verity. I really can." She placed fresh grilled chicken on one of the pizzas. "I can make a living with my own business."

"I always knew you could." The lunch crowd in Sugarland was lucky to have her.

Melody strolled down the library steps and moseyed her way

past Ellis, who smiled at something Beau said. She made her way toward us.

"Can you handle a big order from the library?" Melody asked Lauralee, waving a notebook scrawled with orders.

"As soon as I take care of my line," she said. If my friend smiled any more, her face was going to freeze that way.

It wouldn't be a bad thing.

"That was real nice what you did for Beau," I told my sister, "offering to display his pictures like that."

"It wasn't kindness," she told me plain. "I can't stand the guy. But he's talented, and we need an entry into the Great Libraries Town History competition. I think Beau could win us a ribbon."

"That would be amazing." For him and for Sugarland.

Melody stiffened, and I followed her gaze.

Virginia Wydell had pulled up in her Cadillac. There were no open spaces, so she double-parked.

"Somebody needs to drop a house on her," Melody murmured.

Lauralee snickered. "Order up!" she called, pulling pizzas off the grill.

Virginia wrinkled her nose as she exited her vehicle, whether from the smell of street food or from the crowd around the library, I couldn't say. She squared her shoulders, bypassed her sons, and strode straight for me.

"Why don't you give Lauralee a hand?" I asked Melody.

"And miss this?" My sister balked. "Not on your life."

Virginia stopped inches away from me and just stared. I let her. I was used to her intimidation techniques by now, and they didn't faze me.

When I didn't blink first, she did.

"Beau has returned to the firm," she stated.

"He told me," I said. "I think he made a good decision."

She snorted as if to say of course it was. Then, with stiff fingers, she reached behind her neck and unlatched the necklace she wore.

I could only see the chain, but still I froze. I hoped against hope that this was the necklace I'd missed like a piece of me. And as she lifted it from under her smooth white silk shell, I saw my grandmother's cross.

"I believe this is yours," she said, dropping it into my open palm.

"It is," I told her, running my fingers over the gold and silver filigree. "Thank you."

"I still don't like you," she said.

At the moment, I didn't care.

"We have time," I said to myself. "People change." I'd seen it firsthand, with Beau, with Frankie, even with the crooked judge who'd died so many years ago. People could surprise you for good and when you least expected it.

And so we enjoyed lunch outside, with good food, good friends, and one almost- mother-in-law.

The necklace felt right once again on my neck, and I couldn't stop reaching up to touch it. This was a sign of good fortune to come. I felt it in my bones.

I allowed myself to relax, to simply *be*. Until Frankie shimmered into view next to me.

"I thought you were taking Suds to the bank." It was right across the square. Frankie's old friend liked to visit his death spot sometimes. They'd hang out down in the tunnel Suds had started under the bank in 1932.

"Yeah, but I thought you might want to see this," Frankie said, letting his power flow over me, tingling my arms, making the hair on the back of my neck stand up.

"Stop it," I said, even as it washed completely through me. "I'd like a break from ghosts."

"Hold that thought," Frankie said as I heard the faint tinkle of a familiar laugh coming from behind the trailer. It couldn't be...

I ventured around the corner and stepped smack-dab into quite the celebration between Marjorie and Shane.

"Excuse me," I said, attempting to make a graceful exit.

"Get back over here, you goof," Marjorie ordered.

I did. A bit slower this time. "I'm glad to see you can leave the Adair property now."

"Marcus isn't holding me back anymore," she said, beaming. "Thank you."

"You were as much a part of that as I was," I reminded her. She'd directed me upstairs on the night of the second party. She'd saved my hide a few times in the menagerie.

"I do what I can." Marjorie winked and adjusted her hair and the straps on her dress as Shane wrapped his arms around her from behind. The stoic diamond dealer still wasn't someone I'd want to cross, but he appeared softer now, less tortured. I supposed it would be hard to watch the woman you love be controlled and abused for so long. As for Marjorie, she seemed to have chiseled away some of the hard edges and unearthed the man.

She linked her fingers in his. "We wanted to say goodbye."

"Really?" That surprised me. I'd imagined they'd be as tied to the Adair property as the Adairs themselves. "No more parties?" I asked. "No more crazy costumes? You were quite the natural."

She laughed. "We're taking a break. Although we may drop in for the Christmas Casino Bash."

"Good for you," I said.

She leaned back into Shane. "We're getting away, moving to Shaney's family home in Memphis. I've cut all spiritual ties to Marcus. We're making a fresh start." She took a deep breath and owned it. "Marcus is in prison. He can't touch me now."

And then it struck me. We hadn't just helped Frankie, we'd changed the game for Marjorie as well.

"I'm free," she said, testing out the idea, reveling in it. "I mean I'm truly free."

"You deserve it," I told her. "You earned it the hard way."

"I'm working up the courage to go to New York. There's no

telling what will happen next," she said, her image fading. Then
suddenly, her eyes went wide, and she came back full force. "Shaney,"
she said, gripping his arm, staring past me as if she'd seen a ghost.

I turned and saw an unfamiliar black Lincoln Navigator
pull up.

A driver emerged and hurried to open a door with a tinted
window. I couldn't see who was behind it, but I'd bet money
Marjorie could.

The man held out a hand to help an older woman out of the
back. She wore a fashionable dress with red and tan swirls—
definitely not from Sugarland—and big black sunglasses. Her
snow-white hair hung straight down her back in an avant-garde
style, and when she pulled off her sunglasses, there was a twinkle
of keen interest in her eyes.

"It's her," Marjorie said, gasping. Tearing up. And I knew
exactly whom she meant.

"Eliza Jean," I said. EJ, the woman from New York—Marjorie's
daughter.

"I-I don't know what to do," Marjorie said as I hurried to greet
our most honored—and unexpected—guest.

EJ shook my hand. She was no spring chicken, but she looked
and acted younger than her years. "I had to come back and see this
place," she said, her gaze traveling over the library and the square.
"The nice ladies at the heritage society said I might find you here."

Whoops. It appeared they'd backed my story at least. Or
perhaps had believed it themselves.

"May I have a moment?" she asked, directing me to a quiet
place away from the crowd. She withdrew an envelope from her
purse with fingers that shook, from age or from excitement I
couldn't say. "I know you're with the heritage society, and that's
why I'm letting myself hope..." she said, opening the envelope. "As
I was looking for pictures for you, I found this among my
mother's things." She withdrew a copy of her adoption

paperwork, signed by Judge Larry Knowles. "Have you ever heard of a woman named Marjorie Gershowitz?"

"I have," I said gently as Marjorie drew close to her daughter and gazed down at her with enough love to last the rest of eternity. "You know her, too. As Marjorie Phillips."

A smile lit her features. "I'd wondered…I'd hoped."

She looked a bit unsteady. "Let me help you," I said, leading Eliza Jean to a nearby park bench.

"Marjorie truly was a mother to me," she said, leaning on me, letting me help seat her. She looked down. "I wish I could have told her that."

"She knows," I said, sitting next to her, watching Marjorie take the seat on the other side. "She's here."

"I can feel her in this place," EJ said, closing her eyes as if she could absorb the moment, as if she knew on some level Marjorie was close by.

"Your mother has always loved you," I told EJ. "I know that firsthand. And I'd like to tell you how."

I took a deep breath and began my story. I wasn't sure how she was going to take this, but I owed it to her. EJ deserved to know the truth. And now that I had her comfortable and sitting, I told her everything—about my ability to see ghosts, about her real parents and how much everyone cared about her.

EJ drew a hand to her chest as I spoke. She didn't interrupt. She didn't ask questions. She didn't say one word. I wasn't even sure if she believed me until I'd finished and directed her attention to the empty spot on her other side, the place where her mother sat.

It was then that the lines at the corners of EJ's eyes deepened. "If you'd told me this last week in New York, I never would have believed it." She shook her head slowly. "But here? In this place…" She closed her eyes briefly and drew a deep breath of warm summer air, tinged with the scent of magnolias. "There's something about being in Sugarland that almost makes it possible."

"I'm telling you the truth," I assured her. "Your mother is here. She's as real as you or me."

EJ chuckled. Maybe it was my phrasing or the very idea.

She pursed her lips together and looked, truly looked at the empty place where her mother sat. "Not a day goes by that I haven't loved you," she said to a glowing, radiant Marjorie, who promptly burst into tears.

EJ turned to me, and a slow, brilliant smile burst over her like a sunrise. "Oh, how I've missed my home."

"You can go back. Anytime," I assured her. "It's not too late."

EJ blinked back tears. "And you'll show me?"

I looked from her to Marjorie, to the solid red bricks and gleaming limestone that made up the town square of Sugarland. "Nothing would please me more."

CHAPTER 26

The following morning, EJ and I visited the Adair estate. Graham and Jeannie had been overjoyed to see her. Marjorie took over as tour director, and I simply interpreted everything for everybody, with Frankie looking on and rolling his eyes a lot. I think the old gangster feared this would be a new career direction for me. But it wasn't. It was my gift to a family who had already lost too much time.

Later that week, I sat on my back porch swing, listening to the sound of Ellis working with power tools. Lucy curled next to me, asleep despite the racket.

"Nobody is going to be able to get through this," Ellis said, drilling my new lock into the back door. It was a security-grade Mul-T-Lock, sturdy as the ones they used in military high security zones. He'd bought more locks for the front door and the windows, and at this point, I wouldn't be surprised if he attempted a barbed-wire fence à la De Clercq.

True to his word, the detective had left us in peace.

He had gone to a better place, knowing his job was done.

I paged through the *Sugarland Gazette*, admiring old photos of the Adair mansion in its heyday. Eliza Jean had brought them with her, and so much more.

By that time Eliza Jean had returned to her family home several more times, with city officials, historical experts, and various contractors. Knowing that this was her family home, her parents' legacy, made all the difference. And, with her connection to the town renewed, she wanted to invest in it.

Turned out she'd amassed a sizeable fortune in New York, with no children or heirs to bequeath it to.

According to the paper, she'd pledged two million dollars to restore the Adair Mansion and Menagerie to its former glory, with her remaining fortune secured to create the Adair Preservation Society. The estate would become a permanent animal park and Sugarland Heritage site.

Once again, children would visit animals at the menagerie. Families would picnic on the grounds. I imagined weddings at the old mansion and fireworks over the lawn.

She'd even promised a giant cuddly snake: Sir Charles II.

The Adairs were back.

This was the biggest gift the town had ever been given for historic preservation and city pride.

It was a legacy that would last for generations.

And there, in black and white, she'd credited me and the Sugarland Heritage Society for making it all possible.

It was the biggest coup for the Sugarland Heritage Society in its one-hundred-and-ten-year history, and I had to think it might go far in repairing my reputation in this town.

I folded the paper over to read it again.

"You did it," Ellis said, blowing the sawdust off his drill. "I'll bet you win the Sugarland Heritage Society Lifetime Achievement Award." He grinned. "My mom's been after that one for years."

I caressed my necklace. "I can't believe EJ sent me a check." She'd delivered it by courier not even an hour ago, from the new

Adair Preservation Society. Made out to me for "historical preservation services rendered."

It was much too much, more than I'd ever made for a single job. I'd immediately called her and said I didn't earn it, but EJ had insisted. She had this idea that when I'd brought her back home, she'd found a piece of herself she'd always felt was missing. She wanted to spend the time she had left in Sugarland, bringing life back to the mansion, making her parents proud.

I was sure she'd accomplish that and then some.

Heck, her father had been over the moon just to see her again —and watch her use her phone. I felt complete. Everything was right with the world. Except...

Frankie lounged under the apple tree, staring out at nothing. Whatever Lefty had said had put him on edge. He hadn't wanted to talk much since.

Well, I'd given him his space. Now it was time to see what I could do to help.

I walked down to him. "How are you doing?" I asked when I'd drawn near. "I'm surprised Molly isn't over here," I added, taking a seat next to him in the grass.

"She came by earlier," he said, slouching deeper against the tree, pushing his hat down farther over the bullet hole in his forehead. "She thinks I need to go after Lefty."

"What? That ghost is bad news." Then again, Frankie had probably told Molly more than he'd told me. "Does Lefty know something about what went down the night you died?"

Frankie didn't speak for a long moment. He was always tight-lipped about the night of his death. It was a sensitive subject, one he'd been unwilling to explore before now.

"Frankie," I said, "you know I care."

His gaze drifted to a spot over my shoulder. "It's a delicate matter. I'm not sure I'm up to it."

"Believe me, I'm not a fan of Lefty." The guy gave me the

creeps on about a hundred different levels. "But I'm starting to think your freedom might hinge on addressing your death."

Most ghosts weren't so tied to their ashes like Frankie was. It was like he clung to his past, unable to acknowledge what had killed him.

"Was Lefty really with you the night you were shot?" I asked.

Frankie glanced at me. "More than that. He knows who did it."

I sucked in a breath. "Did he tell you?"

"No." Frankie's jaw flexed. "He wants a favor first."

No, thanks. "You don't need to be doing his dirty work while he's in prison."

"Not prison. Worse. He's been transferred to the Pikesville Sanatorium."

"I know that place. It's been abandoned for years."

"Not by the dead," Frankie said. He turned and looked at me. "It might be worth giving him what he wants if he's willing to talk."

I hated to admit he might be right.

"I'll probably need help with the favor, though," Frankie said, not exactly asking for my help. "You seem pretty good with people, dead and alive."

"I have my moments," I admitted. I'd prefer to stay away from Lefty Scalieri, and whoever else haunted that sanatorium. But Frankie was my friend. I'd stand by him. "If you want my help, you have it."

"All right then," Frankie said, nodding, trusting me, coming to his decision. "I've got a story for you."

NOTE FROM ANGIE FOX

*T*hanks so much for exploring a whole new side of Sugarland crazy with Pecan Pies and Dead Guys. These characters are such a kick to write and can't wait to see where they "grow" next. In fact, I'm already hard at work on the next book in the series.

There's no release date for the next one yet, but you like these mysteries, and want to know when each one comes out, sign up for new release updates at www.angiefox.com. You'll receive an email on release day, and in the meantime, your information will be kept safe by Lucy and a pack of highly-trained guard skunks.

Thanks for reading!

Angie

ABOUT THE AUTHOR

New York Times and *USA Today* bestselling author Angie Fox writes sweet, fun, action-packed mysteries. Her characters are clever and fearless, but in real life, Angie is afraid of basements, bees, and going up stairs when it's dark behind her. Let's face it: Angie wouldn't last five minutes in one of her books.

Angie earned a journalism degree from the University of Missouri. During that time, she also skipped class for an entire week so she could read Anne Rice's vampire series straight through. Angie has always loved books and is shocked, honored and tickled pink that she now gets to write books for a living. Although, she did skip writing for a week last fall so she could read Victoria Laurie's Abby Cooper psychic eye mysteries straight through.

Angie makes her home in St. Louis, Missouri with a football-addicted husband, two kids, and Moxie the dog.

If you are interested in receiving an email each time Angie releases a new book, please sign up at www.angiefox.com.

Be sure to join Angie's online Facebook community where you will find contests, quizzes and special sneak peeks of new books.

Connect with Angie Fox online:
www.angiefox.com
angie@angiefox.com